CATH FERLA is a Melbourne-based writer with a background in screenwriting and script editing, educational publishing and arts writing. Also a trained teacher, Cath has taught English as an Acquired Language (EAL) in Melbourne, Sydney and Beijing. She has a keen interest in regional Chinese food and once took a solo food pilgrimage to China's Sichuan province. Ginger, chilli and garlic are her favourite flavours.

CATH FERLA

GHOST GIRLS

echo

echo

Echo Publishing
A division of The Five Mile Press
12 Northumberland Street, South Melbourne
Victoria 3205 Australia
www.echopublishing.com.au

Part of the Bonnier Publishing Group
www.bonnierpublishing.com

Copyright © Cath Ferla, 2016

All rights reserved. Echo Publishing thanks you for buying an authorised edition of this book. In doing so, you are supporting writers and enabling Echo Publishing to publish more books and foster new talent. Thank you for complying with copyright laws by not using any part of this book without our prior written permission, including reproducing, storing in a retrieval system, transmitting in any form or by any means, electronic, mechanical, photocopying, recording, scanning or distributing.

First published 2016

Cover design by Sandy Cull, gogoGingko
Cover image by Kutay Photography/500px
Page design by Shaun Jury

Printed in Australia at Griffin Press.
Only wood grown from sustainable regrowth forests is used in the manufacture of paper found in this book.

National Library of Australia Cataloguing-in-Publication entry:
   Creator: Ferla, Cath, author.
   Title: Ghost girls, Cath Ferla.
   ISBN: 9781760401177 (paperback)
   ISBN: 9781760401184 (epub)
   ISBN: 9781760401191 (mobi)
   Subjects: Students, Foreign–New South Wales–Sydney–Fiction.
   Language teachers–New South Wales–Sydney–Fiction.
   Organized crime–New South Wales–Sydney–Fiction.
   Ghost stories.
   Dewey Number: A823.4

Twitter/Instagram: @echo_publishing
Facebook: facebook.com/echopublishingAU

*For Mum and Dad
and for Eugene*

THE ROOM smelled like wet onions.

This was the first thought to filter through Han Hong's fear. She inhaled the musty, sour scent again and dissected it. She knew the smell. It reminded her of the leeks stored for too long in the damp cellar below her childhood house in her hometown. At the end of a long winter, the cellar took on an acrid smell that would linger until the last days of the following summer. Like the mildew on their perennially damp sheets or the pungent scent of shit emanating from their latrine, the cellar held a particular scent memory for Han Hong; one whiff of rotting onions and she was back there.

How she wished she were back there.

She remembered how, as a young girl, she held her nose between pinched fingers on her visits to the space below the house. She'd tried in vain to smother the scent, gulping earthy air into her lungs. Later, with hard soap, she'd scrubbed at her skin in an effort to release the stink from her pores – always unsuccessfully, she'd felt. She'd been self-conscious in her English classroom where the teacher, a perfectly groomed Western woman, smelled of fresh peaches. Han Hong had once caught the teacher wrinkling her nose as she'd bent over the desk to help her with an assignment. She'd known then that she'd never smell sweet, like peaches, until she found her way out of her hometown. That day she'd promised herself to study harder than ever before, to work hard so that she might one day escape her family home and its cellar and damp sheets and backyard toilet. She would make it out of her hometown and into the wide world, find success and money and the opportunity to make everything in her life smell sweet.

That night she'd taken to her skin with her mother's scrubbing brush. And she'd scrubbed so hard she'd caused her arms to bleed.

Now here she was.

Han Hong inhaled deeply. The scent of her cell brought a small comfort in the memory of home. But before long, she felt the bite of hot tears in her eyes. She knew she was trapped here, but to be trapped in a place so reminiscent of everything she had left behind made her situation all the more unbearable.

Han Hong shifted, hoping to restore some feeling to her buttocks, which had numbed long ago. Some sensation remained in her legs and, through her thin stockings, she felt the damp and dimpled concrete floor scrape like sandpaper. Occasionally she heard the rattle of an animal, its claws clattering somewhere nearby. She heard voices, distant, and the occasional rush of fire mixing with the roaring in her head.

Han Hong was blind to the eye of the digital camera that watched her. It recorded every movement. Every groan. The blindfold around her eyes was secured so tightly her eyelids hurt. She couldn't breathe deeply because of the cloth in her mouth but she forced air into her lungs through her nose, inhaling with it the damp, sour scent of her prison.

She knew life could be tough. But she never thought it would end like this.

IT'S THE small things that cause panic.

A dumpling dropped into a dish of soy. A bowl of tea splashed over a lap. Losing the practice tests in a classroom full of expectant students on the final teaching day before exams, ten pairs of eyes staring her down. Small things.

These thoughts occurred to Sophie Sandilands as she hunted desperately for the practice English tests that had performed a disappearing act among the papers on her desk.

The eyes regarded her silently. Those ten pairs of eyes were making her panic.

Where the bloody fuck ...

Sophie dumped the pile on the floor and got down on her hands and knees. Chuck had done it to her. He'd handed her this disorganised bundle of paper, telling her he'd done her copying as a favour. She'd failed to check what lay beneath the pink cover page where he'd scrawled a long-winded note that she hadn't had time to read.

Always do everything for yourself. She breathed the mantra quietly before inhaling deeply though her nose. She wasn't one to easily accept favours. In Sophie's experience, it was better to learn first how to serve yourself and forget about anybody ever serving you. If Chuck's gesture reinforced anything, it was that she was better off getting on with things on her own.

Pushing the locks of her black hair behind her ears, Sophie rifled through the mess, ignoring the occasional titter but noticing the warm heat of embarrassment that crept up her neck and smoothed itself over her cheeks in a caress. A gift from her mother, that flush. In moments of discomfort, or at the first sip of a beer, it stained Sophie's skin.

'I'm glad you don't look like me,' her mother had confided once, long ago. 'But that pink in your skin comes from my blood. Avoid wine and rose petal tea if you do not want to blush.'

She'd avoided neither for a long time and had embraced the pink. Disorganisation, on the other hand ...

Disorganisation suggested a lack of control, showed weakness and allowed emotions to be laid bare. Seamus taught her that, way back when she'd been small enough to perch on his knee. Flustered people, her father had said, find it harder to hide their true self from others. Panic opens up a person's body and allows it to speak through involuntary language: a nervous flick of the hair; a rap of knuckles against a desk; the grinding of teeth. In panic, a person's weaknesses are on display for observers to read. Only organisation, regimen and control can allow a person to hide in plain sight.

Sophie forced a smile onto her class. 'I'll be there in a sec,' she murmured.

The students stared back, dissatisfaction on their faces. She had to take control of the situation immediately or they would begin to complain. And a collective of complaining language students was not something Sophie needed right now.

She glanced across at Wendy, a lanky Chinese woman with bobbed hair. She'd assumed her usual position, slumped over her desk, no doubt attempting to sleep off the rice wine she'd consumed the night before. Party girl. Unlike her classmates,

Wendy approached study with minimal effort. More often than not these days she seemed only to want to sleep.

Outside, through the floor-to-ceiling windows, the Sydney winter presented its ugly face. A thick mist hung over the rooftops, obscuring the narrow slash of sky visible between the skyscrapers on a clear day. In the foreground, a mess of construction scaffolding and yellow cranes explained the tinny clank of metal on metal that played the soundtrack to most of Sophie's days.

'Gotcha.' The pile of practice exams appeared from inside the sleeve of a manila folder. Chuck had practised organisation after all. He'd slipped the folder containing the tests under a pile of recycled copier paper. Now that Sophie read the cover note, she saw he'd intended for the students to use it 'as scrap'.

Su Yuan leaned forward in her chair.

'Hey Sophie,' she said, her eyes sparkling.

Sophie straightened herself out, dusted her corduroys and began distributing the tests to the students. She ignored the groan from Enrico, the Brazilian sandal merchant, who had clearly been hoping for a bludge.

'It doesn't matter if you lose things, as long as you find them again.' Su Yuan stretched out a slender arm for her paper, her smile widening as Sophie handed her the sheet.

'My thoughts exactly,' Sophie said as she prodded Wendy awake and slipped the practice test onto her desk. 'Although I'm not sure you'd be reassuring me if I'd eaten ten minutes into your real exam.'

She returned to the front of the room.

Wendy yawned, stretched and began drawing circles on the corner of her test sheet.

'Sophie?' Su Yuan again, her clear voice cutting the silence.

'What's up?'

'Just one question.'

Sophie flicked open the spare practice test on her desk. 'Yes?'

'How can you eat an exam?'

If I'd eaten ten minutes into your real exam. The turn of phrase. At best you created confusion and at worst you created a group of people who went out into the streets of Sydney complaining about their 'blue mood' or interrupting conversations with a 'burning question'. But when Sophie looked up at Su Yuan, the young woman's smile was broad: a joke.

'I dunno, Su Yuan,' she said, as the tension between her shoulders began to fade. 'I guess it'd taste okay if you added a lot of salt.'

鬼

AT LUNCHTIME, Sophie joined the crowd in a staffroom that smelled suspiciously like a fridge. The room, small and windowless, had space to seat only ten – inadequate when the school employed a staff of forty. Most people skipped downstairs to the sushi bars or the food court for lunch, cramming into the elevators alongside hordes of rowdy students. Not an option for Sophie. Standard food court food was the pits. If she allowed herself one indulgence in her life, one safe thing to remember her childhood by, it was interesting, eclectic food: the kind that didn't involve sweet and sour sauce.

She squeezed past the line for the microwave and took a seat at the laminex table next to Chuck, her fifty-something Kentucky-born colleague, who was as camp as he was heavy, the proud king of the photocopier and the owner of one mother of a smelly lunch.

'It's onion salad and it's good for me,' he said to Sophie

when he caught her eyeing his plate. 'I'm trying to lose pounds for Pattaya. Two weeks and I'm in party town.'

'Hope your onion breath's cleared up by then.'

Chuck smiled and pulled a pack of chewing gum from the pocket of his polo shirt. 'Juicy Fruit,' he said. 'Besides, the Thais eat so much chilli they've destroyed their scent receptors.'

'Don't you mean their taste buds?'

'Those too.' He sneaked a peek into Sophie's brown paper bag. 'What you got there?'

Sophie's lunch was a large steamed bun she'd picked up from a tiny Chinese breakfast cafe opposite Central Station. She'd stopped in on her walk to work for a bowl of hot soy milk with sugar and an oily fried dough stick on the side. She'd seen the buns, lined up in rows in giant bamboo steamers, and that had been it.

She bit into the steamed bun, cold now, but still delicious. Fluffy white bread encased a filling of mushroom, tofu and bamboo shoots. She dunked it into the container of chilli dipping sauce and offered it to Chuck.

He held up a hand and shook his head. 'No thanks, sweetheart. I'm off carbs.'

Sophie shrugged. 'Suit yourself,' she said, biting off another chunk. 'All the more for me.'

'Don't talk with your mouth full.'

Sophie flipped a finger. Chuck feigned shock. They laughed.

A sudden collective shriek from outside the room jerked their attention to the door. They heard the thump of footsteps in the corridor.

Sophie's colleague Tim filled the doorway, his great frame heaving with effort.

'It's one of the students,' he said. 'Wendy Chan. For fuck's sake, she's just bloody well jumped!'

It was true, then – people really could turn to stone. Life could jam like a disc with a scratch. The moment probably only stretched three seconds, but it felt as though the room hung suspended – fingers raised to mouths, forks resting against salad leaves, hands clasping spectacles, knives sunk into butter – as people digested Tim's news. Then, with the beep of the microwave, life returned. Chuck was out first, his chair thrown back, slipping past Tim through the door and down the corridor. The others followed, leaving spilled drinks and remnants of lunches and the sour stink of onions.

女孩

OUTSIDE, A crowd had gathered. Sophie pushed through the thick fog of faces to where Wendy lay. She looked strangely intact, not at all like she'd just fallen from a city skyscraper. There was her head, yes, a bloody, spongy mess, but the rest of her lay neatly against the footpath, whole. Sophie opened her notepad. A young police officer had his eyes on her and the expression on his face conveyed a mixture of anxiety and distaste, like a new teacher on his first day of class.

Get the details. Always get the details.

Seamus had taught her that. *It's amazing how quickly the mind forgets*, he'd said. *Self-preservation. The mind knows that remembering horror can drive it insane.*

For years Sophie had concentrated on writing down the details: an encounter with a traffic inspector; harsh words exchanged with a lover; vehicle descriptions of the cars driven by her dad's clients. She'd thought the practice would come in handy one day when she followed in Seamus's footsteps and started her own private investigation business.

But then it had all unravelled.

Her mother disappeared in the night. Her father removed his mask.

Sophie ran.

She'd gone to Beijing to forget the details, forget her past and discover something different. And the more she distanced herself from the details, the more she started to feel renewed.

You like it here in Beijing?

More than what I left behind.

We're all running away from something. Can I buy you a beer?

Only if you want to see me blush.

You're a one-pint screamer?

It's my Chinese blood.

You don't look fucking Chinese.

You don't look like an arsehole.

You're funny.

I'm not even drunk.

Can I kiss you?

Please.

And then it happened. A crime on her watch. And because Sophie had failed to write down the details, she'd been unable to provide any more information than the bits she could sieve from her confused brain. She'd muddled her memory with nightclubs and booze; she'd lapsed in her judgement and let go of Seamus's rules. And because of those things she'd been unable to help solve a terrible crime for which she felt responsible.

Now, a teenager tried to break around the privacy barrier, his mobile phone poised to shoot.

The cop saw him and moved quickly, catching the kid by the elbow.

'Buddy, I said move off.' He gave the kid a gentle shove. 'The woman's dead. Show some respect.'

The kid shook his arm free and muttered something under his breath before scuffing across the street. Sophie watched him pass Chuck and some other teachers. They were hugging each other and crying. She scanned the remainder of the crowd and recognised several students as hers. She should probably offer comfort, but her feet felt fused to the earth.

Maybe she was in shock.

That was Wendy on the concrete, the girl who'd sat a practice test in her classroom not an hour before. Had she given any indication that she planned to take her own life? Sophie scanned her memory for details. Wendy had been sleepy and uninterested, but Sophie had never known her any different. She'd completed the test in a barely legible cursive and smiled politely at Sophie when she finished. On the hour, she'd untangled her limbs from her desk and bee-lined for the door. She'd sauntered away wordlessly, books clutched to her chest.

The police officer turned to address Sophie. 'Which paper are you from?'

Sophie slipped the notepad into her back pocket. 'I'm not.'

He frowned. 'You're not officially reporting on this?'

She shrugged. 'More taking notes for the record.'

The cop cleared his throat and glanced away. When he looked back his eyes were cold. 'Well, that's a bit sick, isn't it?'

'What?'

'Are you some sort of private investigator or are you just taking notes and photos for kicks?'

Private investigator. In another life, maybe.

'She was my student and she's dead,' Sophie said. 'Her parents might want to know the details and I want to be able to tell them.'

The cop raised an eyebrow. 'You can probably leave that to the police.'

Sophie smiled. 'Yeah, right,' she said. 'I have this thing about uniforms.'

The cop leaned in, like she'd asked him out on a date. 'Oh, yeah?'

Sophie let her eyes lock with his. What was that she saw in his irises? Hope?

'Can't be trusted,' she said.

She felt the cop's gaze follow her as she moved to a nearby bench and sat down. Depending on the size of his ego, he might try to write her up. Let him. She didn't give a shit.

People around her were crying now. Sophie spied Su Yuan and Enrico. The tall girl embraced the rough, muscular Brazilian. Tears cascaded down Enrico's face and tangled in his beard.

Sophie retrieved her notebook and wrote down the time. She flicked back through the pages and tried to decipher her scrawl. What had she seen? Wendy's face, a slick of colours and textures: the magenta sheen of her blood and black matte of her hair; a white gleam of bone splintered through flesh; her pale pink brain oozing onto the concrete.

She'd noted Wendy's fingernails, painted orange and still intact.

She'd described a shopfront sign, now dented and damaged from the force of Wendy's fall.

She'd sketched the angle of Wendy's forearm, crooked and dislocated from the elbow socket.

Sophie closed her eyes, contemplating what she'd seen and what it meant.

'You've done a lot of work there.'

She whipped her head up. A man leaned on the bench behind her, his arms folded neatly across its curved back. He wore a grey suit, white shirt and black tie. His sandy hair was cut short, parted neatly and combed. Sharp. He examined Sophie with clear blue eyes and the slightest smile on his lips.

Sophie flipped the notebook shut. 'Do I know you?'

The man shook his head, drawing Sophie's eyes to his strong jaw, a hint of stubble just visible on sun-loved skin.

'I overheard you saying you have trust issues,' he said. It sounded more like a question than a statement.

Sophie stood up.

'Hey, it's all right, I'm not into uniforms either.' He smiled and extended a hand. 'I'm Damian Sommers.'

Sophie eyeballed him. 'You're a plain-clothes'.'

Damian reached into the breast pocket of his jacket. Sophie's body tensed as though he were going for a gun.

He offered a card. 'Nah, just a PI.'

This had to be some kind of joke.

Instinct kicked in and Sophie stepped back. 'You know who I am, then?' The question was out of her mouth before she had time to catch herself.

'I overheard your conversation with the cop and I saw you taking some serious notes.'

'The girl's only just jumped,' said Sophie. 'You can't be on the case already.'

'Nope. Just here on my lunch hour.' He pointed to a nearby Japanese restaurant. 'But it always pays to talk.'

Sophie stuck her hands in her pockets, gripped the top of her thighs. 'If I was a private detective, I'd hardly want to share any information I had with a competitor,' she said. 'But I'm not and I don't have any information worth talking about.'

'That's what they all say,' he said with a smile.

'I told that cop I don't trust uniforms,' Sophie said. 'But I trust suits like you even less.'

She sensed a hint of defeat, despite the smile still patiently painted to the man's face. He pushed the card towards her.

'It's fine,' he said, his voice quiet. 'But do me a favour and take this. You might decide you feel like a conversation some time.' The blue eyes glinted. 'Or, you know, maybe just some food.'

'There's a dead girl on the concrete and you're asking me out?'

He offered the card again. 'Just take it, please.'

They stood looking at each other. He had a freckle above his lip.

Sophie grabbed the card. 'Fine.'

Damian rocked back on his heels, slipped his hands into his suit pockets. 'See you,' he said.

She watched him melt his way through the crowd, unhurried and in control. People stepped aside for him. The faintest flutter of curiosity stirred within her. But he was a private detective and God knows she'd had enough of those in her life to last the rest of it.

She flopped down on the bench and took out her phone. She scanned through the images of Wendy, noting that they matched the descriptions in her notes. Then a detail jerked her upright. Why hadn't she noticed it earlier? Wendy's demeanour, her sleepiness and lack of interest – it all made sense now. Possibly her suicide did too.

The skin on Wendy's arm was pale, translucent and covered in needle tracks.

HE GOT there as fast as he could. The news was all over the radio. The jumper had attended a language school in the city and it hadn't taken long for him to find out which. Foreign language students were a tight bunch – they attended schools scattered throughout the CBD but they all seemed to know each other. It was a community; friendship forged by dislocation, alienation and an unfriendly city. It worked for him and his business. The students' bonds meant they worked together to keep each other's secrets.

And these students had many secrets. Behind the smiles, eager faces and shyness that a language barrier naturally brings, lay a range of complex, ambitious people with little to lose and everything to gain. Some of them would do almost anything if it meant getting ahead.

Including unprotected sex for money.

This reality had served him well in his brothels and clubs over the years and had made him a lot of cash. But cracks had begun to appear. If the girl on the pavement was who he thought she was, he'd have to authorise his first kill. And he didn't like it.

He knew he'd arrived because of the crowds. A couple of police officers were doing their best to prevent a bottleneck but people still stood six deep. The general public's thirst for horror both shocked and excited him. Perhaps his associates were right, perhaps there was a market for something harder than vanilla sex.

He swam his way through the bodies and fake Gucci shoulder bags, slipping easily to the front of the plastic barricade. He could smell cabbage and garlic on the breath of the students around him. He also detected a top note, cloying, like fresh meat.

He caught the attention of the nearest cop. The young man looked as though he wished he were somewhere else. But before he had a chance to flash his card and proffer his excuse for viewing the body, he saw the shoes. They poked out from beneath the white sheet, bright red like fresh blood. The shoes were unmistakable because he'd bought them himself. They'd been a gift from one of his associates for his favourite girl. And now she was dead. He gritted his teeth and backed away into the crowd.

The fact she was gone meant only one thing: soon there'd be a hunt on. The hunt would lead to him. He reached into his breast pocket for his phone.

It was unfortunate, but to protect the business and his freedom, a different woman would have to die.

THE CROWD dispersed quickly after the ambulance left. Sophie picked her way up the street to Su Yuan. The girl rested in a flat-footed crouch in front of a shop window. She held her chin in one hand, eyes wide and unblinking.

'Are you okay?'

A stupid question. Had Su Yuan known Wendy? Had the two women been friends? They were both Chinese, but aside from that, they appeared to share little in common. Bright, bubbly Su Yuan breathed light into Sophie's classroom. Wendy had sometimes snored.

Su Yuan stared up at Sophie. 'I don't think I am okay,' she said, her voice little more than a whisper. 'I've never seen a suicide before.'

Sophie squatted beside her and stared out at the passing foot traffic. She twisted the ring on her finger. 'Me neither,' she said. 'It's bloody awful.'

Su Yuan slumped against the window. 'Poor Wendy,' she said. 'I'll always wonder why she did it.'

Heroin. 'I don't know if it makes you feel better,' said Sophie, 'but you're not alone.'

Su Yuan grunted a disagreement. 'That's what you think.'

'We can talk about it if you want,' Sophie said. 'There won't

be any classes this afternoon, we could get something to eat...'
She sounded like the PI.

Su Yuan shot her an irritated look. 'The last thing I can think about now is food!'

Sophie cringed. She should remove herself and her runaway mouth from Su Yuan's pain. 'I'll go,' she said. She pushed up from her squat and her hand brushed Su Yuan's knee. The girl shot her hand out and clutched Sophie's fingers, pulling her close.

'We're all connected,' she said.

The words hit Sophie like bullets. 'What?'

Su Yuan gave a small smile. 'I'm sorry,' she said. 'I'm just upset about Wendy.' She squeezed Sophie's hand. 'Some noodles would probably do me good.'

The Happy Chef restaurant at the top of the Sussex Centre was Sophie's happy place. It was more a series of authentic hawker stalls than a typical shopping-centre eating spot, and the air smelled of ginger and pork broth and dried shrimp. Clutching her receipt in one clammy hand, Sophie watched a shop assistant ladle spoonfuls of wonton laksa and seafood noodle soup. The surfaces of the bowls shimmered with oil. Finally, it was her turn. Sophie willed her hands not to shake as she collected her tray and its boiling resident: five-spice beef noodles with extra chilli.

The first spoonful burned her mouth. Then the chilli hit the back of her throat. She coughed loudly. Diners at other tables stifled grins against chopsticks. But the carbohydrate did the trick and Sophie felt her body coming back to her. The pounding in her head and her heart began to recede. She relaxed.

Around her, the food court heaved and pushed. Fluorescents lit up the stalls but the tables themselves sat in shadow.

Patrons, a mix of casually dressed business people, sharply dressed shoppers and gaggles of students, queued six deep at the more popular outlets. Others watched midday television, without sound, from the flat screens screwed into the roof. She listened to the buzz of chatting patrons punctuated by the ringing of service bells and the occasional sneeze. Smells of beef broth and fried garlic, shrimp paste and chilli laksa, seeded themselves into her nostrils, pores and clothes.

Su Yuan placed her tray on the table and slipped into the chair opposite. Her bowl brimmed with an elegant clear broth. A few prawns, curled neatly into orange crescents, floated alongside the white flesh of scallops without roe. A pile of gleaming choy sum stems, cut on the diagonal, glistened like precious jade.

'These are the best,' Su Yuan said, pulling wooden chopsticks from a packet and snapping them apart with a quick flick of her wrists. 'Noodles like my hometown.' She rubbed the sticks together to shave off stray splinters.

'You eat seafood noodles in Kunming?' Sophie asked. The city was many miles inland.

'For sure. With frozen fish, not fresh. Here it's the same.' She took a mouthful of soup and closed her eyes. A faint smile curled the edges of her lips. '*Hen hao chi*,' she said; *delicious*. Her eyes drifted open and settled on Sophie's. They were deep brown and wide, a gaze you could drown in.

'I think maybe this place reminds you of home, too,' Su Yuan said.

Sophie considered the girl sitting across the table. Her heart beat a faster rhythm at her breast. A memory scorched through her.

Her mother's kitchen, the air thick with steam. Bone broth rolling in a pot, garlic dry-frying in a wok. Sophie at the sink, her shirt sleeves protected by floral-patterned sheaths. A leek, pale and creamy on the outside, is slit to reveal inner rings blackened with dirt. Her mother shows her how to wash it. Sophie's fingers are in the water, in her mother's hair, at her mother's neck. Wet. A gentle admonishment. A laugh and a kiss. The soup is ready. Five-spice beef with noodles.

Sophie pulled away from Su Yuan's stare, busying herself with her soup. She scooped noodles with chopsticks. 'I don't know what you mean,' she said.

For a while they ate in silence, but for the sounds of their slurping.

'The true thing is, I'm not surprised she did it,' Su Yuan said finally, resting her chopsticks against the rim of her bowl.

'You're not surprised Wendy killed herself?'

Su Yuan's eyes fixed on Sophie. 'It's not easy here,' she said. 'This country is not so friendly if you are a foreigner. It's easy to feel alone in the crowd.'

'But Wendy wasn't alone,' said Sophie, scanning her memory for everything she knew about Wendy Chan. 'She had her classmates and a boyfriend. I even went out with them once. She probably partied too hard, but she didn't seem unhappy.'

'She was alone,' Su Yuan said.

Sophie twisted her chopstick wrapper between her fingers. 'It doesn't seem a strong enough reason for Wendy to kill herself.'

'Loneliness is a real reason.'

So is heroin.

'Wendy could have gone home,' said Sophie. 'She could have returned to her family. She didn't have to jump.'

Su Yuan shook her head. 'If she'd done any of those things, she'd have failed. Her parents probably paid all they had to send her here. Or maybe she won a scholarship that would have gone to waste. If she went home early, people would know she'd failed.'

'So you think she killed herself to save face?'

'Chinese people care a lot about other people's opinions,' said Su Yuan. 'It's not a simple thing to save your family embarrassment. But it is important.' She bit her bottom lip. 'I'm sure you know something about this, Sophie. You may not have a Chinese name, but I know you are one of us.'

Sophie screwed the wrapper into a ball. She curled it into her palm and squeezed. Her nails dug into her skin. She wrestled with the feeling she'd been slit open like a fruit.

'My mother came from Hong Kong,' she said finally. 'But people don't usually guess.'

'That's because most people here don't know how to use chopsticks properly,' said Su Yuan. 'But I can tell that you've used them your whole life.'

Sophie debated whether to tell Su Yuan about the track marks she'd seen on Wendy's arms. But for what? The information would only highlight even further Wendy's obvious fall from grace. She flicked the ball of paper across the table.

'What about you?' she said. 'Do you care about what other people think?'

The girl opposite shrugged. 'No,' she said. 'And I don't care about the difficulties in this country. I'm not here to make friends.' There was hostility in Su Yuan's voice. In her eyes, though – sadness.

'Why are you here, then?'

Su Yuan pushed her bowl to the side and folded her fingers together in a white-knuckled grip. 'To find my sister.'

Sophie's stomach lurched. 'Your sister's lost?' she asked, hoping the emotion didn't show on her face.

'Yes,' Su Yuan said. 'But I will find her. I can't say any more about it now.'

'Is your sister in trouble?'

Su Yuan shook her head. 'Don't worry. I will find her.' She plucked her bag from the floor and pushed back her chair. 'Thanks for showing me this place,' she said with a grin. 'Next time I feel sad, I know where to come for noodles that remind me of home.'

'Where are you going?'

Su Yuan shrugged. 'My room,' she said. 'I'll see you at school.'

She watched as Su Yuan disappeared down the escalator. Tomorrow afternoon, the students would sit their tests at an external exam hall and most wouldn't show for revision in the morning. The new teaching term would begin next Wednesday, following a break. Sophie hoped she'd find Su Yuan's name on her list.

鬼

SOPHIE CLOSED the door of her rented Paddington terrace and slumped against it with relief. Her shoulder hurt. Afternoon classes had been cancelled for counselling and an emergency staff meeting. Then Sophie had walked across Hyde Park, down Liverpool Street, and through the Five Ways junction. She'd carried a bag of books and now her body screamed for a wheat bag and a cup of tea.

Sophie moved through the small lounge room crammed with potted plants and bookshelves and into the dining space. She dumped her book bag on the dining table, ignoring the mess that spilled out of it onto the floor. In the kitchen she disturbed three baby cockroaches: Sydney friends. They scattered across the green bench top as she reached for one of the many canisters lining the wall. Tea. She needed it like a drug. Thank fuck for Jin Tao.

Her housemate claimed the title of household tea king. Whatever the variety – Darjeeling, lapsang souchong, Indian chai, pu-erh, oolong – Jin Tao kept the house in plentiful supply. Sophie reached for the longjing – dragon well – a strong Chinese green that tasted a little bit like rice.

Three years ago, after attempts at juggling the expectations of housemates – for cooking sessions, Scrabble nights, Tuesday trivia, and girls' nights in – with her own needs, Sophie had resolved to move to the suburbs and live alone. Then she'd seen Jin Tao's newspaper ad and had decided to give the inner-city house share one more go. So far, so good. Jin Tao was a shift worker who shared Sophie's taste for Chinese food and for balancing personal time with the schedule of a busy life. He left her alone but shared his tea and his balcony when she needed to chat.

Sophie chucked her wheat bag into the microwave and watched it rotate. At the sound of the bell she took the bag and her cup of tea into the lounge room and collapsed onto the couch. Outside the wind had picked up. The newspaper stuffed up the chimney rustled and scratched. A dreary winter Wednesday. And Wendy was dead.

The needle tracks on her arm.

When had she first met Wendy? Sometime earlier in the year. Sophie had been assigned a new class. Although none of the students had known each other, many had studied at the school in the previous level, and understood the structures and the routine. Part of the routine was an English-language name: some students chose to use one, to save the repeated agony of listening to their teacher mangle the tonal sounds of their birth name. Often these were literal translations. Hence, Sophie had taught a Stone, a Tiger, a Golden and a Field. Wendy was from China, and it was in China that He Wen Yi had first selected the English name, *Wendy*. She'd told Sophie dryly that she'd decided to reject her language teacher's initial suggestion of 'Winnie'. She hadn't wanted to be named after the noise made by a horse.

Wendy had been funny. But most of the time she'd been quiet, sleepy. More than once, Sophie had had to prod Wendy with the whiteboard marker, gently reminding her to lift her drooping eyes. Could Wendy have been on the nod all those times? Was there a drug problem that she just hadn't noticed?

Dad would be so proud. Not. She'd been brought up to look for the cracks in stories and appearances, to seek out anomalies in the otherwise mundane. Yet she'd missed this. And now Wendy was dead.

Just as little David Qin was still missing.

Thorny pain tore through Sophie, engulfing her as it so often did in the moments when she let her guard down and allowed herself to think of David. She would never forgive herself. Sophie had resigned herself to that fact. She would do anything to bring David back. But at the same time, she could do nothing. He was gone and his beautiful mother, Li Hua, had forgiven her. Li Hua had set Sophie free to move on with her sterile, Western life, away from the pain and the constant searching and the false hopes. And Sophie had seized the opportunity, had run from Li Hua and Beijing; fled back to Australia, to Sydney, where she was unknown. In Sydney, neither Seamus's mistakes nor David's disappearance could haunt her. Sophie's past could remain buried.

And now this.

Sophie sipped her tea, blinked away tears, allowing the leaves to work their soothing wonder. Wendy was dead: a limp body on the concrete, face mashed to a paste. Who would grieve for that girl? Would Wendy's mother double over and howl in pain, the way Li Hua had? Would she accept the fact that her daughter had travelled all the way to Australia only to throw herself from her language school window?

Loneliness is a real reason.

Sophie scanned her memories. She pulled up a rainy night in June. A Sichuan restaurant. Sophie and Jin Tao on one side of a corner table, Wendy and her boyfriend on the other. White tablecloths and peach napkins. A feast of a meal: shiny jellyfish salad, hot boiled beef, whole barramundi fried in chilli bean sauce, pickled snake beans and fire-exploded lamb kidney. The fierce afterglow of the Sichuan peppers danced on their palates. She remembered Wendy, happy, drinking Tsingtao and placing soft kisses on her boyfriend's neck. She remembered Jin Tao, unruly.

Sophie searched her mind for the boyfriend's name. He might be able to help. The memories of the night's scents and textures were crisp but the name escaped her. Was he still friends with Wendy? Could he offer some explanation for the marks on Wendy's skin?

The revolutionary Mao Zedong clock on the mantle read six. Jin Tao would be preparing for dinner service.

Sophie chucked the wheat bag on the coffee table and collected her helmet from the shelf by the door.

The wind bit as she wheeled her bike into the night.

HAN HONG woke from a terrible dream. Someone had put her in a box, loaded her into a vehicle and driven her away over some very rough terrain. She'd been smashed against the sides of the box and the rough wood had splintered her skin. Scratchy hessian, damp and tied tight, rubbed at her eyes.

She smelled eggy methane fumes mixed with the tangy scents of onion and garlic. She could hear music, dark and electronic, like something from a video game.

'I'm at the restaurant, sorting supplies.'

Han Hong stiffened, her mind rushing full throttle to complete wakefulness. This wasn't a dream. Someone else was here with her in the darkness. She recognised the voice – it was one of them.

'What time will she be leaving?'

A one-sided conversation. Han Hong's heart leapt. This meant a phone.

Han Hong scoured her memory for details of her time in the box. The dream had prompted memories of her transportation here, to this dark place. Had the trip taken one hour or two? Or had they driven all night? She couldn't remember. But they were obviously somewhere with mobile coverage. And that meant a chance.

Fully awake now, Han Hong tried to assess her situation.

She was cold, dressed only in a T-shirt and underpants. She couldn't feel her arms. She forced her mind to seek out the different parts of her body, assess herself for pain and injury, discover whether she was still whole. Her hands were pinned behind her, tied together with some kind of thin cable. Her fingers ground into the concrete, mashed into the floor by her weight. Her legs were crossed and strapped at the ankles. She rolled to her left. There was space here, in this place that smelled like her dad's cellar.

At least she was no longer stuck in the box.

Han Hong bashed her head against something hard and metallic. Ripples of pain washed through her temples and jerked down her spine. She groaned and rolled to her right. She felt more metal; it pressed into her forehead, its mesh pattern sinking into her skin.

'Shut up!'

The voice again, from somewhere ahead of her. Raised, demanding. Talking to her.

'I wish it hadn't happened.' The voice softened again as the man returned to the phone. 'But business is business and we need to clean this up. If they find the real girl and she talks, we're done.'

Han Hong struggled to make sense of the conversation. The real girl?

And then he was beside her and she could smell the garlic on his breath.

'It's your lucky night,' he said. 'I've got some business to attend to. You get the night off.'

She listened to his footsteps as he moved back across the room. Then the creak of a hinge and the slap of wood against wood as a door slammed shut.

She was alone.

Han Hong mustered all her strength and stretched her neck high. Her abdominal muscles screamed in outrage and her head felt heavy but, through the fuzz, she recognised the sensation of the top of her scalp touching a ceiling of some kind.

Exhausted, she lay back against the concrete and allowed a tear to run down one cheek. It touched her mouth and she savoured the moisture, even though the salt stung her lips.

So this is what it feels like, she thought, to be caged.

THE ROAD shone slick with the evening's earlier rain. Sophie hung a right into Victoria Street, cycling past her favourite gelato store and an enoteca exuding Darlinghurst cool. At the Cross, she admired the giant Coke sign in spite of herself. Kings Cross was no Siam Square, no Wangfujing Street, but something about the electronic billboard suggested good times, party times, ahead.

She skirted down Darlinghurst Road, past the sex shops, porn shops, pizza joints and ragged junkies looking for a score. Around the corner was Blue Lotus. The restaurant sat on a leafy side street behind the main drag. Home to expensive real estate, a couple of exclusive clubs and some sophisticated dining options, this was where the trendy came to enjoy the sense of danger promised by Sydney's seedy side without actually having to dabble in it. Blue Lotus served food inspired by the cuisines of China's Yunnan, Sichuan and Guizhou provinces. In his role as head chef, Jin Tao used locally sourced ingredients, organic produce and only sustainably farmed fish. This marked his prices up but gave his restaurant an edge, allowing the cocktail set to indulge with a conscience.

After decades of ginger-steamed scallops and sweet and sour pork, Sydney had begun its love affair with China's sultry heart. Foodies flocked to restaurants specialising in the tastes of China's peasant cuisine, relishing the tang of the Sichuan peppers, the punch of pickled chilli and the salty heat of fresh black beans. Blue Lotus matched this food with its atmosphere. The long, narrow dining area featured a single dark wood table and smooth benches running along either side. The no-reservation policy meant diners turned up early to bag a space at the communal dining table and indulge in a drink at the bar out the front. Jin Tao's sommelier was famous for his detailed knowledge of Old and New World wines. And for his mandarin-infused vodka.

Sophie chained her bike to a pole in the alley behind the restaurant. She scuffed across the cobblestones to the kitchen door. Through the window she saw benches laden with food: chicken breasts, shallots, baskets of dried chillis, giant carafes of brown sesame oil. She jerked open the door. Cooking scents hit her: garlic, star anise, cinnamon, chilli oil.

The sous chef, Stu, nodded hello. His hands were buried deep inside a fish. He indicated the burners at the back of the kitchen where Sophie spied Jin Tao's shiny head. 'Go on through,' he said. 'He's checking the pork belly.'

Sophie strode over the tiles to where Jin Tao stood examining the contents of a clay pot.

'You have to try this,' he said. He held out a spoonful of glistening pork belly for her to taste. The skin gleamed black from a reduced soy glaze. A white sliver of fat separated the skin from the meat.

'Hello to you too,' said Sophie. She took the spoon into her mouth. The pork tasted like velvet. 'That,' she groaned, 'is sensational.'

Jin Tao winked. 'I got it right tonight,' he said. 'The crowd is going to go sick. You want some more?'

Sophie waved the spoon away. 'Already eaten,' she lied.

'You'll be a celebrity one day, I know it.' She paused, watching a faint pink creep into Jin Tao's cheeks. 'Can I talk to you for a minute?'

Jin Tao put the lid back on the pot and washed his hands at a basin. He jerked his head towards the storeroom. 'Step into my office.'

The storeroom smelled like garlic and shrimp paste and its shelved walls were lined with tins and jars: pickled tofu, deep-fried shallots, dried seaweed, nuts, peppers. Jin Tao slid the door closed. He picked up an open bag of sunflower seeds, shook some into his palm, and offered it to Sophie. 'My secret stash.'

She took a handful, putting a seed in her mouth and cracking the shell between her teeth. The kernel slipped out easily and she ground it to a paste. 'Do you remember that dinner we went to a couple of months ago, with my student?'

Jin Tao chewed thoughtfully. 'More information. There've been loads.'

'At the Sichuan place.'

Jin Tao picked some more seeds from the bag. 'The jellyfish salad,' he said. 'It rocked.'

Sophie smiled. Jin Tao remembered anything, as long as he could associate it with food. 'Do you remember my student Wendy?'

Jin Tao nodded. 'And the other guy, Tae Hun.'

Sophie held out her hand for more seeds. 'That's it, I'd forgotten his name.'

'Lucky bastard.' Jin Tao scowled. 'That Wendy's cute. Bit weird, but cute.'

'What do you mean?'

Jin Tao cracked a seed between his teeth. 'She spent the whole night cacking herself, like she was stoned or something. She reckoned the walls had ears.'

I don't remember. I've forgotten the details.

'All I really remember is the food,' Sophie said. 'And I wasn't even drinking.'

'You want to go out with them again? Have a night on the tiles with wacky Wendy?'

In her mind, Sophie saw Wendy's mangled face. Blood on the concrete. Her stomach lurched. Her legs felt weak. She dropped the sunflower seeds to the floor. Took a step back.

'Soph?'

Behind her, a bag of dried shiitakes provided support. Sophie leaned into it, feeling the sharp ends of the mushrooms stick into her back.

'Wendy died today,' Sophie said. Her words came out in a croak. 'She jumped.'

Jin Tao's face was perfectly still, a sunflower seed perched neatly between his teeth. He blew the shell from his lips. Sophie watched it flutter to the ground.

'Holy shit,' he said. He rubbed a hand across his head. 'Are you okay?'

Sophie bit down on her tongue. Now was not the time to cry. 'Actually, I can't stop thinking about her.' She brought her hand to her pocket, wanting to ram it in. For the second time in a day she felt raw, exposed. Jin Tao reached out and touched her fingers. Then he took her hand and pulled her gently to him.

'You need a hug,' he said.

'It's all right,' she said. But Jin Tao's arms were already around her, holding her.

Sophie surrendered. In the fluorescent bright of the storeroom, she actually felt safe.

At the end of the long hug, Jin Tao stepped back. He lifted

Sophie's chin with a slim finger. 'I should take you home,' he said.

She dropped to the floor to gather the spilled sunflower kernels. 'I have my bike.'

Jin Tao didn't miss a beat. 'I'll dink you.'

'It's fine, you've helped me by giving me Tae Hun's name.'

Jin Tao retrieved a dustpan from the corner and squatted beside Sophie. 'Poor bastard,' he said. 'You going to write him a note?'

'I need to find him first,' she said. They finished clearing the seeds. Sophie stood up and slid open the door to the kitchen. The sounds of the evening rush hour swept around them. 'You'd better get back to your pork.'

Jin Tao raised an eyebrow, held up a forefinger. 'One minute,' he said. 'Wait here.'

Sophie hovered in the doorway and threaded the toggles on her coat. Jin Tao reappeared and pressed a plastic bag into her hand. She didn't have to look to know what it held: a container of rice, some sticky pork, probably some vegetables.

'You'll want to eat later,' he said.

Sophie left the warmth of the kitchen and headed back out into the night.

A GIRL named Wendy Chan left the noodle shop at ten. Thoughts of a strange woman's afternoon suicide sluiced through her mind's eye. In the little restaurant across from Central Station she'd tried to enjoy a beef tendon soup, the broth thick and heady and almost as good as her mother's. The flavours had made her homesick. What she wouldn't give for an evening in her mother's apartment, sipping tea, eating crackers and watching soap operas on the TV.

Wendy pulled her coat collar closer to her neck. No matter how many layers she wore, the chill always found its way into her bones. She had thought Australia would be dry and hot. This had turned out to be a myth, along with the idea that the people were friendly. Wendy found that most people ignored her or stared impatiently at her mouth as she stumbled over her English when asking for directions. On the bus out to the beach, a woman in a tracksuit had shouted at her and called her a nipper. She'd looked the word up on the internet and found it meant surf lifesaver; odd, given she could barely swim.

And then there was her job. Wendy marched on into the night, noting the tickle in the pit of her stomach that even the hot noodles hadn't managed to calm. If her mother knew what she'd been up to, she'd probably collapse to the floor in tears.

Her mum hadn't slaved away at the factory all these years for her daughter to turn into a common prostitute. Not that she was quite there yet.

But serving drinks semi-naked to leering men was almost as bad. She'd done it because of the money, cash in hand, and because so many other students seemed to be doing it too. She didn't want to miss out. And it seemed a foolproof system was in place. Nobody had noticed her absence from school and her student visa remained intact. If this was the opportunity Australia offered, she needed to seize it with both hands.

But it made her feel dirty.

Wendy turned onto Harris Street and slouched past the ABC building. Streetlights bounced shadows along the deserted road. The postcard brilliance of Sydney Harbour seemed a long way from here. She had so looked forward to her trip to Australia. Space and freedom lived here, she'd been told. But, encaged in a small foreign-student world, excluded from the wider community, she felt trapped.

That night at the Cheers bar. She'd drunk too many beers and decided becoming a waitress with benefits was a good idea. It seemed every second person she met there was talking about the same thing. She heard about the money they were making and the ease of flouting the visa regulations. Wendy had just wanted to fit in. She'd agreed to go to an audition, and the rest was history.

Her apartment was close. It would be closer still if she cut through the TAFE. Wendy skipped through the campus gates and headed down the lane between two buildings. The walls formed a narrow passage. She increased her speed as she thought of her bed and her hot water bottle. Soon she would be warm. She would pull the blankets over her head and try to forget she was here in Australia, a long way from home and from everything she knew. She would try to forget she felt so terribly ashamed of herself and so terribly alone.

The wind whistled through the tunnel and Wendy's ears. Lost in her thoughts, she didn't hear the footsteps behind her. She felt only a warm surge of adrenaline as a gloved hand closed over her throat and her nostrils filled with a chemical burn.

Wendy's last sensations before the darkness were not fear, but resignation and disappointment. It was all going to end here.

This Australian adventure had not panned out as she'd hoped.

SOPHIE EMERGED from the lift to the smell of burned toast. The school's director of studies ran past her and down the corridor. She noted he wore a yellow fire warden's hat.

'Don't worry, there's no major emergency.' Chuck smiled, falling into step with Sophie on the way to the staffroom. 'The police were in early with Pete and he decided to eat breakfast here. Somebody should teach the guy how to use the grill.'

In the prep room, people worked without the usual pre-class chatter. Teachers perched quietly behind their desks, correcting papers, assembling files, avoiding eye contact and conversation. The burnt toast had tripped the heating system. The air clung, cold and damp. Motion fell in time to the photocopier's slow, grinding beat. Sophie's lips prickled from dehydration and nervous energy. She walked slowly to her desk at the back of the room.

Lenny, Sophie's desk companion, cleared his throat. He wiped a grain of rice from the corner of his mouth. 'They don't know how to deal with this,' he muttered, his voice laden with contempt.

Sophie looked around the room. Several teachers sought to share her gaze, severity in their glances. 'Deal with what?'

'Life,' spat Lenny. 'This is the real world. Teaching English in a Japanese cram school can't prepare you for it.'

Sophie unloaded her shoulder bag. At sixty-eight, Lenny looked better than most men did at forty. He'd lived in seven countries. He spoke four languages and had forty-five years of teaching experience. And didn't everyone else know about it.

'Look at them,' Lenny continued, between mouthfuls of California roll. 'Shocked into silence for once in their lives. Oh, for this peace and quiet every day of the week.'

Sophie opened her lesson plan and tried to concentrate. But all she could think of was Wendy. Her face on the concrete. A pink and red mash.

'Lenny, did you know her?'

He finished his breakfast and snapped his lunchbox shut. 'Who?'

'Wendy. The girl who died.'

He stood up. 'To tell you the truth,' he said, opening his arms wide in a stretch, 'I'm not interested in trying to remember.'

Sophie watched him walk to his locker and stash the lunchbox.

'Talk about losing it,' whispered Chuck, sitting opposite. 'The guy helps Pete with the timetables but he doesn't know one student from the next.'

Pete entered the prep room still wearing his fire warden's helmet. Beside him stood an older man in a well-cut wool suit. The two of them scanned the room. From his chair at the front, Tim made a face and pointed at Pete's head. Pete snatched the helmet away.

'Some important information,' Pete said. Sophie strained to hear. It sounded less like an announcement and more like the second part of a sentence. Pete spoke softly at the best of times; frailly, like an older person who's lost their sense of self. More than once she had wondered how a bloke like Pete – shy, disorganised, unable to delegate – had made it so far in this business. Teachers like him usually got demolished in their first month in the classroom. But perhaps that's why Pete had succeeded as an administrator: his job meant he didn't often have to engage with people.

He cleared his throat. 'Firstly I'd like to introduce you all to a visitor,' he said, indicating the man in the suit. 'This is Michael Disney, from the Association of English Language Centres. He'll be with us for the next few days, running an audit of the school's attendance records.' He paused. 'I trust you'll make him feel very much at home.'

It sounded like an order.

Disney raised his hand in a wave. 'I'll do my best to keep out of your way,' he said, his voice booming.

'Which brings us to the matter of the day,' said Pete. 'The apparent suicide – and the police are calling it that until they've had a chance to finish their inquiries – is a matter of great concern.' He spoke louder now, his confidence returning. 'Of greater concern is the revelation that Wendy ...' Pete faltered, glancing around the room.

From his position by the lockers, Lenny exhaled. 'We can't bear the suspense, Pete,' he drawled.

'Wendy was not who we thought she was,' Pete said, his glare falling on Lenny.

Sophie registered a collective intake of breath as the staff processed Pete's words. Her mind replayed the final images it had captured before the screen went up around Wendy's body – that pale, lifeless arm. Needle marks, brown and definite, like a snakeskin tattoo.

'Actually, we don't know who the girl on the footpath was,' Pete said. 'What we do know is that she wasn't Wendy Chan.'

A confused murmur rose above the sound of the photocopier

as people turned to colleagues, concern and confusion etched on their faces.

'Let me make this clear,' Pete said, his voice raised above the din. 'The girl on the footpath yesterday attended this school and some of you may have taught her. She went by the name of Wendy and she was enrolled here under that name. But the police have, this morning, informed me that what we have is a case of mistaken identity.'

'Hence the audit,' muttered Lenny.

'How have they established that?' Sophie's voice carried above the chatter.

Pete paused, ran a thin tongue across his lips. 'The police have their methods,' he said. 'I'm not an investigator.'

Sophie sat back in her seat, rocked. What other secrets had 'Wendy' been hiding? And where was the real Wendy Chan?

Pete's voice drilled into Sophie's thoughts.

'... a very serious matter and I need each staff member to exercise extra vigilance when it comes to the roll. I shouldn't need to remind anyone that these are legal documents. Should you note inconsistencies in student attendance this week, please draw them to my or Michael's attention immediately. We'll pass the information on to the police.'

Pete glanced across at his companion. 'Did you want to say a few words?'

Michael Disney cleared his throat. 'I'll be interviewing each of you individually over the course of the next week as part of my investigation into visa regulation adherence among the language schools in the city,' he said. 'This is nothing for you as teachers to worry yourselves about – we haven't singled your school out specifically – but because of Wendy Chan's disappearance, it was decided that United English is a good place to start.'

A few mumbled questions. Pete held up a hand, pleading for quiet. 'There'll be time for questions over the course of the week. Feel free to bail Michael up in the staffroom or by the coffee machine or wherever you happen to catch him. He doesn't bite.'

Pete nodded and the two men backed out the door. Sophie felt the tension lift as she watched her colleagues shake their heads and discuss Pete's announcement, making jokes, again beginning to jostle in the queue for the photocopier.

Across from her, Chuck had noted the change in atmosphere as well. 'Hear that?' he asked Sophie.

'What?'

'The chatter.'

'People talking, yeah.'

'It's relief.'

Sophie stared at Chuck. 'Relief from what?'

'From thinking she was somebody we knew.'

A hoot of laughter sounded from the corner of the room. Chuck leaned forward, beckoning Sophie closer. 'I know it's sick, but somehow it doesn't seem so awful now. Don't you think?'

Sophie swallowed the bile rising to her throat. 'I'm sorry, Chuck,' she said, pushing back her chair. 'I absolutely disagree.'

Over in student administration, Sophie found the intake officer, Maria, eating banana bread with her morning coffee.

'Want some?' Maria held out a thick slab of the stuff, its surface glistening with butter.

'Pass,' Sophie said.

'You're too skinny,' complained Maria, licking a finger and then wiping it on her pants. 'But if you won't let me put some meat on those bones, what else can I help you with?'

Sophie handed her a slip of paper. She'd written Tae Hun's

name on it in black pen. 'I think this guy is a student at our school,' she said. 'I need to talk to him.'

Maria took the paper. 'Not ringing any bells but it's a fairly uncommon Korean name, Sophie.' She shook awake her computer. 'You must know that, though. Being Asian.'

Right.

'Pretty sure my birth certificate says I'm an Aussie.'

Maria smiled, like Sophie had told a joke. 'Got a family name too?'

'Nuh uh.'

Squinting as she pushed her spectacles up her nose, Maria typed the name into her database. Her forehead furrowed into a frown.

'What do you know,' she said.

Sophie moved behind the desk to peer over Maria's shoulder. 'Tell me.'

'We've had two Tae Huns enrolled in the past six months,' said Maria, pointing to the screen. 'One is currently a student in lower elementary ...'

'That's not him,' said Sophie. 'This guy's English is stronger.'

'The other guy ...' Maria scrolled the cursor down the computer screen. Sophie saw a panel on the right side of the screen flash red.

'... here it is.' Maria highlighted the information. 'He left the school a couple of months back. It says he fell behind in fees.'

Sophie rocked back on her heels. 'Any idea where he went?'

Maria studied the computer screen. 'We don't keep records of the competition, Sophie,' she said. 'But here's something that might help. He's down as working at Seoul Cafe in Haymarket. If he's still in Sydney, you might find him there.'

Sophie grabbed a piece of paper and scribbled down the name of the restaurant.

Maria reached for her banana bread. 'What's this guy done? Broken some girl's heart?'

Sophie smiled. 'Maybe,' she said. 'That's what I want to find out.'

HE'D BROUGHT her broth again. He fed it to her with a flat-bottomed spoon. It reminded Han Hong of the blue and white porcelain soup set her mother kept at home, under the bed. The thought made her want to cry. She pushed it far away and concentrated on the task at hand.

She leaned forward, rested her forehead against the bars of her cage and parted her lips. If she bent her head down to an awkward angle, she could find the rim of the spoon with her mouth and sip delicately at the soup. She'd been slow in developing her technique. In the beginning, she'd knocked the spoon frequently, spilling its contents and wincing – not from the physical pain but from the emotional distress of wasting her nourishment. But hunger made her resourceful. She'd started to get the hang of it. She remembered the story her father told her, about his time living through the great famine. He and his brothers had taken to the fields, following mice to their burrows. They sought not only to eat the mice but to steal the few precious kernels of grain that the creatures had stored carefully for the winter. That had been a time of great hunger, and her father and his brothers had used their resources to survive. Now was her time to do the same.

Han Hong swallowed a mouthful of broth. It tasted rich, the result of long-simmered pork bones with generous amounts of ginger and spring onion. She detected notes of white pepper and Chinese rice wine. She guessed, from the thin texture, that he was feeding her a master stock, a base broth yet to be turned into a soup.

Oh, to strike out at her captor and spew the hot soup over his face.

The bars of her cage prevented it. She had no choice but to take the small sustenance he offered, use it to build her strength, so that when the opportunity arose she could use it to escape.

It wasn't much of a plan, but it was the only one she had. Han Hong leaned forward again and sipped.

STUDENTS DOMINATED the lunch crowd at Seoul Cafe. They sat in groups, sporting hip-hop gear, gold chains and dyed hair.

Sophie stopped at the entrance to the dining room and scanned the interior. The restaurant had been difficult to find – she'd entered via a lift hidden within a newsagent on Liverpool Street. A young waiter hurried over with a menu. Sophie indicated she wanted a table for one, and he led her to a small booth by a window. The restaurant smelled of pickled cabbage and meat. Sophie leaned into her seat, tuned to the sizzle of fat hitting hotplates. The steam from the barbecue settled into her shirt. She already felt clammy and by the time she got out of here, she would reek.

'Something to drink?' Most of the diners were indulging in midday soju sessions. They held thimbles of the potent spirit in the air with gusto.

Sophie nodded. 'Some tea.'

She looked out the window and down to the street below. Lunchtime pedestrians headed west. She flipped through the picture menu and, when the waiter returned with her tea, she selected rice cakes and kimchi soup.

'And I'm looking for one of your staff,' she said, handing back the menu.

'Excuse me?' The waiter studied Sophie, his face a furrow of confusion. 'My English is not so good.' He smiled apologetically.

'A waiter,' said Sophie. 'His name is Tae Hun. Do you know him?'

Sophie watched a vein pop out on the boy's temple as he leaned in closer. 'Excuse me?'

'Tae Hun,' said Sophie, raising her voice above the noise of a rowdy table beside her. No doubt she'd mangled the pronunciation. 'I'm looking for Tae Hun.'

The boy shook his head, miserably. 'My English is not so good,' he mumbled. 'One minute.'

Sophie waited. She took a sip of her tea. Her muscles relaxed.

'Can I help you?'

Sophie looked up. In front of her stood Tae Hun.

'Sophie.' Tae Hun's face drained of colour. He placed a hand on the table, as though to steady himself. 'Do you remember me?'

'I came looking for you.'

Tae Hun slid onto the bench seat opposite.

'Have you heard the news?'

'You mean Wendy?' He looked at the table, straightened the mat with smooth fingers. 'I didn't know she felt so ...' He searched for the right word. He looked up at Sophie, his eyes wide. 'I didn't know she felt so sad.'

'Did you see her the day she died?' Sophie asked. 'Had anything changed?'

Tae Hun leaned forward. 'Oh no,' he said quickly. 'You don't understand. I hadn't seen Wendy for many weeks.'

'I thought you were friends?'

'She dumped me.'

'She wasn't who she said she was.'

Tae Hun scratched at his chin. 'I heard this,' he said. 'But to me, she was Wendy.' He paused, as though searching for something. 'For foreign students,' he said, 'this city is not so friendly. It's not easy.'

'I know.'

'It's not easy to be a foreigner,' he continued. 'We are students together. We share our experiences here, not our history.'

Sophie looked at Tae Hun. She knew how it felt to be a foreigner.

Laowai! On ice-cold Beijing days, she'd wandered the streets, inhaling China's fragrance: drain water, coal dust, chicken fat and skin. The place was part of her heritage and yet she'd felt so lonely and pined so much for home.

'I wish I could have helped,' Sophie said.

Tae Hun examined her closely, like someone trying to unlock a code.

'Can I tell you something?' he asked. 'A secret?'

Sophie nodded. 'I'm good at those.'

'Nine o'clock tonight,' he said. 'The Three Monkeys.'

JUSTIN HOLMES entered the store from the laneway. The shop took up space behind a Chinese butcher and backed onto the lane. He wrinkled his nose in distaste. The lane reeked of garbage and the refuse from the butcher shop. It hadn't rained, but he'd had to leap over several puddles to avoid ruining his shoes.

The entrance led to a narrow passageway. A single bulb glowed from its metal cage. Justin pushed through the plastic flaps at the end of the passage and stepped into the shop. It smelled of fried food, a relief to his nostrils after the scents of blood and offal in the lane. House music played quietly from speakers mounted high above his head. At the counter stood the shopkeeper, a man of about thirty – built, tattooed, shiny metal sticking out from his face. He flicked Justin a momentary glance and looked away again, more interested in his dinner.

At the back of the room, a man in a cabbie's uniform examined the range of dildos. Disgusting. Justin unbuttoned his suit coat and headed for his usual shelf – the DVDs.

Making a selection. This part was always exciting. Justin liked to take his time, picking each case up, examining the cover. But tonight the experience was tainted by a growing sense of disappointment – he'd seen many of these titles before, and the others looked tame. Justin realised he was growing bored with the usual fare. He wanted something harder.

Justin sensed the shopkeeper's eyes on him. Shit. He preferred to keep his exchanges to a minimum. It was bad enough that he had to see the same guy behind the counter every week. He never made eye contact and he'd kidded himself that the guy didn't remember him, never recognised him. But clearly that was untrue. Justin decided he would have to start going somewhere else. The question was, where? No other adult store had as wide a range as this one. No other store provided the convenience of proximity to work combined with privacy and the pure visual exhilaration of such a premium product. He didn't trust the internet. He didn't want to be tracked.

As he considered this, Justin realised that the shopkeeper had approached. He turned his head. The guy had a neat silver pin through the pink flesh connecting his upper lip to his gum. Ouch. Justin liked pain, but not that kind. What would possess a man to do that to himself?

Justin realised he was staring at the shopkeeper's lip. The guy didn't seem to mind. He just stood there, smiling. Justin put his hands in his pockets, eyeballed the guy.

'What?'

The shopkeeper took a folded piece of paper from his shirt pocket and offered it to him. Justin glanced at it, his hands still firmly stuck in his pockets.

'In case you'd like a bigger selection,' the shopkeeper said. 'For special clients. We deliver, pick up, whatever. More discreet than online.'

Justin took a moment to digest the shopkeeper's words. The last thing he wanted to become was a *special client*. He'd have to find another store, a place where he could again be anonymous. But the idea of a bigger selection appealed to him. The possibilities were tantalising.

At that moment, the cabbie approached. He carried a massive black penis-shaped contraption in his hands.

'Is this the biggest you've got?'

The shopkeeper turned towards the cabbie. Justin seized his courage, grabbed the paper from the shopkeeper's hand and pushed past him, shoving the cabbie roughly to one side. He stalked through the plastic flap, increasing his pace as he fled along the corridor and out into the alley.

He cursed as garbage water splashed around his ankles and seeped into his shoes.

SOPHIE ENTERED the Three Monkeys hotel on George Street at ten minutes to nine. She scanned the room. A few suits mingled over the last of their after-work drinks. A group of men in rugby jumpers watched the final stages of a game on the telly. Sophie ordered a soda and sat at a table by the window. Took out her notepad and pen. Outside, George Street buzzed with young people dressed up for a night out. They walked in groups of five or six, heavily made-up girls hanging onto the arms of their boyfriends, young men with trendy mullet cuts and skinny jeans. They smoked cigarettes, sipped bubble tea and laughed.

Then Sophie saw Tae Hun. He mooched along the footpath, an American baseball cap on his head, headphones jammed to his ears. A boy.

And then he was across from her, placing a schooner on the bench. Sophie smiled, raised her glass. 'Cheers.'

Tae Hun clinked his glass against hers. 'It's true,' he said. 'Australians make better beer than Koreans.'

'Is that right?' Sophie laughed. 'I can't believe you'd admit it.'

Tae Hun shrugged. 'We make soju,' he said. 'And better food. And our women dress best.' He motioned to a group of girls standing outside the pub window. They wore short skirts and sloppy, off-the-shoulder knitted jumpers, loads of jewellery, ankle boots, dangly earrings, pretty printed scarves. 'Korean girls dress more like women.'

Sophie looked down at her jeans and purple sneakers. 'How about Chinese girls?' she asked. 'Is that why you liked Wendy? Because she dressed well?'

Tae Hun took a sip of his beer and placed the glass carefully on the coaster. 'Wendy liked to have fun. That's what I liked about her,' he said. 'And I liked her smell.'

'What do you mean?'

'She had this perfume, very sexy, like spices. Now when I think about her, all I can remember is her smell.'

'Scent can do that to you.'

Tae Hun gazed out the window. 'We had fun together but we dated for two weeks only. She dumped me and I don't know why. And what's the matter about it? I don't even know who she was.'

He took a long drink from his glass, draining it.

'You said you wanted to tell me something,' she said. 'Was it about Wendy?'

'I want to forget her.'

'Okay,' said Sophie. 'So, what did you want to say?'

Tae Hun looked around. The bar had filled and electronic music pumped through the speakers from the space upstairs. 'I need more to drink,' he said. 'Can I buy you one?'

Sophie tapped her glass. 'I'm okay.'

'You're an Aussie who doesn't drink?'

The image of Su Yuan, so perceptive, flashed through Sophie's mind. 'It doesn't agree with me,' she said. She took a breath. Fuck it. 'It's an Asian thing.'

The boy looked puzzled. 'But you're not Asian.'

'Buy me a beer and I'll blush rose for you.'

Tae Hun pushed off his stool. 'It's fine,' he said, uninterested. 'I think it's good when girls don't drink.'

Sophie watched him – a skinny kid trying to act like a man.

After his third beer, Tae Hun began to open up. He played with a coaster as he spoke.

'After Wendy broke with me, I didn't know what to do. I really liked her, you know?' He looked into his drink. His voice became a mumble. 'I went to a dancing club.' His face turned a shade of red.

'It's okay, Tae Hun,' said Sophie. 'Whatever you tell me, I won't repeat it.'

'This club, it's a place where girls dance without their clothes.'

'You're not the first man on the planet to do that, Tae Hun,' said Sophie. 'It's not that big a deal.'

An impatient scowl crossed the young man's face. He pushed the hair out of his eyes to give Sophie a deliberate stare. 'Yeah, I know it's okay,' he said, with a sudden sarcastic drawl. 'We do this in Seoul, too. I have no problem with it.'

Sophie felt her own blush creep. She'd patronised him and he'd called her on it. 'What's the problem then?'

'At the club I saw a friend from school.'

'In the audience?'

'No. A woman. Dancing on the table.'

Sophie sat back. 'Is this a classmate from our school, the place where I teach?'

Tae Hun shook his head. 'No, my new school. I go to Central English. It's cheaper. She's not a classmate but just someone I know from the school. This woman, her name is Han Hong. She didn't see me, but I took a photo of her. I went back to the club the next night and I saw her. And again and again. It was like I was keeping an eye on her. Making sure she was okay.'

Sophie sipped her drink and regarded him. 'You're a nice guy, Tae Hun.'

He waved away the compliment. 'Not nice,' he said. 'I liked Han Hong. I could not understand why she would do this job. Could she need the money that bad? I decided I would speak to her. I'd find her a job in my restaurant. She would never have to work at the club again.'

'Told you. What a nice guy.'

Tae Hun leaned closer. 'But then our term changed and she didn't come back to school. I saw her at the club a couple more times but then she stopped turning up there, too. At first I thought she'd moved into another class at a different time, but I looked and looked and I didn't find her.'

'Did you ask?'

He pulled off his baseball cap and placed it on the table, scraped a hand through scruffy dyed hair. 'Something's wrong but I don't know the details,' he said. 'She's been working at this place and it's illegal ... I didn't want to draw attention, get her into trouble.'

'Maybe she's taking a break.'

He shrugged. 'Maybe. But I went back to the club and she didn't arrive there, either. She's disappeared.'

'When was the term change?'

'Two and a half weeks ago,' he said. 'There is something strange going on and I'm worried.' He peered out the window onto George Street. 'Maybe she has done to herself like Wendy. Maybe she's killed herself.'

Maybe she's become a junkie. Sophie kicked her feet against the narrow rail running under the table. 'Why are you telling me this, Tae Hun? A regular person would just contact the police.'

'No.' His voice was defiant. 'These kinds of places aren't legal. I cannot tell the police I went there.'

'If you really cared about Han Hong, you would tell someone.'

'Yes,' said Tae Hun. 'So I am telling you.' He pulled out a phone and scanned the menu. He pushed the screen across the table to Sophie.

'This is the picture I took,' he said. 'This is Han Hong.'

Sophie glanced at the picture and took a breath. A chill settled between her shoulder blades. Not because the girl in the photo was naked or because the girl's make-up was smeared and smudged. But because the girl in the photo looked so young: a teenager, seventeen at best.

Tae Hun had lowered his eyes to the table. 'I don't know what you think I should do,' he mumbled. 'But I really don't want you to go to the police.'

What to say? If Tae Hun was telling the truth and the club was illegal, then a normal person would take both Tae Hun and his photograph down to the nearest station to make a report. But what of Han Hong then? Would she be charged, imprisoned, fined and deported? And would it stop anything? Would it really make a difference to a trade so long established that the average punter turned a blind eye to the suspect goings-on? It was far better to find the girl and talk to her, try to convince her to turn her back on the seedy world, coax her back to the classroom, offer some friendship and support.

She wrote her number on the back of a coaster. 'Message me the picture and give me time to think about it,' she said. 'I won't involve the police, you can trust me on that.'

Tae Hun smiled something like appreciation and drained his glass. 'Thank you,' he said simply. Then he picked up his baseball cap from the table. 'I should go.'

女孩

GLIDING DOWN the hills of Liverpool Street, Sophie couldn't shake the image of Han Hong. It was something about the eyes. She'd read something in them, an emotion she recognised but couldn't quite recall. Not fear, or loneliness. Those eyes communicated something subtler, but equally powerful. Sophie bent her head against the wind and pedalled hard on the incline towards Glenmore Road. The cold air scoured her cheeks and the hill beneath her wheels made her thigh muscles scream. Then Sophie realised it. In Han Hong's eyes she'd recognised a state she'd seen and experienced – in her students, when language difficulties overwhelmed them; in her dear friend Li Hua, on that dreadful day when everything had changed forever; in herself now, as she rose to the challenge of Liverpool Street. Resignation. The girl in the picture gazed out with dead, fatalistic eyes, resigned to her role, as dancer, entertainer, stripper, naked woman. Maybe she'd resigned herself to her fate.

But surely she hadn't travelled all the way to Australia for that?

By the time Sophie wheeled her bike into the hallway, it was a few minutes past midnight. She moved swiftly to the kitchen to brew a pot of oolong. There, leaning against the bench, she sipped the warm brown brew and let the tea leaves soothe her. She placed the terracotta teapot on a tray with a cup and padded up the steep carpeted stairs to her sanctuary.

The room glowed warm from the bamboo-shaded lamp on the dresser. Sophie cast her eyes around, relishing the immediate nourishing effect on her. She loved this space, not for the high ceiling or the intricately carved ceiling rose or the wide window that looked out onto the slanted roofs of

Paddington. She loved it for the objects it contained, each of which held meanings and memories of different places, people and experiences. She loved the soft lines of the sculpted stone woman she'd watched being shaped on a beach in Vietnam; the red teacups passed down from a beloved grandmother; the glass jewellery dish that glowed orange in the lamplight; the intricately woven pink, purple and indigo wall hangings that she'd bought in a mountain village in Yunnan; the framed photo of her mother; and the shrine to David.

Sophie went to the wooden cube in the corner. She dusted its motley surface and emptied the ash collected at the bottom of the incense holder into the wastebasket. Then she lit the candle positioned in the middle of this makeshift altar and watched its flame flicker beside the framed picture of a little boy in full bloom. Before the candlelight and David's beaming smile, Sophie knelt and closed her eyes, her head bowed in silent prayer. This was her ritual. She imagined taking it with her throughout her life, wherever she wandered, until the time arrived when David returned home.

When she finished, she considered her bed. The turned-back quilt revealed cream flannelette sheets beneath. It invited her. Her body ached with fatigue but she couldn't sleep now. Not with a mind cluttered with images of Wendy's pink brain seeping onto the concrete and Han Hong, naked and dirty, in some backstreet lap-dance bar.

Sophie opened her MacBook and uploaded the image of Han Hong. The girl's face filled the screen. Enormous eyes, clear skin, full lips. Han Hong's youth seemed magnified. What was it that she had seen and how had she come to be involved in the seedy underworld of a foreign city? Surely Sydney had signified a new beginning of sorts: a place for Han Hong to find her independence, come to a new understanding of cultural differences and relationships and to think and dream in a language different from her own. How had this girl's overseas adventure turned so sour?

Sophie's thoughts turned to Wendy. The track marks on her skin.

Wendy had been hiding a secret pain. Maybe she'd been involved in a similar scene. Sophie shivered. If students were resorting to lap dancing to pay their passage to Australia, no wonder they wound up depressed.

'Hey, stranger.'

Sophie turned to see Jin Tao leaning against the doorframe, still dressed in his chef's whites. He held a small porcelain teacup in one hand. 'Another brew left in that pot?'

It was a habit they shared, popping in to each other's rooms, stealing cups of tea and conversation. Jin Tao always drank from the floral-patterned porcelain he held out now. Tea bonded them.

Sophie poured the last of the oolong into Jin Tao's cup. He folded himself onto the woven mat beside the bed.

'You want to tell me what's up?'

Forget reading the tea leaves afterwards, Jin Tao could read her mood by her choice of brew: oolong was for the weight of the world. The dark amber hue and the burnt bitterness of the leaves worked as a catharsis, helping Sophie clear her mind and refocus her senses.

She stared at him, admiring not for the first time his perfect wide eyes, deep pools rimmed with black. Jin Tao had a way of staring into her; his gaze never felt like an interrogation – more like a caress.

Sophie flipped the computer screen closed. She would sleep on what Tae Hun had told her, pick through the details of the conversation and allow her thoughts to ferment until clarity arrived.

'Nope,' she said, and slid down next to Jin Tao on the mat.

He motioned to the candle flickering in the corner. 'You thinking about the kid?'

Sophie reached out to the candle, dipped a pinkie finger into the hot wax. She felt it burn and tighten, a smooth and perfect green cap.

'You know I don't tell just anyone about what happened to David,' she said.

'And I've promised to keep your secret safe.'

Sophie held her capped finger out. 'A pinkie promise,' she said.

Jin Tao touched her pinkie with his own. 'Even deeper than that.'

Sophie leaned against Jin Tao's shoulder. She twirled the wax cap between two fingers. It crumbled. Gone.

'How was work?' she asked.

'Full-on.' The usual response. 'Stuart decided to nick off at a quarter past nine, leaving me a man down. Reckoned he had a hot date and he'd told me about it.'

'I'm sure you had everything under control.'

'You kidding me? We were only halfway through the sitting. Total nightmare.'

'At least Stuart's getting lucky.'

Jin Tao nudged her gently. 'You in need of some loving, lovely?'

'Are you offering?' She regretted the words as soon as they were out of her mouth.

He drained the last of the tea from his cup. 'I certainly am,' he said. He disentangled his warm body from hers. 'A lovingly prepared breakfast for you first thing in the morning. You can have it in bed.'

Sophie grinned through her relief. 'Make my eggs runny,' she instructed.

'Yes, chef.' He planted a kiss on her cheek. 'Sweet dreams.'

'Goodnight.' She watched him go. The skin on her cheek burned from the touch of his lips, and continued to tingle long after he pulled shut the door.

HAN HONG blinked and tried to see. He'd removed the blindfold but she remained in darkness – in here it was as dark as shit. She was out of her cage, she knew that much. He must have moved her while she slept.

The soup. From the throbbing in her temples, she guessed he'd laced it. She didn't know how long she'd been out for, or what had happened while she was down for the count, but at least she was out of the cage.

She tried to stretch her arms. They were behind her. As she jiggled her wrists, she realised they were secured loosely to a thin post. She tried to think straight, assess her position. Bare legs, no underpants, cold concrete chafing at her bottom. Irritation trickled through her, threatening to overpower fear. She wished she were clothed, not for modesty's sake, but for comfort and warmth.

She'd thrown modesty out the window a long time ago. The first time she'd made a video, she'd let it all go.

Han Hong shifted and discovered that her neck was held flat against the post by a thin cord. It bit into her skin and drew tighter if she turned her head to the side. Her captor was forcing her to stare straight ahead. She'd made videos for them before – why the sudden change and the imprisonment?

The light flashed on.

She closed her eyes against the brightness. Her mind registered patterns, all orange and red, the blood vessels in her head.

When she opened her eyes she saw a man in a mask, a simple black stocking stretched tightly across his face. It distorted his features, but she could tell that he was thick-lipped and pudgy. He sat on a camp stool, his belly bulging from under his windcheater to hang over his tracksuit pants. Just behind him was a light. It looked like a professional cinematography lamp, thin and straight. It had a powerful burn. The man held a video camera. She saw the red light – it was on. This, at least, was grotesquely familiar. But she'd not yet made a film in this room, before a man in a mask.

Han Hong crossed her legs. She tried to scan her surroundings, but the cord around her neck prevented movement. He'd tied her to her mark.

'Smile for the camera, baby,' he said. The voice came thick and slightly muffled through the stocking. An Australian accent.

Nausea built in Han Hong's stomach. She fought to control it. If she vomited she would choke.

'Come on, you're a movie star.'

She wanted to scream. She tried to think clearly. Where was she? What was this?

'I said smile.' Her captor sounded in no mood for games.

Han Hong had no option. She stretched her mouth into a thin grin, cringing as the dry skin on her lips cracked.

JUSTIN HOLMES'S wife tucked him into bed and kissed him on the top of the head. She zipped her bag, gathered their daughter and hauled her out the door. An average day, the school run followed by work. On the bedside table, she'd left a tray holding a glass of orange juice, a plate of buttered brown toast and a pot of tea. In the fridge she'd left a plate of chicken sandwiches, in case he felt up to eating something more later.

Justin settled back under the covers and allowed his head to sink deep into his pillow. Relaxed. He hadn't pulled a sickie on his wife in a while. And she'd bought it, smothering him with kisses and back rubs and goodwill. He deserved a day in, she'd told him. He worked so hard, after all.

Justin's hands felt clammy with the hot anticipation of what might unfold in the hours to come. For a while he lay there, savouring the possibilities. Then he leaned over and opened the drawer in the bedside table. From the coin jar, Justin fished out the slip of paper. On it was scrawled a mobile number. Justin licked his lips, picked up his mobile and dialled.

'*Wei?*' A curt greeting, as though Justin had interrupted something important.

He hesitated. 'Uh, I think I have the wrong number.' He took the phone from his ear, and moved his finger to the end-call button.

'You want DVD?'

Justin caught the words just as he pressed disconnect. He dialled again.

'Yes?' the voice said in English.

Justin swallowed. 'You sell DVDs?'

'We sell DVDs and private appointments. What do you want?'

Justin massaged his wedding ring. A private appointment sounded interesting. But he supposed it would involve sex. That would mean cheating on his wife.

'DVD,' he said.

'Yeah, yeah, DVD. What kind?'

He thought hard. How to put it? 'Something ... unconventional.'

Peals of laughter carried down the phone line. Justin forced himself to release his grip on the handset. He watched as the blood flowed again under the skin of his knuckles. He took some deep breaths, willing calm to return.

'Unconventional?' the voice said finally, between squeaks of laughter. 'We only do unconventional. What do you want? Naughty or nice?'

This time he didn't hesitate. 'I want the naughtiest you've got.'

'Depends how far you want to go.'

Justin felt an erection stir against the flannelette of his pyjama pants. He glanced at the snatch of sky visible through the chink in the curtains. The storm clouds had gathered grey and black. If he was going to go through with this, he may as well go hard.

'I want to go all the way,' he said, surprised at the nervous tremor that crept into his voice.

At the end of the phone line, more laughter rang out.

When Justin finished on the phone, he slipped into a dressing gown and some slippers. He took the tray of toast and juice into the kitchen, binned the toast and took a bottle of vodka from the freezer. He added a generous splash to the orange juice. Rain shot darts against the windowpane. Justin sipped his drink. From the kitchen he could see the driveway and the road. He would wait here for the delivery. For a split second, he wondered whether handing over his home address had been a good idea. His wife and child lived here. What if a delivery arrived when he wasn't at home? But the anxiety slipped away as the vodka penetrated his bloodstream and left him basking in its warm glow. He watched the rain beat down outside and decided it was a good day for curling up in front of the telly.

SOPHIE CHAINED her bike to a pillar outside Sydney Central English School. She pulled the collar of her jacket tight and made a sharp dash through the rain for the sliding door at the entrance. Inside, the narrow stairwell smelled of blackcurrant chewie and cardamom. She took the stairs two at a time.

The small foyer on level three smelled strongly of damp. Sophie took in the brown carpet, grubby yellow walls and vinyl sofa set. The receptionist talked with a crowd of disgruntled students. The phone rang nonstop. Sophie took a seat on the sofa and waited.

At 10.45 the class bell sounded. The students milling in the foyer began to filter away. Sophie stood up and walked to the front desk.

'Can I help you?' the receptionist drawled.

'I'm a teacher up the road, at United English,' said Sophie.

The receptionist nodded. 'On poaching duty, are we?'

'I'm looking for a student of yours,' Sophie said. 'I tutor her privately. Her name is Han Hong.'

The receptionist entered Han Hong's name into her database.

'I'm only doing this because I'm about to leave this crappy job and I couldn't give a stuff,' she said in a low voice. 'Student information is confidential but they can't sack me because I already quit.' She found the information she was looking for. 'Han Hong is in English Two. I can call her to student admin at the next break. You can sit tight, or come back. It's a forty-minute wait.'

Sophie fought to keep her face blank. Tae Hun had said that Han Hong had been missing for two weeks. Perhaps the girl really had been on holiday; maybe she'd taken it upon herself to make some extra money in underground girly bars while studying on the side. Or maybe Tae Hun had been mistaken; perhaps the girl in the photograph wasn't Han Hong at all.

'You can come back or sit tight,' the receptionist repeated.

Sophie opted for a corner of the couch, next to a young woman with perfectly straight hair. The girl smiled, her eyes meeting Sophie's briefly before flitting away. She twisted a cotton handkerchief between her fingers, balancing a new student manual on her lap.

The details. Pay attention to the details.

'Are you new here?' Sophie asked.

The girl nodded.

'Where are you from?' As though she didn't already know.

The girl's eyes flashed with pride. Her smile became a beam. 'I come from China,' she said, her back suddenly straight, her head high.

'It's a beautiful country,' Sophie said.

'Yes,' the girl exploded. 'Five thousand years of history.'

Five thousand years of history. Sophie had heard this expression so many times before – but never from her mother.

'I hope you'll be happy here,' she said.

The girl lowered her eyes again. 'It is very different,' she said. 'I remember my last day in my hometown. I took a picture with my, how do you say ... memory. Now, when I close my eyes, I see the picture of my hometown and it brings me some kind of peace.'

Sophie stared at the girl beside her. She'd captured beautifully the sense of a last glance, that last snapshot of a place. A memory settled.

'Excuse me.' The girl stood and moved to meet a teacher at the reception desk. She walked away with him, turning once to wave.

I took a picture with my memory.

On the morning of Sophie's last day in Beijing, she woke early, rolled creakily onto her back and stared at the cracks in the ceiling of her first-floor apartment. She lay there for some minutes, one hand behind her aching, hung-over head, the other on her stomach, completing her morning ritual – counting the noises of her neighbourhood. These were the sounds she would take with her, the noises that would bring her back to her Beijing apartment in a flash, should she hear them in another place and at another time: the voices of old women gathered by the bicycle stand in the yard; the crackle of bicycle spokes wheeling past her window; the rasp of the gate as it opened and closed; the fizz of moist dough sticks connecting with oil; the chatter of budgerigars. Five sounds to remember this morning by. Sophie counted them, threading them into her memory. She allowed a tear to escape onto her cheek. She would not cry more than this one tear. This leaving was what she wanted, what she had prepared and waited and burned for over and over. This was it, and Sophie was surprised at how much it hurt. But she would not cry any more. Too many tears had already been spilt. And none of them had brought David back.

Sophie brushed the wet from her cheekbone. Her bags had been packed for weeks. Since deciding to leave, Sophie had felt like she'd been treading water, waiting patiently for the days and weeks to pass so that she might finally say farewell and shut the door on this wide ragged land with all its beauty and pain and contradictions. Her only hesitation was in saying goodbye to Li Hua.

Dear, sweet, giving Li Hua, who'd lost so much.

Sophie shuffled into her slippers and padded into the galley kitchen that she'd used only for boiling water and rice. She made herself a cup of dragon's well tea and wandered through the flat as it brewed. Empty of her personal touches and knick-knacks, the flat felt like a stranger. All that remained were lonely pieces of furniture and the traces of last night's simple farewell: a burned-down aromatic candle, a leftover plate of pumpkin seeds and some empty wine bottles by the TV. Sophie gathered the candle and the plate of pumpkin seeds and threw the lot in the bin.

Li Hua would arrive to collect her in an hour.

As she shut the door on her flat, the one across the concrete landing opened. Mrs Lu stepped onto the landing, steadying herself against the pile of winter cabbages. She held a paper bag out to Sophie.

'For your trip,' she said in rolling Putonghua. 'For tea.'

Sophie took the crumpled bag and peeked at its contents. A pile of dried hawthorn berries.

Mrs Lu's eyes shone. 'Before you came here we'd never had a foreign person in this building,' she said. 'You are the first foreign person I've met. You are ... not so bad.'

Sophie's arrival had caused a scandal. The old ladies by the bike stand hadn't smiled at her for months. She'd listened to their chatter from her window and noted that they stopped talking whenever she walked past. When she finally plucked up the courage to speak to them, in stilted and broken Mandarin, their mouths had gaped.

From then on, they'd smiled.

Sophie shook Mrs Lu's hand. 'Look after your body and your health,' she said. 'And thank you.'

Mrs Lu watched from her open door as Sophie lugged her suitcase down the steps to the courtyard outside. Sophie turned once, raising her hand in a wave. Mrs Lu stood still, her back against the cabbages, her arms folded against the cold.

Sophie walked across the courtyard, the eyes of the apartment block on her back. Nobody shouted goodbye and nobody offered to help. Her time here had been only an interruption, a scratch on the ebb and flow of decades.

The gatekeeper emerged from his watchhouse, his wrinkled face squinting up at her for one last time. The ever-present cigarette dangled loosely from one hand. In the other, he held a piece of torn card. He pressed the card into Sophie's gloved palm.

'In case you forget something. Just call.' The simple kindness made Sophie want to sob.

Li Hua stood beside her car at the gate. Sophie swallowed her tears and muttered a farewell to the man she'd spent hours with, drinking brown tea from chipped cups, discussing small topics in smaller words: food, pets, family, tradition.

'Hello?'

Sophie snapped alert. A lank-haired girl stood before her, hands fiddling with the strap of a plastic carry bag.

'I am Han Hong,' she said, her English heavily accented.

Sophie stood. The girl, thin-lipped and skinny, was taller by a few centimetres. Heavy make-up caked her face but couldn't disguise the traces of acne or the sores around her mouth. Without question there'd been a mistake. Even in the age of digital enhancement, photographs didn't lie this much.

The girl twisted the bag strap. 'I am Han Hong,' she repeated.

'I'm sorry,' Sophie said. 'I was looking for somebody else.'

The girl began to back away. 'Okay.'

She turned and walked a few unsteady steps down the corridor. Strapped to her feet were a pair of wedge heels, bright yellow patent leather – more suited to a nightclub than a classroom.

Sophie pulled her phone from her pocket. 'Excuse me,' she called. 'Han Hong?'

The girl turned. 'Yes?'

Sophie approached. 'I'm looking for the girl in this picture. Her name is also Han Hong. Do you know her?'

The girl stared at the image. She swept a finger around the circle of her eye, as if brushing away a tear. When she looked up, her eyes gleamed.

'I do not know this person,' she said, her voice a fierce whisper. 'I'm sorry. I cannot help.'

Clutching palms to elbows, the girl walked quickly away. Sophie watched the shopping bag swing from one finger. She seemed so definite.

Sophie's phone rang. Jin Tao. She brought it to her ear. 'Hey, you.'

'Lunch date. You and me. Dumplings.'

'Sounds great,' she said. 'But it's pouring and I'm on my bike.'

'Leave it chained, I've got the car. Where are you?'

'Central English,' she said. 'Pop it into your GPS. I'll be down in five.'

She hung up and returned to the receptionist's desk. The stench of tuna salad hung around it like a noxious gas.

'How'd you go?' the receptionist asked through a mouthful of her lunch.

Sophie tried to speak without inhaling. 'Actually that wasn't the girl I was looking for,' she said. 'Are there any other Han Hongs in your database?'

The receptionist tapped at some keys, scanned the screen, took a mouthful of tuna. 'Nope,' she said, finally. 'She's the only one listed. A consistent student. She's studied here for six months.'

'That can't be right,' Sophie said. 'I know for a fact the girl I'm looking for was enrolled at this school.'

The receptionist shrugged. 'I can't tell you any more than what I see here,' she said. 'I guess if you're looking to poach our students you should try someone else. From the look of her records, this girl's a stayer.'

HE WATCHED her from the glass window of an interview room. Her legs seemed to stretch to her chest, but she didn't know how to dress. She looked vaguely familiar but too much like a man in those brown corduroy pants and heavy worker boots. Freckles across her nose. Brown eyes, something different about them, striking but too strong. At least her hair feminised her. Thick and black it flowed over her shoulders, the locks held out of her face with an emerald green clip.

He'd heard her ask the receptionist for Han Hong as he wrapped up his check of the timetables. He'd been pleased with the receptionist's response but agitated at the inquiry – Han Hong didn't have an English tutor. He knew that for sure.

But she *was* missing.

He hadn't seen her for a couple of weeks and a familiar anxiety flipped his stomach.

This was not the first time he'd lost track of one of his girls.

He scanned the paperwork, looking for a clue.

For years, the business had operated without a hitch, aided by a few dodgy language school employees who'd helped him play the system in exchange for cash. The girls enjoyed the opportunity he gave them for a decent income; they sent it home to their parents and spent a decent portion on designer handbags and eyewear. They made better money with him than working in a convenience store – and they didn't need to worry about the language. As willing participants in his game of mix and match, his workers knew the rules and they played by them, manipulating only the system in order to get ahead.

But things had gone so well and the operation had seemed so safe that perhaps he'd got lazy. He'd allowed the drugs to seep in and for his workers to become dependent like common East Sydney hookers. Worse, he'd let his associates convince him to move away from simple sexual service work and into darker markets ... clearly, the girls didn't like it.

The question was: where had they gone? If they'd returned home to China he would know about it. And if they'd set up somewhere else in the city, surely word would have filtered through. But he'd heard and seen nothing. Three women had already vanished, and now so had Han Hong.

He twisted his hands together as he watched the woman in the brown cords tap out a message on her phone. Everything was falling apart. He'd ordered the real Wendy Chan killed out of necessity. A one-off to cover his tracks. Sooner or later, the police would have found her, questions would have been asked and she'd have led them back to him. The order had been a self-preservation decision but murder was not his main game.

As for Han Hong, she'd disappeared, not shown up at the club for over ten nights. When he called her phone it went straight to message bank. He'd visited her apartment, rapped at the metal security screen and tried to peek around the venetians. Soon a landlord somewhere would start worrying about unpaid rent.

As usual, his associates didn't seem worried. This was a cause for concern in itself. It meant they'd also become over-confident and slack. Or that they knew something he didn't.

Things weren't going to plan. In the space of a fortnight

Han Hong had gone missing, the substitute had committed suicide and the woman in the emerald green clip had begun nosing around.

Something would have to be done.

SOPHIE WAITED at a bus shelter a few doors down from Central English. The footpaths glistened, wet and streaming. Jin Tao pulled up in his Audi, honked the horn like he'd won a football game.

Sophie headed for the kerb. As she pulled on the door handle, she noticed a willowy figure emerge from the English school. The girl walked along the pavement towards them.

Sophie slid into the car. 'Jin Tao,' she said. 'See that girl?'

Jin Tao flicked a glance. The rain blurred the windscreen. 'Not clearly,' he said.

'Her name is Han Hong. Do me a favour and call to her.'

'Call her yourself.' Jin Tao began pulling out from the kerb.

A surge of adrenaline surfed Sophie's system. In a moment, Han Hong would pass. She pressed the button controlling the sunroof. The black plate slid back, welcoming the rain.

'Hey,' said Jin Tao. He slammed the brakes. 'It's leather upholstery, Soph.'

'Call to her,' she said. 'It's important.'

'Fuck me,' groaned Jin Tao. He unbuckled his belt and climbed onto the driver's seat. He stuck his head out the sunroof. 'Han Hong!' His voice boomed over the patter. A pedestrian turned to stare.

Sophie watched for Han Hong's reaction. The girl didn't

flinch. Blank-faced, she scurried away, head bent against the weather, arms wrapped tightly around herself.

Jin Tao clambered down and shut the sunroof. 'She didn't hear me over the rain,' he said. 'Are you satisfied?' He pulled off his jumper and began wiping down the leather.

But Sophie had her eyes on the girl. 'Or maybe she didn't recognise her own name.'

Jin Tao dumped his jumper on Sophie's lap and put the car into gear. A white T-shirt clung to his chest. 'Don't know what you're talking about,' he said. 'But when we get to where we're going, I'd like you to wipe the water off your seat.'

They drove to the restaurant with the heater on full blast. Sophie flipped over the encounter in her mind, unable to shake the feeling that something was very wrong. If the thin woman on the street wasn't Han Hong, then who was she? And as for the real Han Hong – where had she gone?

By the time they reached Chinatown, the rain had cleared and the air was redolent with pig fat. Along Dixon Street the tables were crowded with tourists; they ploughed through plates of sticky sweet and sour pork and braised vegetables with pineapple. Chirpy waitresses in red aprons wiped down wet seats and tabletops, poured scrappy tea and cracked cans of beer.

'Yuck,' breathed Jin Tao in Sophie's ear. 'Smells like your mum's chop suey.'

Sophie dodged a teenage girl holding a laminated picture of a king prawn. 'Knock Mum's chop suey and I'll chop suey you.'

Jin Tao grinned. 'Take one can of pineapple, half a kilo of diced pork, some sweet chilli sauce, capsicum and prawn crackers and you've got a disgusting concoction that far too many people would call a meal.'

Sophie stuffed her hands in her pockets. He was right about the chop suey. Ironic that her mother's most popular dish, the one she'd cooked in bulk for Sophie's primary school fetes, had been some Australianised version of the Chinese food she cooked at home.

'I just give them what they like,' her mother used to say. 'If I gave them chicken feet they would laugh.'

But the Australian palate was changing. Even suburban mums and dads kept Sichuan peppercorns in their spice racks these days. Still, whenever Sophie made her mother's chop suey, it gave her a small taste of home.

'About these dumplings, then.' she said. 'What's this secret venue you're excited about?'

Jin Tao grabbed Sophie's hand and threaded her through the throng. 'This way, m'lady. A feast awaits.'

They crossed Goulburn Street. 'In here.' Jin Tao ushered Sophie through a narrow doorway. They climbed stairs that smelled of cumin. At the top, plastic grapes covered the ceiling of the restaurant and a fake green vine wound across the far wall. Groups of people sat around wide tables. They slurped noodles and shared plates heaving with food.

Sophie smiled, breathing in smells of spices and lamb. 'Xinjiang.'

'Been there?' asked Jin Tao, grabbing a chair at a table.

'I once pretended to be Uyghur.' Sophie ducked for a passing tray of lamb kebabs. The scent of chargrill soaked into her. She slipped into the chair opposite Jin Tao.

'A half-Irish, half-Chinese Australian chick?' said Jin Tao. 'How did that work?'

'It was Beijing in the late nineties, just after I first arrived,' Sophie said. 'I wasn't supposed to live where I did.' She massaged the plastic grapes in the fruit bowl on the table.

'Fearless foreigner.'

'The complex had guards,' she said. 'I wrapped a scarf

around my head whenever I left the apartment, hoped they would take me for a Uyghur and not ask for my paperwork.'

'You pretended to be Muslim?'

'Gave it a shot,' she said.

Jin Tao grinned. 'They would have been onto you,' he said. 'They probably just turned a blind eye because you're gorgeous.'

Heat in her cheeks, like the warm rush of too much wine, Sophie flipped open the menu. Jin Tao did the same.

'Tea?' A tall waiter with an unfortunate mullet offered a copper teapot. Its long, thin spout stretched the length of the table. Sophie turned her teacup. The waiter poured tea, hot and steaming, into her cup. Jin Tao pointed to a bandage on the waiter's hand.

'A burn?'

The waiter filled Jin Tao's cup. 'Surfing accident. Had a fight with a coral reef. You should see the reef.' He spoke with the fluency of a local, but his accent told a different story.

Jin Tao blew on his tea, cooling it. 'She reckons she'd make a good Uyghur. What do you think? Reckon she could pass for one of you lot?'

The waiter assessed Sophie, a smile on his lips. 'You like mutton?'

'Love it.'

'And cumin?'

Sophie nodded.

'Can you dance on a table?'

'Even when I'm not blind drunk.'

'Then yes, I say you pass,' he said. 'You should give me your number. I'd make a good husband.' He took Sophie's hand in his bandaged one, brought it to his lips.

'Hey!' Jin Tao pushed his chair back. Face dark, like he wanted to punch the guy.

The waiter laughed, stepped sideways. 'Don't worry, man, she's not my type.'

Jin Tao's mouth gaped.

Sophie stretched out a hand to him. 'His name's Brad,' she said. 'He's my friend.'

The waiter winked at Jin Tao. 'Sophie gave me my English name,' he said. 'A good, solid surfer name for the new Aussie in me.'

Jin Tao rolled his eyes, returned to studying the menu.

'Your friend,' said Brad, 'he's speechless.'

'He's only disappointed,' Sophie said. 'He thought I didn't know about this place or that you serve the best potato slivers in Sydney.'

A serving of big plate chicken arrived for the customers at an adjacent table, its aroma thick with onions and peppers.

'Then your friend doesn't know you as well as he thinks,' Brad said. 'Now, what will it be? The usual?'

Sophie smiled. 'Dumplings,' she said. 'Jin Tao's got a hankering.'

Jin Tao, head in the menu, said nothing. Brad moved off towards the kitchen.

Sophie poked Jin Tao's arm with a chopstick. 'Are you going to talk to me?'

He stretched back in his chair. 'I always felt like Chinatown was my hood,' he said. 'But it seems you know it better than me.'

'Does that upset you?'

'Makes me feel old,' he said. 'I used to come down here with my *yeye* when I was a kid. Saturday mornings. Early.'

'To do what? Hang out with your grandpa?'

Jin Tao nodded. 'He'd play mahjong and smoke cigarettes with his mates. I'd eat steamed bread, drink soy milk and play hopscotch with mine. Bet that doesn't happen now.'

'Have you checked out Chinatown in the early morning recently?'

'That's exactly my point. I'd end up getting stabbed.'

'Rubbish.'

Sophie knew the blocks between Goulburn Street and Paddy's Markets like a birthmark. She knew every hand-pulled noodle shop both on and off the map. 'You want seedy, you've got it in the Cross. Up there you've got junkies and prostitutes on every corner.'

'Yeah, they're on the corner where you can see them. Down here, it's what you don't see that's the problem,' Jin Tao said. 'You must know what I'm talking about, Sophie. You must have picked up on the vibe?'

A waitress arrived with their dumplings. Sophie pushed aside glasses and a tissue box to make room for the dish. She didn't know what Jin Tao meant, not really. She'd never found herself looking over her shoulder in Chinatown, not in the same way she did in parts of East Sydney and Surry Hills.

Jin Tao pinched a large dumpling with his chopsticks and dumped the glistening white parcel into his bowl. 'So what were you doing hanging out at Central English?' he said. 'Looking for more work?'

'God, no,' said Sophie. 'That school's the pits.'

'So?'

'I was checking out something Tae Hun told me.'

'Is this about Wendy Chan?'

'Maybe.'

Sophie watched him shovel food into his mouth as though it were his last meal. Usually she'd be able to compete, but today the urge to eat had left her.

'A girl commits suicide and nobody knows who she is,' Sophie said. 'Why not? Because she was pretending to be someone else. You don't think that's strange?'

Jin Tao chewed over a mouthful. 'Yes,' he said. 'But maybe that's why she topped herself.'

'What do you mean?'

He laid his chopsticks down across his bowl. 'One thing about these dumplings is they're made from lamb.'

Sophie suppressed an urge to swear. 'You bring everything back to food,' she said. 'The Uyghurs are Muslim and that means no pork. What's this got to do with anything?'

'Food has to do with everything,' said Jin Tao, serious. 'You see, these dumplings are made from lamb, which is less fatty than pork. So, while these dumplings are tasty, quite nicely spiced, scented with cumin and just a hint of chilli, they are, in essence, a poor imitation of their juicier, fattier, more succulent cousin.'

'I'm insulted.' Brad stood beside them. He held the teapot in one hand and a plate of shredded potato in the other. He eyeballed Jin Tao. 'What do you people know about Uyghur cooking anyway?'

'Sorry, man, only making a point,' said Jin Tao, his hands in the air.

Brad placed the potato slivers on the table. The spout of the teapot floated dangerously close to Jin Tao's cheek. 'It's cool,' he said. 'We Uyghurs are used to you Han people stealing our culture, bastardising it with pork fat and calling it yours. Of course your pig dumplings are better.'

Jin Tao rocked back in his chair. He rubbed a hand across his head. 'Dude. You need to make like a surfer and chill.'

The two men eyeballed each other. Pleasure tickled Sophie's insides, a buzz better than beer. She put a hand on Brad's arm and leaned across to Jin Tao.

'He's fucking with you.'

Brad placed the teapot on the table. He gripped the edge of the tablecloth and leaned in. 'Don't tell my boss or my mother, but the best thing about going for a surf is the beef and bacon burger on the way home.' He straightened again and moved off through the restaurant.

Sophie stuck her chopsticks into the plate of potato. The thin slivers had been braised in vinegar, salt and chilli, a Chinese version of the salt and vinegar chip. She felt the sour of the vinegar hit the back of her throat, and the chilli catch as it made its way down. She reached for her teacup. Jin Tao sat still, staring into the space Brad had left.

'He's a cheeky bastard, and he likes sticking it to the Chinese,' Sophie said.

Jin Tao poured some vinegar into his bowl. 'Maybe you could let him know I'm Australian next time you're talking to him.'

Sophie bit into a dumpling, felt its hot juice run down her chin. 'Finish your lamb versus pork analogy.'

'What fun is it being a substitute?' he said. 'I'd rather top myself than walk around pretending to be somebody else.'

Sophie turned the words over in her head. Wendy, for some unknown reason, had been playing the role of somebody else. Perhaps it had become too much for her, and she'd killed herself. But then, where was the real Wendy Chan? Was she missing, just like Han Hong?'

Sophie pulled out her phone and pushed it across the table. 'Take a look,' she said. 'That's Han Hong. She's young.'

Jin Tao pushed the screen away. 'It's a racy picture,' he said. 'Not sure what it's doing on your phone.'

'She's supposed to be a student at Central English but she hasn't been in class for a couple of weeks. I went to the school this morning on the chance she might be there.'

'That girl you wrecked my upholstery for?'

'She claimed to be Han Hong, but she looks nothing like the girl in this picture.'

Jin Tao bit into a dumpling. 'So there are two girls with the same name at Central English?'

Sophie shook her head. 'There's only one Han Hong on the books. You saw her. She didn't even turn her head when you called. My guess is she's an imposter.'

Jin Tao put his chopsticks down. He raised his hands to his forehead and drummed his fingernails against his temples. 'What are you doing?'

His stare gouged Sophie, chilling her.

'You're the one spooking me out about Chinatown,' she said. 'All this talk about strange vibes and watching your back.'

'I was referring to muggings,' he said. 'You're talking about missing people and imposters. Real life isn't that interesting.'

Could he be right? Could she be imagining things, making links where there were none?

She swiped her phone. Han Hong's face stared back at her. The girl's haunted eyes scraped her soul.

'This is real,' she said.

'Maybe,' said Jin Tao. 'But you've never met this girl. You're just going on what some jaded kid says. He could have the wrong name or the wrong idea. You don't know.'

'And what about Wendy? We know she wasn't who she said she was.'

'It's not that unusual, Sophie,' Jin Tao said. 'It happens in the cooking world too.'

'What?'

'Visa fraud.'

'What do you mean?'

'I mean these kids, they want to come out here and the only way they can do that is on a student visa.'

'So?'

'A student visa says you have to study at your nominated institution for at least twenty hours a week.' Jin Tao studied her. 'You do know that, right?'

Visa obligations, a source of irritation to teachers and students alike. For students, visa obligations became the ball and chain that tied them to a school building. For teachers, student visa obligations meant extra hours monitoring 'free study periods', classes acknowledged by everyone as a waste of time and a sham to help students and the school meet government obligations. The teachers of these classes were glorified minders; they were not expected to teach, for this would mean increases in weekly salary packages that the schools could not afford. The teachers' only responsibility during these classes was to take the roll and account for all their students.

'But students have to eat too, yeah?' Sophie said. 'So they need to work and some work long night shifts and take three-hour power naps before heading back to school in the day.'

'And the others engage in visa fraud.'

Jin Tao picked a toothpick from a plastic box on the table. He covered his mouth with a hand as he picked. 'Happens in the cooking academies all the time,' he said. 'It's often easier to pay someone else to sit in on their classes. That way, they don't lose their visa credits, they earn their schooling qualification and they can also afford to feed themselves.'

'It's *how* they're earning their extra money that worries me,' said Sophie.

'I reckon that part's up to them,' Jin Tao said. 'Besides, if these girls were really missing, don't you think their families would have kicked up a fuss by now?'

HAN HONG squinted at the phone screen. She'd spent so long in the dark, the slash of light hurt her eyes. He'd undone the blindfold so she could key the number in to the pad. She could have told it to him, but he hadn't asked. He rarely spoke to her. She held the phone to her ear and imagined the scene at the end of the line. She'd called the grocery store down the lane from her parents' new apartment, the one they'd moved to after the government demolished their village. Her mother would be waiting at that grocery store, perched patiently on a red plastic stool beside a glass-topped counter containing cigarettes. Han Hong pictured the packets, all red and gold and white; beautiful designs, nothing like the cigarette packets in Australia – no images of death and destruction. No warnings of death and sickness. Only pretty things: birds, stars, flowers, mountains.

Han Hong wanted to smoke. She wanted to step out from her mother's apartment and onto the concrete balcony where two bamboo chairs sat beneath a low-hanging clothes line. She would sit on a padded cushion and pour hot water from the thermos into her teacup. She would watch the chrysanthemum flower unfold into bloom, add some rocks of sugar, lean back and light a cigarette. She would watch the red sun set on her town, its light softening the hard lines of the apartment blocks that were the view from the balcony.

How Han Hong missed the view. But more than that, she missed her mother. She'd be waiting beside the counter at the grocery store, waiting for the phone to ring; wanting to know that Han Hong was all right. And again Han Hong would lie.

She would lie because she had to. She would lie because they knew where her mother lived.

The call rang out. Han Hong stared at the phone in her hand. She looked up to the man in the mask. Even if she were able to overpower this man, stick her fingers into his eyes and gouge out his eyeballs, she would not be able to escape. He'd locked the door from the inside upon entering – she'd heard the padlock snap shut. And even if she could somehow find the key and manage to escape, who knew what terror awaited her on the other side? It was better to play their game. She was good at it and they would keep her alive because of that. She would find a moment for escape and take it. But that moment was not now.

She dialled the number again, gripped the phone to her ear.

'*Wei?*'

Han Hong thought she might cry. She bit her bottom lip and tasted blood.

She imagined night falling, the light soft. She smelled burning coal and potato skins from Mr Xie's tin drum on the corner. Mrs Tan, who ran the bric-a-brac shop next door, would be bringing in her plastic buckets, tin pots and mops. Her mother would be wearing her best blouse, the pink one that brought out the rose in her cheeks.

Han Hong imagined herself beside her mother, chopping cabbage, breathing the sour smell of pickle, savouring the warm comfort of tea in her belly; the comfort of home.

She forced a smile onto her face and closed her eyes. 'Hello, Mama,' she said. And once again she began to lie.

JIN TAO pulled up at the language school and leaned across Sophie to push open the passenger door.

'No offence,' he said. 'I have to hoof it to the restaurant – all your talking has made me late.'

'Have a good afternoon, housey,' Sophie said. 'Hope Brad didn't freak you out too much. Perhaps he has a crush on you.'

Jin Tao stared at her. 'He's gay?'

'He appreciates Australia.'

Jin Tao considered her. 'A gay Uyghur surfer who eats pork is an interesting human being. Now, I like him.'

'Why exactly?'

'Because he clearly doesn't have his eye on you.' Jin Tao grinned and revved the engine. 'See you tonight,' he said, raising two fingers in a street salute.

Sophie climbed out and watched Jin Tao speed down the street, his wheels taking the corner with a screech. Tough guy. At least, he liked to play like one. So why had he seemed so fearful of Chinatown? And why had he been so quick to dismiss her concerns? Sophie shivered. She pulled a scarf from her bag and wrapped it around her neck. She crossed the slippery street and arrowed for the artificial warmth of her building.

FROM THE front of a car parked further down Pitt Street, someone else watched the Audi roar away.

He'd made some inquiries, found out where the woman worked, and waited. It had paid off. He fingered the camera strap at his neck. Something familiar about the woman still gnawed.

He studied the images he'd snapped. Up close, through the zoom, he recognised something almost Chinese about the shape of her eyes and in the bridge of her nose.

How had he missed it?

The vice squeezing his insides loosened, breath came easier, relief trickled.

He slipped the camera strap over his head, rested back in his seat. That must be the familiarity: she was Asian.

A thought crashed through his calm.

Perhaps she spoke Mandarin and had overheard a conversation. Perhaps she knew these girls or one of his associates and had been told more than was safe.

He'd already had Wendy Chan killed to protect his business. He'd been surprised to discover that he hadn't felt anything – no guilt, fear or regret. He'd issued an order and his team had carried it out – no fuss, no emotion.

It was like they'd done it before.

He loosened his collar, touched sweat as he brushed his thumb along the curve of his neck. The air hung thick. How well did he know the men he worked with? Were they more experienced than he thought?

He brought the camera close, switched his mind back to the woman, focused on solutions.

He could have her killed.

A sudden shiver, the tickle of a thrill ...

Or perhaps he could put her to work.

With a slim fingertip he traced the line of the woman's jaw, imagined how it would look in a bridle.

He punched a name into the dash, stared across the road at United English.

It made perfect sense. She was an English teacher and she taught at the school where the suicidal bitch made her last stand. He could watch her now.

'Need to arrange a meeting,' he said, when the call connected. 'There's some rubbish that needs dumping before it starts to smell.'

鬼

THE LOLLY selection arrived late afternoon. Justin pushed back his chair. The baskets on the table contained a variety of cheap sweets, the type he used to find in twenty-cent bags as a boy. He selected some strawberries-and-creams and a couple of milk bottles. With two fingers he pulled the strawberry cap off a lolly and chewed it slowly. The sugar worked on his blood and his mood.

Justin took in the trading room filled with hard-faced men, heavy drinkers and gamblers full of confidence and cock. All except Salvo, the guy stockpiling pink musks by his hard drive.

He'd eat them later, four at a time in sets of five. Twenty musks an afternoon seemed Salvo's only vice. The guy was a serious weirdo, what with his lolly habit and love for pink shirts and jewellery. He also brought in his own salami and occasionally butterfly cupcakes, complete with cream and wings. Salvo insisted his wife made them, but Justin had met Salvo's wife and she didn't seem the baking type. He suspected Salvo liked to whip them up himself after work. Seriously strange. But genuine. And perhaps just a little too innocent for his age.

Justin had better things to do in his non-working hours. Last night, though, he'd been unable to sleep. The images he'd viewed on his day off had seared his mind like a torch. It had all seemed so real. The thought brought acid to his throat. He had a wife and a daughter and he absolutely loved them both. But love changes. In recent times, Justin's lust for his wife had turned to platonic affection, which had since turned to mutual boredom and distance. It seemed they both agreed to tolerate their marriage for the sake of convenience and their daughter. It wasn't difficult to play-act happy families; how many of the men in the trading room did the same thing? Justin watched Salvo head out into the corridor, his newspaper in his hand. Perhaps the only guy on the floor who didn't pretend. The guy was heading to the bathroom to hang a dump. He'd taken the paper with him and he didn't care who knew.

Salvo and Justin had very different relationships with toilet cubicles.

Justin recognised a familiar stab of jealousy. Salvo appeared so full of hope: new job, new wife, new goals. No kids. It would only go downhill from here. Soon enough, Salvo would find himself locked into the never-ending cycle of debt repayments, supermarket shopping, nappy changing, kick-to-kick in the park, sock folding, bed making and night after night of reality television. Suck the soul out of you, suck the life out of your marriage, suck the sex out of your bed. That is what happens.

That was why Justin needed another outlet. Why he'd found himself turning to movies. His wife was the mother of his child – he couldn't ask her to fulfil his fantasies. How could he look at her the same way if she did? No. What he needed was unknown, unnamed bodies; canvases for his dark desires. He needed escape from the reality of this dull, dogged life and the chance to find some peace.

He had to get some more.

THE AFTERNOON before a term break meant chaos in the staffroom.

Sophie scanned the class lists pinned to the noticeboard. Teachers occasionally bagged the same class two terms in a row, but not often. While continuity benefited both learners and teachers, Pete argued that it didn't please everyone. Younger students liked change and, in the competitive language teaching business, student satisfaction drove revenue. 'We give them what they want to pay for, and hopefully they learn something along the way,' Pete had informed Sophie when she interviewed for her position.

This was why Pete worked as the director of studies, a glorified administrator, and not as a teacher.

Sophie checked her class list. Disappointment settled. A new class and Su Yuan was gone.

The line by the photocopier was six deep. Sophie avoided it and headed for the library.

Chuck stepped out from behind a bookshelf. 'My favourite time of the month,' he said, his voice booming with enthusiasm.

'You sound like a sanitary pad commercial.'

Chuck pulled a face. 'You know what I mean. A new term! New class! It's exciting!'

'I've got elementary students,' Sophie said. 'Need to teach them how to speak.'

'That old challenge.'

'I'm going to miss my favourite student.' Sophie flicked through the books on the shelf. 'You know how there's one person who brings the whole class together?'

Chuck nodded. 'I know it, sister. That student is the lifeblood. Without them, the class is dead.'

'Well, I'm missing my lifeblood,' said Sophie. 'Her name's Su Yuan.'

Chuck picked up his selection of books. 'Oh good,' he said. 'I've got her.'

Sophie stared at him.

'I already memorised my list,' he said, a touch defensive.

'Lucky bastard.'

Chuck held up two fingers in peace. 'You want to get a coffee or something? Hear about my Pattaya plans?'

Sophie checked her watch. Joy Lin would be rapping her knuckles against the front door in an hour. 'Tute night at my place,' she said. 'I'm biking home and my student's never late.'

'You work too hard,' said Chuck.

Sophie shrugged. 'Stops me from thinking too much.'

女孩

THE FIRST shades of evening had painted the streetscape pink. Sophie pulled her scarf tight, tucked her collar against the wind. She dodged afternoon shoppers balancing bags against blown-out umbrellas and splashed along a footpath shiny with water and headlights. It took only ten minutes to reach Central English. Her body glowed warm from the afternoon exercise.

Then she saw her bike.

Tyres slashed, deflated rubber pooling against concrete like wax. Somebody had bothered to drag a knife right through each tyre, slitting the rubber in two clean, slim arcs.

Fuck me.

Sophie looked around, hoping to spy a laughing street kid or lounging student who might have seen something. But the language school had emptied its classrooms an hour ago and the few stray pedestrians scuttled through the weather like sand crabs.

Sophie removed the lock. Leaving the bike now would be a mistake; she'd have nothing to collect in the morning. Water dripped down her coat collar, mingling with the cooling sweat on her skin. Sophie hauled the bike slowly along the pavement. Spokes cackled. Bare wheels rasped. It was going to be a slow journey.

But I'll make it.

'What happened to you?' Jin Tao held the gate open wide as Sophie limped her bicycle into the garden and over to the front steps. 'You look like you went swimming with your clothes on.'

Sophie shivered hard. A fierce cold pierced her. 'I thought you were supposed to be at work?'

Jin Tao examined the bike. 'Ducked home for some cloves,' he said. 'Shit, someone really went to work on your tyres.' He picked up the bicycle and carried it up the steps.

Sophie followed him into the hallway. He leaned the bike against the wall. 'You got any enemies?'

She tugged at her jacket. 'Not that I know about. Maybe next time they'll leave me a note with an explanation.'

Jin Tao rubbed his head. 'You don't think it's a bit weird that it happened outside the English school?'

'Why?'

'You were there this morning, asking after Han Hong.

Maybe somebody saw you poking around.'

She pushed past him. She needed the hot pins of the shower. 'You've been at my Trixie Belden collection, haven't you?'

He broke into a grin. 'You're right. It's probably just a case of wrong place, wrong time. But are you OK?'

'Yep,' said Sophie. 'And I know a bike-shop guy. No worries. I'll sort it.'

She jumped up the stairs, hit the landing and turned. Jin Tao stared back at her. What was that she saw? Concern or suspicion? For the first time in a long time, Jin Tao's face was unreadable.

THEY MET as they always did, high above a butcher shop in Haymarket. The room smelled faintly of old blood.

He surveyed the men in front of him. The Butcher sat cross-legged on a spring mattress on the floor, like a monk in contemplation. The other guy lounged in the leather armchair; with careful accuracy, he worked on painting his fingernails black.

The Chef would arrive soon. He'd pant and blame his tardiness on a busy night at the restaurant. The usual.

He considered the two men. Things weren't going to plan and the stakes had changed. He'd asked them to take Wendy Chan's life and they'd done it. No questions asked.

A familiar pinch in his belly, clammy hands, the twitch of the muscle above his lip.

Why no questions? He'd ordered the murder to protect his business, but why had these guys jumped so quickly into action? The money?

Or did they also have something they needed to protect?

Rushed footsteps on the stairs. The door flew open. The Chef barrelled in. 'Sorry I'm late.' Little more than a mumble.

He nodded to a wooden chair beside the wall. The Chef collapsed onto it, mopped his brow with a handkerchief.

'Busy night ahead?'

The Chef pulled a flask from his backpack. 'The restaurant's fine but the traffic's a shocker.' He flipped the lid on the flask, took a long drink.

'Scotch?'

The Chef raised his drink in a mock toast. 'Pu-erh,' he said. 'Scotch of teas.'

The other two men laughed but as usual he'd missed the joke. He hated tea, only drank water or booze. In this room right now he was supposed to be the leader, but as usual it was clear he remained on the outside.

A thought made his skin creep. These men were killers now. What if they decided to turn on him?

He opened his briefcase and removed a manila folder containing the photos he'd snapped in the early afternoon.

'I've called you together to alert you to a potential problem,' he said.

The men stirred, curiosity piqued.

'Two problems actually,' he said. 'First, another one of our ladies, a beauty called Han Hong, has disappeared.'

He looked at each of the men, hoping to read something in their faces. The three sets of eyes gave nothing away.

'The last I know is she finished a shift two weeks ago and went home,' he said. 'She hasn't been seen since and I want to know where she is.'

Bored expressions. They either didn't know and didn't give a shit, or they had some information they weren't sharing.

The Chef yawned. 'Sounds like she's done a runner,' he said. 'Not much point sending the substitute in for her any more, if she's not bringing us in the bucks.'

True. But he needed to protect the system. If the girl had done a runner, they'd need to officially withdraw her from study. He'd need to talk to his contact at Central English.

'The second part of the problem is that a young woman has started nosing around asking questions. She's someone we need to deal with before everything unravels.'

The men sat up. He had their attention now. This was good. He passed around the photographs.

'She's an English teacher whose care and concern for her students can only be commended.'

The Butcher, sitting on the mattress, caught his eye and smiled.

'Our problem is she's a little too caring and a little too concerned,' he continued. 'She visited Central English this afternoon, looking to speak with Han Hong. Somehow this teacher has become aware that Han Hong is missing and she's taken it upon herself to find her.'

The man with the nail polish blew on his left hand. 'Did she find the substitute?' he asked, as though talking about a point on a map.

'I spoke to the substitute,' he said. 'Somehow this teacher had obtained a picture of our Han Hong and realised that the photo didn't match with the girl in front of her. I can only guess that she's suspicious.'

The Butcher stared deep into the photo. 'Where'd you take this?' he asked.

'Outside United English. The scene of the suicide.'

At this, the Butcher flinched.

The Chef raised a hand. He'd looked at the picture only briefly. He leaned in to the group.

'I know this woman,' he said, his voice soft. The others stared back at him.

'You have an idea how to stop her?' Finally, luck on his side.

'I know her weakness,' said the Chef. 'I know how to get right under her skin and drive her sick.'

THE BEST thing about sharing a house with a chef, Sophie decided, was the leftovers. She'd spied crispy skin duck in the fridge earlier. It would go down a treat with some salad once she'd ushered Joy Lin out the door.

The schoolgirl slipped her mountain of a bag onto her shoulders. 'I'll write the essay again, another two or three times,' she said.

Sophie snapped to attention. 'That sounds a bit much.'

'I want to get it right.'

She had to give the girl points for stamina. Joy Lin had a voracious appetite for study. Already a whiz with numbers, she also maintained a B+ average across the humanities; she hoped to push this to an A, with Sophie's help. They'd spent the last hour analysing Monet's *House Among the Roses*.

'It doesn't always pay to practise things too often,' said Sophie. Joy Lin stood lopsided, the heavy schoolbag dragging one shoulder down.

'Practise makes perfect, don't you know?' she said as Sophie adjusted her straps.

'Some things have to come from the soul.'

Joy Lin snorted like a horse. 'That sounds like something from the horoscopes!'

Sophie laughed. 'I think the best writing happens when

you forget all the rules,' she said. 'The question is asking you to interpret a particular painting series. You can know the technical and historical details, but if that's all you include in your writing, it won't be very interesting, will it?'

Joy Lin frowned. 'It will be interesting to people who don't know those details.'

'But your examiners do. You need to give them something more. You need to convey emotion and passion. How can you express these things in your writing if you've planned every word before you even begin?'

Joy Lin shook her head. 'I couldn't write an essay without planning.'

'I'm not saying don't prepare,' said Sophie. She turned to the bookshelf, an idea sparking. 'Know how you plan to proceed, but you don't need to memorise every word.' She scooped a pair of earrings from the dish on the bookshelf and held them in her palm: roses, perfect red buds. Perhaps a little quirk would catch Joy Lin's inner spark.

'Here.' She held the earrings out to Joy Lin. 'I never wear them. Take them on loan as a good-luck charm.'

Joy Lin picked the earrings out of Sophie's hand. 'They're pretty,' she said. 'Cheers, I'd love to borrow them. But good-luck charms are as useful as reading tea leaves. I prefer facts.'

Sophie smiled and opened the bedroom door. 'Which is why you'll probably make a very successful scientist.'

Joy Lin grimaced, slipping the earrings into her pocket. 'Couldn't think of anything worse,' she said. 'Sitting in a lab all day, peering through a microscope stinking of mould and chemicals for hardly any money? No thanks.'

Sophie followed the girl down the stairs. 'Career plans, then?'

Joy Lin stopped by Sophie's bicycle. 'My parents want me

to do medicine,' she said. 'They are the ultimate Chinese cliché.' She ran a hand along the ridge of one busted tyre. Her fingers brushed the jagged flaps of split rubber. 'Be careful, Sophie,' she said, her voice husky. 'I think someone has it in for you.'

A chill snaked across Sophie's shoulders. She pulled her cardigan tighter. 'Pardon?'

The faintest trace of a smile played on Joy Lin's lips. 'Your tyres got slashed,' she said. 'I'm doing what you said. Interpreting the facts.'

Sophie tugged at the latch on the front door. The heavy wood swung open. Outside, rain fell. She picked up a polka-dotted umbrella from the coat rack and handed it to Joy Lin. 'Your interpretation is very creative, Dr Watson. But I think it's more likely this tyre attack was random.'

'Probably,' said Joy Lin. 'But that wouldn't be very interesting.'

Sophie leaned against the doorframe and watched the spotted umbrella bob down the street, tightness in her shoulders, a circus in her belly, a sudden urge to drink something stronger than tea. She'd dismissed the slashed tyres as a piece of random vandalism, a case of rainy-day bad luck. But both Jin Tao and Joy Lin had seen something sinister.

Sophie climbed the stairs to her bedroom. She stood quietly on the carpeted step, her eyes drawn to the wooden shrine in the corner. The small boy in the photograph smiled at her. What was it about the missing? No matter where she ran, they haunted her still.

It's all connected. Li Hua had taught her that and Su Yuan had echoed it, her hand clutching Sophie's fingers like a clamp.

Sophie lay down, closed her eyes. In a moment she was back in Beijing.

Neither of them spoke as Li Hua drove through the construction site that would one day become the Olympic Village. Sophie watched the shop-fronts of her neighbourhood slip past the window: a shoe store next to a shop selling guitars; a kebab stall next to a barber; a merchant selling sixty varieties of cigarettes.

The sky billowed grey and blended into the concrete. And then they were at the underpass that turned onto the fourth ring road. Sophie had watched the underpass birth itself. In Australia, construction projects moved slowly, took months or years. But China had felt like a living time-lapse movie. Whole freeways, skyscrapers and transport terminals could appear in a matter of weeks. The pace was frenetic, the air choked with dust. But things got done.

Li Hua drove east along the ring road. She slipped a hand onto Sophie's thigh, stretched her fingers wide. Sophie leaned back into her seat, tried to settle the pounding in her head and heart. They travelled in silence, Li Hua's hand on Sophie's leg, until they reached the airport.

At the baggage check, Sophie fought hard not to crumble. She fumbled through the check-in, dropped her passport, blurred her signature with tears.

Li Hua rubbed her back. 'Breathe,' she said.

They walked together to the departure gates. 'I hate goodbyes,' said Sophie, a rock in her throat.

Li Hua took Sophie's hands in her own. 'It's not goodbye,' she said, her own voice soft with emotion. 'You and I, we are connected, we have a *guanxi*. Even though you will move, the connection will not break. It will change, but it will not break. Distance may even make it stronger.'

Li Hua released Sophie. She held her right palm in the air. 'Hold up your hand,' she said.

Sophie held her left hand up, so that her palm faced Li Hua's.

'Closer,' said Li Hua. Sophie followed. Their hands floated, only millimetres apart.

'Close your eyes,' said Li Hua. 'Feel the energy, think about your hand and mine. Feel the energy between us.'

Sophie tried. She felt nothing.

And then, a gentle warmth, soft but electric. It pricked Sophie's nerves, like the faint tingle of Sichuan pepper on the tongue. Sophie concentrated. It felt as if their delicate, shared energy created a bridge between them.

'This is our connection,' Li Hua said, her voice even. 'Keep your eyes closed and focus on it. I will move my hand – try to follow.'

Sophie concentrated on the warmth between her palm and Li Hua's. She felt a magnetism as Li Hua moved her hand slowly backwards. Eyes closed, Sophie tracked the movement and her hand moved forwards. She imagined a tangible object, thin as a sheet, separating their cells. It was true. She could feel it. They were connected.

'Open your eyes,' said Li Hua.

Sophie raised her lids. She saw her hand moving in fluid motion, as if connected to Li Hua by a thread. If Li Hua pulled back, Sophie's hand followed. When Sophie's wrist flipped under, carrying the weight of the energy, Li Hua's palm floated on top, caressing the space between them with her fingers. Sophie watched. The energy they carried felt strong enough to see. She strained. What was that?

Li Hua brought her hand closer to Sophie's. Their palms met. The electricity faded, leaving a warm glow.

'You see,' Li Hua said, 'there is a connection between us. It doesn't matter where you go, no distance can break it.'

She leaned forwards so that their foreheads touched. For a moment they stood there, breathing in each other's scent. Calm pulsed through Sophie like a slow-moving river. She knew that the time had now come.

She picked up her cabin bag and walked towards the departure door, turning once. Like Mrs Lu against the cabbages, Li Hua stood motionless – stoic and strong.

Sophie lifted her hand in a wave. Li Hua raised hers. They stood like that, distance between them, hands in the air, an imaginary string binding them tight. Then Sophie lowered her arm.

She walked through the doors to the departure lounge without looking back.

FIRST DAY of the new term. Early enough for weeknight clubbers, hospitality workers, backpackers and hopeless party-drug addicts to be making their way home. Sophie walked the backstreets of Surry Hills, warm coffee in its paper cup taking the sting out of her hands. She passed kids in wide-legged reflector pants, a couple of drunks. She inhaled the smell of piss mixed with the straighter, kinder scents of coffee and baking.

Sophie sipped hard on her coffee, savouring its temperature and caffeine kick more than the slightly metallic taste. She'd spent four days in bed with a cold. The fever had pitched and rolled and she'd faded in and out of dreams until yesterday, sometime in the afternoon, when the fever broke. Last night had been sleepless. In the cold hour before dawn, a decision had formed. The slashed tyres may well have been a coincidence, but the connection between Wendy and the girl posing as Han Hong seemed more significant. Two imposters at two separate language schools. One girl dead and another girl missing – there had to be a connection.

She had forty-five minutes before class and she intended to spend them asking questions.

The familiar scent of fruity chewing gum greeted Sophie in the stairwell of Sydney Central English. She mounted the stairs fast, ignoring the protest in her lungs.

In the foyer, the receptionist welcomed Sophie with a roll of her eyes. 'You're back,' she said through a mouthful of breakfast muffin. 'What exactly did you say to her? Here's me the other day telling you that Han Hong girl was a stayer, then I'm eating my words. She withdrew.' The receptionist licked her short fingers.

'You mean she's disappeared?'

'She withdrew.' She eyed Sophie over the top of her glasses. 'I'm assuming whatever poaching strategy you used worked. Like I told you last week, I'm leaving so I don't care, but I am curious – are you back to steal more of our students?'

Sophie rested her elbows on the top of the desk. 'I came back to speak to Han Hong again,' she said. 'Do you have any idea where I could find her?'

'No idea, love. She's gone.'

Sophie watched the receptionist's pink tongue flick at brown crumbs. This woman cared little for the students she encountered within these walls. They represented numbers on her computer screen and countless administrative tasks. These people were her weekly pay cheque, the money that poured out of her purse and into breakfast muffins. They were the gradual dent she chipped in her mortgage. No overtime for her. No drinks at the student bars down the road. No eye contact in the elevator. These students meant nothing. Their accents had no meaning other than making the arduous task of listening that little bit more difficult. To this woman, Han Hong was a number.

Sophie opened her satchel and grabbed her phone. She laid it on the counter. Han Hong's image appeared on the phone's screen. 'Do you know who this is?'

The receptionist peered at the image. 'Should I?'

'This is Han Hong,' Sophie said. 'She stopped attending this school a fortnight ago. I'm trying to locate her.'

The woman grunted, took a long time to confer with her records.

'You're mistaken,' she said. 'Han Hong has attended class regularly. You know that because you spoke with her yourself.'

'Whoever that girl was, she wasn't the girl in this picture,' said Sophie.

The woman sniffed. 'That's good,' she said. 'That picture isn't very nice.'

鬼

MICHAEL DISNEY sat alone at a student desk in an empty classroom, laptop open in front of him. He looked up when Sophie knocked and waved her over.

'Help yourself,' he said, pointing to a white paper bag resting on another seat.

Sophie moved to the bag, picked it up, peered inside. 'Pumpkin seeds?'

'Salted.'

'I haven't eaten these since China.'

Disney smiled. 'English teachers love them. Reminds us of the fun times we spent in Asia.'

Sophie popped a seed into her mouth. She cracked it between her teeth. Nostalgia flooded her senses, along with the salt. 'They remind me of my mum. She liked these.'

'Most Chinese people do.'

'Come again?'

He flashed a grin. 'Your mother came from Hong Kong. Pete told me.'

'I didn't know he knew.'

'I'll make this quick,' said Disney, flipping open a folder on the desk. 'I've had a look at your roll book and everything seems to be in order. No unreported student absences. I assume you follow school policy in relation to absenteeism?'

Sophie nodded. 'I'm a play-by-the-rules sort of girl.'

Disney grinned. 'All of the time?'

No. 'These days.'

Sophie noticed laugh lines at the corners of Disney's eyes. He had a kind, open face. Slightly weathered skin told of someone who liked the outdoors. He was older, somewhere around fifty-five, she guessed.

'Did you know her?' he asked.

'You mean Wendy?' Had she known her? Clearly not very well. The girl she thought she'd known had a life outside the classroom that Sophie had become a small part of. And yet she'd been a fake, a woman pedalling another's identity and hiding some very dark secrets of her own.

'I taught her and I guess you could say I befriended her,' Sophie said. 'We went out to dinner.'

'Did she give you any indication that she was unhappy?'

'None that seemed obvious. She had a boyfriend and a sense of humour.'

'Other teachers have said she was always sleeping.'

Sophie nodded. 'That's not unusual,' she said. 'So many of our students work night jobs.'

Disney made a note in his exercise book.

Sophie watched him. 'Do the police have any ideas who she was?'

'Her real name was Lisa Zhu. She entered Australia on a tourist visa but ...'

'Her reason for coming here had nothing to do with the Barrier Reef.'

'It doesn't appear so.'

'Are there records of what she's been doing all this time?'

Disney shrugged. 'In China she worked in administration but she wasn't overly qualified. If she was working, I doubt the job was glamorous.'

Silence for a moment, heavy.

'Sex work,' said Sophie.

'Unfortunately there aren't many records of the names of sex workers in this city's brothels. But if there were, we'd probably find Lisa's name on some of them.'

It made sense. The student's style, her carefree attitude, even the track marks on her arms. She'd been working as a prostitute and perhaps she'd become addicted to drugs in the process.

'What was she doing, pretending to be Wendy Chan?'

Disney cracked a seed between his teeth. 'That I don't know.'

'Do the police have any ideas?'

'If they do they're not going to share them with me. I'm asking these questions out of curiosity. Amateur detective work.'

Sophie smiled. She knew about that.

Disney leaned forwards. 'We all know amateur detectives rarely get it right,' he said. 'I should mind my own business. My real job is to make sure something like this doesn't happen again.'

But it had. At Central English. A girl named Han Hong was missing. Another girl was there in her place.

'Do you think the visa fraud goes further than this school?' she asked, taking a chance.

Disney nodded. 'All I can say is I'm working on it and we're going to bring those responsible to account. Relax, I'm confident we'll sort all of this out.'

He pulled out a card, green like a leaf. 'Here,' he said, pushing it across the desk. 'My business card. I'm giving it to all the teachers. If you notice anything suspicious, please give me a call direct.'

女孩

IN THE common area, students mingled over morning coffees and snacks. The scent of dried papaya made Sophie's stomach turn. She passed Chuck's room, heard the boom of his voice. Had Su Yuan turned up today? Sophie spun back and rounded the corner into Chuck's room. Several students sat in chairs, forming a circle around a whiteboard. Su Yuan was not among them.

'Hijacking my class now?' Chuck said from the whiteboard.

Sophie waved a hello. She felt foolish standing there in the middle of his classroom. She had students of her own to prepare for. 'Looking for Su Yuan,' she said. 'When she gets in, ask her to come see me in Room 302?'

Chuck nodded. 'I'll pass it on.'

She brushed past a couple of girls as she moved out into the common area, headed to her class. As she reached the closed blue door to her room, the sound of Chuck's voice calling her floated above the buzz. Sophie turned and spied Chuck at the door of his classroom. He beckoned her.

'Are you blind or something?' he said. 'Su Yuan's here. You passed right by her on your way out.'

Sophie's stomach lurched. She dumped her books on a lunch table and stepped into Chuck's room.

Chuck pointed to a girl in the corner. 'She's one of the early birds, eager like you said.'

The girl in the corner didn't look eager. She sat bent over her desk, hair draped across her face. Sophie noticed a hand poking out from a sleeve, pale and scabbed. Not the same hand that had gripped hers and held on tight. Not Su Yuan's.

Sophie reeled back.

Chuck prodded her. 'Well?' he said. 'Did you want to speak to her or not?'

It's happening again and I don't know how to stop it.

Sophie pulled Chuck out the door. His face darkened.

'Sophie, honey, what's wrong?'

'Bring me your roll book.'

'What's going on?'

There was no time to explain. Any attempts to make sense of the jumble in her head would fail. She needed to know that the adrenaline coursing through her veins like vodka was based on something real.

'Just bring it.' Her voice, raised, sounded panicky. Chuck registered it and closed the door on the classroom. Sophie took a seat at a lunch table and brushed some grains of cooked rice from the tabletop.

'I'm guessing you know what you're looking for?' Chuck slid into a seat opposite. He passed Sophie the roll book.

Sophie flipped to the back section of the folder. She skimmed her finger down the list of names, mostly Korean and Japanese. There it was. Su Yuan's full name, printed officially in twelve-point font. Sophie turned to Su Yuan's file. Fire in her gut, hot and raw.

The plastic pages slipped through her fingers. Before her, Su Yuan's familiar script looped and rolled. She skimmed through Su Yuan's test results and essays and found the application story she'd written about her hometown, Kunming. She saw another script, too. There, signing off on the file in blue ink, was Sophie's signature, the one she'd developed as a teenager when she still had dreams of joining her father in his private investigation business.

Before it all went to shit.

Sophie closed the file. 'The girl you have in your class is a fake.'

The words escaped as though spoken by another. She felt removed from herself, from the hard plastic chair and the table with its specks of rice and soy; from the building, with its faint smell of ammonia; from these students, who still crowded and jostled and breathed sweet fruit smells in through their nostrils and out through their mouths. And in the moments before Chuck responded, Sophie registered a rush of thoughts: she sounded hysterical, affected by Wendy's death, irrational, confused.

Chuck chewed the inside of his lip.

'I'm not with you, honey,' he said. He reached a hand towards her, tentative, like he thought she might strike it.

He was right. She'd gone mad. Sophie sensed a ringing in her ears. The noise around her became muted. The rush of air through her nostrils seemed to boom with each breath.

'That girl,' she said, her voice echoing through her eardrums. 'She's not Su Yuan. I don't know who she is, but she's not Su Yuan.'

'Sophie, honey, what are you saying?'

'I'm saying that the girl in your classroom is a fake. She's pretending to be Su Yuan.'

Chuck placed his hand on Sophie's arm. With the other, he pulled a neatly folded handkerchief out from his pocket and offered it.

'Honey, you're sweating. A woman should never sweat.'

The knot between Sophie's shoulders loosened. She accepted the handkerchief and pressed the cool, clean cotton against her forehead. She inhaled its scent. Oranges and musk. Masculine with a hint of something sweet. She leaned back into the plastic, felt the chair mould into the curve of her back. The ringing died to a faint buzz. Thoughts crawled into focus.

'It's all so strange ...' Her voice cracked. She glanced at Chuck.

He traced a grain of rice around the table with a finger, screwed up his face as he became aware of himself. 'Gross,' he said. He flicked the rice away, wiped his hands on his pants. 'Maybe admin got the class list wrong. Did you think of that?'

'That would be one explanation.'

He folded his hands. 'I know it's terrible to have somebody die and to not know who they were,' he said. 'But why do you think Pete made such a fuss the other day?'

'He wants us to be on top of it.'

'Wrong. He wants to cover his butt in front of the cops, make it look like his school is following the rules.'

'But Michael Disney's running an audit. Pete can't exactly hide from that.'

Chuck sighed. 'When you've taught as long as I have, honey, you'll know most language school admin is a crock and it goes all the way to the very top,' he said. 'Schools confuse students, often on purpose, to get around visa requirements. Why forgo a student fee just because some kid doesn't want to turn up? Mostly no one notices or cares, and people like Michael Disney are part of the whole flawed system. If it weren't for that girl topping herself, nothing would've changed.'

Sophie pointed to Chuck's classroom. 'So you think Pete knows something about the girl you have in there?'

'I think he knows more than he's told us,' said Chuck. 'And I don't think he was as surprised as he let on when the cops told him Wendy was a fake.'

'You're talking like you're alright with all this,' said Sophie. 'Like you've been turning a blind eye yourself.'

Chuck raised his hands, gave a weak smile. 'I'm not here to make a fuss. I've taught in schools like this all around the world,' he said. 'This job pays my bills and I love it. I don't ask too many questions.'

'But what if something's happened to Su Yuan and she's in trouble?'

'Honey, no offence, but you're more of a drama queen than I'll ever be,' said Chuck. 'More likely she's off working and Pete's agreed to take her money in exchange for keeping her visa intact. But if it makes you feel better, I can go talk to Pete and see what he has to say. I'm not often wrong but there's always a first time.'

Students filled the space around them. Time for class. Chuck leaned in.

'My advice is to let this one go,' he said. 'Forget about Su Yuan and get on with things.'

Get on with things. That was how Wendy had met her death. She'd been hiding something and no one had noticed. Everybody had been too busy getting on with things. Sophie knew this pattern like a favourite tune. Move on and make a ghost.

She couldn't let it happen again. Not to Su Yuan. Even if Chuck was partly right and Pete had pulled a few dodgy strings, surely the records department had some checks and balances. The people pulsing through the classrooms, corridors and stairwells of this language school had paid good money to be here. Intelligent and ambitious, they would revolt if they knew their language learning accreditation could be so easily hijacked. Sophie pushed back her chair.

'Keep the girl here. I'm going to talk to Pete myself.'

Chuck grimaced like he'd just lost a race. 'Sure, Soph,' he said with a tight smile. 'Whatever you say.' He got up, turned towards his classroom.

Sophie gathered her books. The door to Chuck's classroom was thrown back. Sophie whipped her head, caught a glimpse of a tall student pushing out over the heads of others. Su Yuan's imposter was making a dash for it.

'Stop her,' said Sophie, lurching forwards, shoving her hand into the small of Chuck's back.

Chuck grabbed for the girl's arm. 'Honey, you have to stay here.'

The girl twisted free and spun away. She burrowed through the students in the corridor. They parted for her, sealing the passage again with their lazy trundle.

Sophie searched the sea of bobbing heads for another glimpse of the girl. But she'd disappeared.

鬼

CHINATOWN AT midday. Sophie arrived in a sweat. Dirty rain rushed down the gutters. The red-brick monstrosity of Paddy's Markets loomed large, its doors welcoming her into the darkness like a great, yawning mouth.

Inside, tourists rammed the space. The whole place pulsed and heaved. Asian tourists and suburbanites from western Sydney shopped for cheap souvenir T-shirts, Harbour Bridge tea towels, kangaroo-skin purses, fake Gucci handbags and shiny knock-off pearls. Sophie slipped in to the throng and inhaled the stench: spring onions and overripe fruit, damp, incense, body odour. Her ears pricked to the sound of Mandarin all around her. She tuned in to snippets of conversation: animated discussions about the best noodle soup, the benefits of royal jelly, the state of the weather.

And she was back there, wandering the old Dongzhimen marketplace in Beijing, Li Hua slipping a hand into hers, feeding her vocabulary, giggling as Sophie attempted to barter. She saw Li Hua's face before her: clear-skinned, strong-jawed, eyes alight. Sophie's heart throbbed.

'Are you following me?' A woman spoke in a low tone.

Sophie turned, cautious. The young woman, a girl, fingered the satin purses on display at the stall beside them. Sophie recognised her hands: the imposter.

'I think you were following me but I found you first,' the woman said.

Sophie dropped her voice. 'I came here looking for you,' she said. 'I need to talk.'

The girl pulled away into the crowd. 'I want to talk to you too,' she said as she moved. 'But in private. Come on.'

They pushed through the streams of people, the thin girl melting between souls like a spirit. Sophie elbowed her way past the mum-and-dad shoppers, did her best to keep up. They rounded a corner and headed deep into the back of the marketplace. Here, it was darker, the stalls less densely packed. Ahead of them stood a filthy orange dumpster. A row of rubbish bins, overflowing with paper and rotting fruit, lined the wall. The girl stopped and turned around.

Sophie wrinkled her nose. 'You want to talk here?'

The girl nodded. 'You don't have very long.'

'What do you mean?'

'I've told my friend Zhou you followed me,' she said. 'He's coming to collect me and he won't be happy to see us talking.'

Sophie looked over her shoulder. No one. 'Are you going to tell me what's going on?'

The girl flashed a crooked smile, cocked her head. 'First, you need to relax.'

Relax. A strange instruction. 'I'm concerned about Su Yuan,'

Sophie said. 'Where is she? And why are you pretending to be somebody you're not?'

'I am Su Yuan,' the girl said.

'You're not.'

The girl eyeballed her. 'You need to relax.'

'Stop saying that.'

'Listen,' the girl said. 'You don't know what it's like to be us. To be students here in a strange country. Some foreign students are rich but lots of us have very little before we find ourselves here among people who have everything.'

'What's that got to do with Su Yuan?'

'There are many opportunities here.'

'You mean for work?'

'Yes,' she said. 'We can make money. The things we do to make money, they may not be so moral, they may not even be legal, but we don't care. We're ... how do you say ...' she paused, searching for her words. 'We're twenty-first-century kids; you should try working retail here. We send the money home and we support each other.'

'What kinds of things do you do for money?'

The girl shrugged. 'Waitressing, escorting, stripping, sex, whatever.' Her eyes shone with defiance. 'We look out for each other, cover for each other. You don't have to worry.'

'You're saying you're covering for Su Yuan?'

'I'm saying you need to relax. There might be something going on but that doesn't mean anybody is in trouble.'

The girl's eyes flicked away, focused on something behind Sophie, who turned to look. An open palm pushed her firmly and sharply against the dumpster. Her head hit its metal edge with a crack. A man in grubby chef's whites gripped her firmly by the arm. She felt his long fingernails curl into her jumper, scratching at the skin above her elbow. She rode a surge of adrenaline, twisted to free herself. But it was no good. The man's grip held firm and his other hand rested against her mouth. In her peripheral vision, Sophie saw the girl lingering. She relaxed back against the dumpster, willing herself to ignore the germs, trying hard to ignore the pounding in her head.

'What are you doing with my friend?' A pair of sharp black eyes, set wide on a narrow face, stared through her. She registered high cheekbones, the thin whisper of a moustache, thick lips parted in a strange smile. Just ten steps beyond them, business carried on. But even if she screamed, her voice wouldn't carry above the din. For all the people, Sophie felt invisible here in the shadows by the rubbish, the imposter out of reach, a strange man clasping her arm.

'I guess you must be Zhou,' she said, when the man removed his hand from her mouth.

He raised his eyebrows in greeting. 'My friend tells me she's being harassed,' he said. 'She told me she was followed here by a teacher.'

Sophie twisted again under the man's grip. 'Your friend is pretending to be somebody else,' she said. 'She's stolen another student's identity.'

The man pulled on Sophie's arm, bringing her closer. She smelled something sour seeping from his skin. He brought his mouth to her ear.

'Who is this somebody else?'

'A girl named Su Yuan. My student.'

Zhou released Sophie's arm. 'Our business is none of your business,' he said. 'But may I introduce to you my friend, Su Yuan.'

Sophie turned. The girl had gone.

'She's not Su Yuan.'

'Then who is she?'

'A stranger,' Sophie said.

'It's probably better you keep it that way.' The man gave her a prod. 'My friend tells me you're an excellent teacher. Don't even think about reporting this to the school. I'll find out and, who knows, I might just drop by your home sometime for a lesson.'

AGAIN HAN Hong felt the light. This time it crept softly around the edges of her blindfold. It filtered through the blackness, bringing with it coloured shapes that merged and swam. A relief. Tracing the patterns provided a brief distraction from her predicament; a glimpse of colour in a world that had become incredibly black.

But the peace, as it settled, was short-lived. Her captor broke it, his voice menacing.

'Don't worry, baby, you'll do fine, you're going to be a TV star.'

He untied her wrists and then he was upon her. His rough hands grasped her shoulders and pulled her up. She yelled out, took a stab at a fight, and stumbled on weakened legs. Her captor ignored her and half dragged her away from the wall towards the light.

Han Hong struggled, struck a hand out and touched skin, felt stubble: a face unmasked. A change in routine, an identifiable face – it could only mean they had something worse in store for her. And that perhaps her time was running out.

Fear shot through her, charging her body with a strength she thought she'd lost. She thrashed hard against her captor, twisting her shoulders in an effort to escape his grip.

'Shit!'

Hang Hong hit the floor with her face. White pain streaked through the side of her jaw to her neck. But she'd had a win. She'd got her fingernails into his face and dug in hard. She tasted the sticky blood dripping onto her lips from her nose and felt the beginnings of a smile. She hoped she'd made him bleed.

'Bitch.'

Rough hands removed the blindfold. Han Hong blinked, momentarily blinded. He knelt beside her, a deep scratch on his cheek. In his hands he held a leather whip. She'd seen it before; the welt on her thigh stung with the memory.

'Okay, babe,' he said. 'You smile for the camera while I work at making you scream.'

SOPHIE REACHED the intersection of Liverpool and Victoria streets and took a left. Despite the bite in the air, a crowd gathered outside the gelateria. Sophie thumbed a hello at the girl serving the cones. She padded along Victoria Street, head down against a wind that danced at her neck.

If Chuck had told her anything it was that Pete was up to his neck in dodge, and maybe Michael Disney too. If so, how broad was Disney's reach? There were language schools all over the city; a couple of students swapped in and out of classes at each could add to twenty or more. She should confront Pete, make him tell her what was going down. But if her own hunch was right, and Su Yuan was in danger, then opening her mouth would be a bad move. Zhou had made this point very clear.

She saw him as she passed Kings Cross Station. He sat in the driver's seat of a white ute on Darlinghurst Road, a passenger in a hooded windcheater beside him. She'd noticed the cigarette first, watched him flick the still-smouldering butt onto the pavement. She'd raised her eyes to the driver's face, recognised him immediately.

Zhou.

She ducked to the pavement, fiddling with a lace on a shoe.

You suck. Get the fucking details.

Sophie looked up. The lights had changed. The ute had moved on.

She stood and scanned the street. Had he seen her? She cast an eye over Darlinghurst Road. The street hummed with end-of-day commuters scurrying north to Potts Point apartments and early bucks-night revellers trawling pavements for strip joints and beer. A bustle to be lost in.

What had Zhou been doing in the Cross? Was it a coincidence that she'd seen him a second time on the day he'd threatened her? Sydney was a small city compared to some she'd lived in, but not that small. Sophie pulled her coat closer, the late afternoon chill digging in.

女孩

A LONELY paper bag danced a slow jig in the deserted laneway behind the restaurant. The ginger alley cat, usually seen scouring the bins for dinner, was nowhere in sight. With only the grey skies and rubbish for company, Sophie actually felt cheered. A fine way to end the day.

A crash behind her.

Sophie spun around, sure of someone else in the lane. *A fine way to end.*

The green garbage bin lay on its side on the cobblestones. Dead leaves and spilled rubbish filled the space to the road. No one there. She turned and pushed into the Blue Lotus kitchen. She really needed a cup of tea.

'You missed him.' Stuart stood at one of the workbenches trussing a duck with a length of twine.

Sophie took in the kitchen. Two other cooks worked quietly at their stations. The remaining stainless steel benches gleamed, cleared of the rubble that usually indicated kitchen prep. The clock on the wall said four.

'We're understaffed and stuffed for tonight's service,' said Stuart. 'Half the crew are off with the flu and the agency guys haven't shown up. I'll be peeling potatoes for the first time since my apprenticeship.'

Sophie smiled and pulled off her duffel coat. 'I can give you a hand,' she said. 'Where'd Jin Tao go?'

Stuart snorted. 'He said you were coming and then he took off all of a sudden. I'm hoping he's out finding more workers.' He bundled the duck into a tray, swivelled to the sink.

'You went hunting for that duck?' She indicated the scratch on his face.

Stuart touched it, winked. 'See, I had this hot date last night...'

Sophie rolled up her sleeves. 'Enough. Show me the way.'

'Catch.'

Sophie snatched at the plastic potato peeler as it flew through the air. Her thumb collided with the handle. The peeler clattered to the floor.

'Better not put you in the slips,' Stuart joked. 'After you've washed up, try to make quick work of the rest of those spuds. I'll put you onto the onions next.'

'You make that sound like a reward.'

Stuart lifted his arms in mock defence. 'Hey, whoever said a chef's life was glamorous never stepped into a kitchen.'

In the small mirror above the basin, Sophie caught a glimpse of her reflection. Grey crescents below her eyes. During the past few days in her feverish state, she'd conjured David's ghost drifting above her bed. He'd smiled, a shy attempt at connection, and held out a gloved hand. She'd grasped it, felt David's touch firming like wax. She'd tried to hold on but the boy faded back into the darkness, leaving Sophie with only a glove to embrace.

Sophie dried her hands on a paper towel. The pile of potatoes would take her mind off the day. She glanced at the clock. It was so unlike Jin Tao to take off when the kitchen was under pressure.

鬼

WHEN SOPHIE finally kicked the front door shut behind her it was after eight. She'd peeled potatoes until five, and then Stuart had got her started on the onions and garlic. When three burly chefs in agency uniforms had lumbered through Blue Lotus's back door, Stuart had seemed considerably less stressed, although he'd cursed when she'd again inquired about Jin Tao.

At a Korean cafe on her way home from the Cross, she picked up some bulgogi and kimchi soup. The warmth radiated from the brown paper bag as she hiked home against the wind. She took the bag into the kitchen and placed the containers of food on the bench. She unbuttoned her duffel coat and threw it onto the table before she began flinging cupboards open. She collected a saucepan, salt and a jar of rice. She never understood why people bothered to pay for cooked white grains.

Because, by the time you make your own, the rest of the food is cold, Jin Tao told her every time she did this. He'd say it with a smirk and follow with the tease: *Tight-arse.* But Sophie didn't care. She didn't pay for things she could make or do more easily herself. That's just the way it was.

With the rice on and the food making warm condensation on the benchtop, Sophie took her satchel through to the living room and scuffed up the stairs to her room.

She flipped on the light. Something was wrong.

She'd had a housemate at university who swore she could sense spirits. The house they'd shared in Melbourne had been a newly renovated Victorian, far too expensive for two young students on casual wages. They'd scrimped in other ways so as to enjoy ducted heating while their classmates lived in share houses with rotting carpet and holes in the walls. Sophie had known, even then, that it was better to ride a bike to university than waste money on a tram ticket if it meant coming home to a warm house with a decent kitchen. While other students lived on hamburgers and pizza, Sophie and Caitlyn had cooked feasts.

She'd thought Caitlyn had been taking the piss when she first said the house was infested with ghosts. But Caitlyn had insisted that she sensed them; that a presence in the house needed acknowledgement. She'd placed tea light candles down the hallway and a bowl of water by the front door. To welcome the spirits, Caitlyn said: 'And to prevent them from turning nasty.'

Sophie had said nothing. But, in the middle of the night, when Caitlyn's silence suggested sleep, she'd crept into the hallway to extinguish the candles in a bid to prevent the house from catching fire. She'd never felt the presence of the spirits, even though she'd tried tuning in to all her senses while lying on her back on the hard wooden floor. She'd felt nothing. The soot from the candles left black stains on the walls and had cost them their bond.

What Sophie felt now was not so much a presence as a strong sense that her room had been disturbed. The window gaped open like the entrance to a blast chiller. The bedspread had been straightened badly, as though by somebody in a hurry, and was gathered heavily at the foot of the bed, exposing the slip of her pillowcase at the head. A distinct depressed spot suggested someone had been sitting there.

She went to the side of the bed. Directly in front of her sat the little shrine to David. The intruder had looked at this, she was sure. The frame tilted outwards, angled in a way that made it impossible for Sophie to see David's face from her pillow.

The incense stick had burned to its butt and the ashes spilled and curled from the holder onto the wooden frame. Sophie tried hard to remember whether she'd replaced the stick this morning. If so, then somebody had lit it and let it burn to the base during the course of the day. She searched her memory. The morning's events had been catalogued somewhere far behind the more ferocious memories of the imposter, the marketplace and Zhou.

It's possible the ashes are your own. You forgot to clean them up.

A ruffled bedspread. An open window. A photo frame with an unfamiliar tilt. Ash. Were these really things to suggest something sinister? Might Jin Tao have sat on her bed to tie a shoe after sneaking into her room to borrow a book? Might she herself have moved the frame inadvertently? She'd had to leave earlier this morning because of the walk and she'd indeed been rushed. She could easily have left the window open, swiped the shrine with her bag, forgotten to clean up the ash, jerked the cover from the bed. Sophie leaned back against the wall, relieved.

She inhaled, caught the scent of crisping rice. In a minute she'd lose both her dinner and a saucepan. She jumped up from the bed and hurtled down the stairs.

In the kitchen, Jin Tao dished rice into a bowl.

'If I had a dollar for every time I saved you from pot scrubbing, I could open ten restaurants,' he said.

Sophie took a glass from the cupboard and filled it with water. 'Where've you been?'

Jin Tao turned, a wooden spatula in his hand, a happy grin on his face. A deep scratch ran the length of his left cheek. Sophie stared at it, shocked. He looked as if he'd been in a street fight and come off second best. She fought a sudden desire to touch the welt, place her skin against his to take away the pain.

'You and Stuart had a fight.'

Jin Tao turned back to dishing up Sophie's dinner. 'How about I buy you a rice cooker for your next birthday?'

'Only people who can't cook use a rice cooker to cook rice. Am I right about the fight? What happened to your face?'

Jin Tao scraped the brown crust from the bottom of the pot. 'Does that mean only people who can't cook toast use a toaster to make it?'

Sophie took the bowl of rice from Jin Tao and began heaping it with beef and soup. 'Toast isn't cooking. Why are you ignoring my question?'

'I'm not ignoring you,' he said. 'I'm just busy imagining you building a camp fire next time you feel like a bit of burnt toast with your tea.'

Sophie pulled herself up to sit on the bench, her legs kicking back against the cupboards. She spooned the food into her mouth. The bulgogi had gone cold but the kimchi soup carried enough chilli heat to make her whole mouth feel alight. Jin Tao pulled himself up to sit beside her. He pinched a bit of beef out of her bowl with finger and thumb.

'Had a problem with one of my apprentices,' he said, kicking his feet in rhythm with hers. 'Bounced the guy yesterday for losing a bandaid in a diner's cabbage salad.'

'Gross.'

'Tell me about it. Lucky Stuart spotted the thing before it went out,' he said. 'I bounced the kid pretty hard anyway and the little shit walked out.'

'So today?'

'So today we're short a bunch of guys and the apprentice doesn't show up. We need all the help we can get, bad attitude or not. I go round to his house and he's smashed and he comes at me with both fists flying and I don't want to get into a scrap with the little guy so I back off but I'm still looking back over my shoulder at him and I don't notice this big dirty hook hanging out of the wall at the side of the house, you know, like to hang a flowerpot on, and it catches me and it hurt like fuck.'

'Was it rusty?'

'Might've been a bit.' Jin Tao nodded. 'But don't worry, Mum, I've had my tetanus shots.'

He gave Sophie a gentle nudge and she felt a smile creeping to the edge of her lips.

She took a mouthful of her meal, took time to chew. 'So what happened then?' she asked.

Jin Tao held up a finger. He jumped off the bench and swung open the fridge. He grabbed a beer, uncapped it, took a long swig. Half a beer and he'd be giggling like a teenager, his face and torso flushed deep scarlet as though he'd contracted a disease. He only drank when he needed courage, he said.

'So I go back to the restaurant expecting chaos, but Stuart's got it all under control and service is happening and people are eating and the agency guys he's got in seem to know what they're doing.' Jin Tao flailed his arms in the air. Beer spurted out of the neck of the bottle to settle in foamy patches on the floor. 'The place is running smoother than it does on my watch and I'm thinking I'd better watch out here or Stuart will be asking for a partnership.'

'He didn't seem happy that you left.'

'He cheered up when I said he could come over later and take that ridiculously expensive bottle of shiraz that I'm never going to drink. And apparently you were a great help.'

Sophie slipped off the bench and carried her bowl to the sink. 'Yeah,' she said over her shoulder, 'me and the potato peeler, we go way back.'

In two strides Jin Tao was beside her, taking the bowl from her hands. 'Then let me,' he said, his voice gentle. 'Cleaning up your mess is the least I can do after you cleaned up mine.'

He took the bowl from her grasp and his fingers brushed hers, lingered. For a moment they stood there, the bowl between them, fingertips connected. Jin Tao lifted his eyes to take a shy look into Sophie's. She allowed herself to stare back, saw kindness and sensuality in his gaze. Her stomach flipped, breath short and fast. Jin Tao brought his right hand to Sophie's side. His fingers traced a slow dance on her hips. Sophie's whole body fell slack.

Don't do it.

She needed to focus on something else. The dirty bowl. The foaming beer. Anything but the sensation in her stomach, the pulsing of her blood, the wetness between her legs. Anything but Jin Tao's beautiful, damaged face.

'I've got a first-aid kit in the bathroom,' she said, twisting away. 'Want me to take a look at that cut?'

Jin Tao dropped his hands and stepped back with a shrug. 'It's fine,' he said.

Sophie knew she'd done it again – destroyed a moment before it had even happened. She straightened a tea towel on the handle of the oven door. Now was probably not the time to ask him if he'd been secretly visiting her room.

He ran water into the sink and began to scrub at the bowl with a brush. 'You left your incense burning this morning,' he said, his voice low. 'It stank the whole top floor out so I opened your window to let in some air.'

A logical explanation. Not sinister at all.

'Really?' Sophie tried to make her voice sound light. 'I thought it was a bit breezy up there.'

'Yeah,' he said, sharp. 'Must be cold as ice.' He placed the dish in the drying rack, wiped his hands on his jeans. 'I've had a rough day, so I'm going to hit the sack.'

'Sure.'

'Okay.'

They stared at each other.

'And this came for you.' He pulled an envelope out from the inside pocket of his jacket.

Sophie adjusted the tea towel. 'Do you always keep my mail next to your heart?' She tried to make the question light, a joke. The words fell flat.

'I brought the whole lot in together,' Jin Tao said. He threw the envelope on the bench and fished out two more from the same pocket. He waved them in front of her. She could see that they were clearly addressed to him.

He indicated the tea towel. 'You can probably leave that now. I don't think you'll get it to hang any straighter.'

Sophie still held the two ends of the tea towel between her fingers. He had her all figured out. He knew her nervous tics as well as he knew her penchant for burning rice. He knew her better than just about anyone. She looked back, conscious of the sheepish smile on her face. But he had gone.

The envelope waited on the bench. Gone were the days

when mail meant letters from overseas friends. These days it meant bills or eviction notices or letters from the missing persons unit to say that, sorry, her mother still had not been found.

Sophie picked up the envelope and noted its weight. She held it to the light. It contained a small object, about three centimetres in length and a centimetre wide. She tilted the envelope to the left and the object slid to the bottom corner. Curious. She turned the envelope over and looked at the address on the front. Her name was spelled out clearly in black ink. The street and house number were correct. Strange, though, that the envelope was missing a stamp. Sophie took out a butter knife and made a neat slit at the top of the envelope. She opened her right palm and shook the contents into her hand.

Her breath caught in her throat as she stared down at a sleek, silver bullet.

女孩

SOPHIE SHUT the door behind her with a very quiet click.

There are some things I need to do alone.

She understood Seamus's words to her now. For years she'd felt resentful that her father had never truly let her into his personal space. The den, as they'd referred to it, had been Seamus's world: a room lined with shelves rammed with books, papers and cassette tapes. Sophie spent time there on Seamus's lap, learning stories of Irish family history and pride, inhaling the scent of tobacco and red wine mixed with sweeter notes of the oil he'd massaged into the leather bindings of his encyclopedias. In many ways it had been a comforting space, because it was the place of her father, the only room of the house that seemed to *breathe* him. And thrilling also, because in there she'd felt safe while at the same time feeling as though she were at a precipice – she'd always known there was more to her father than he let her see.

Sophie turned the nib on the lock to her door. If Jin Tao wanted access now she knew she would do the same as her father had done to her – shut him out. She needed privacy and silence. There were too many voices already, and they were just the voices in her head. She slipped her right hand into the back pocket of her jeans and fished out the silver bullet.

A thumb drive.

She'd realised what it was as soon as she'd noticed the divide that separated the cap from the body. With relief she'd snapped apart the two components. And then she'd jogged her way through the lounge room and up the stairs. She needed to see what message this bullet brought her. She had a feeling it wasn't going to be something good.

Her MacBook took an age to boot. Sophie drummed her thumbs against the desk and cursed as the screen flashed green and then blue and then brought up the hard drive's various programs one by one until finally coming to rest. It had taken a minute but it seemed like hours. She jammed the bullet into the USB port and waited for it to open.

The drive's name: The Walls. She scanned her memory for links, clicking methodically through the memory tree of her life. She came up blank. She moved her cursor to the file icon. By clicking on the file she risked screwing her hard drive or opening her information up to a hacker. But if she ignored it, she'd never learn the message that this bullet contained.

I've got enough unanswered questions in my life.

Sophie opened the drive. It contained three folders: 一,二,三. She knew enough Chinese to understand the basic text: one, two, three. She opened the first folder and scanned the contents of the files. It contained PDF documents and jpeg images. Sophie pulled up an image and drew a sharp breath.

Staring back at her from the screen was her mother, Helen.

She hadn't looked at it for over ten years but Sophie knew the photo intimately. It was the image she and Seamus had released to the press shortly after Helen's disappearance. They'd chosen the photo because, although dated, it was the only one in the albums that showed a clear close-up of her face. Mothers, Sophie had discovered in the frantic hours and days after the disappearance, are rarely photographed alone. The Sandilands family photo albums overflowed with images of happy children and laughing groups of people. But Helen was largely absent. She'd either been behind the camera or had been made virtually invisible by way of her position in the middle of a throng, the sticky hands of a toddler obscuring her face.

Sophie stared. It had been so long since she'd seen her mother and here she was, in front of her, vivid and real. She loved this photo. It had been taken long before her mother disappeared, although her features had remained very much the same. The woman in the image seemed happy. She held her head aloft, as though halfway through a chuckle, her eyes danced and her face bloomed with good health. Her cropped black hair and straight fringe, combined with a rather wide seventies-style shirt collar, gave her a funky, straight-out-of-the-commune look. Behind her, out of focus, a Hong Kong street: a smear of grey, green and red.

Sophie returned to the folder and flicked through the other files. Each jpeg contained a newspaper image from the time of her mother's disappearance. Snapshots from the press conference her father had given, an image of Sophie taken from the pages of a glossy women's magazine, more pictures of Helen – as a young woman in a party frock, her hand clasped in Seamus's; and another, as a young girl staring up through the lens of the camera, a shamble of exposed pipes and wires running the length of the wall at her back.

The Walls. The reference made sense now. Kowloon Walled City, her mother's birthplace and the place she'd run from: an unregulated, ungoverned vertical shantytown in Hong Kong. Destroyed now, but once home to prostitution, drugs, money laundering and triads. Sophie's mother had witnessed a murder and a mark had been placed on her back. Seamus had rescued her, married her, brought her to Australia and tried to keep her safe. Helen had turned her back on her past, learned a new language and taken a new name; adapted her cooking for the local palate. She'd tried to make herself invisible in her new country and culture. But it hadn't worked. She'd still disappeared.

Sophie moved on to the PDF files, although she could already guess what they contained. Sure enough, each contained a scanned copy of a newspaper article from the time of her mother's disappearance. PI'S WIFE IN DISAPPEARING ACT. PRIVATE INVESTIGATOR'S CASE TURNS PERSONAL. TRIAD INVOLVEMENT IN MISSING MUM? HONG KONG MAFIA LINKS TO MISSING WOMAN.

Sophie sat back in her chair, her mind buzzing. Someone had gone to a lot of trouble to collate this data. The State Library would contain the newspaper clippings from the time of her mother's disappearance and it wouldn't be difficult to find the articles and scan them. But why go to the effort? Did the collator of the information hope to spook her in some way, to threaten her with a triad link? Sophie's past was something she kept to herself in Sydney. She'd gone to great lengths to create a new life here and she'd told only a couple of trusted friends about her troubled history.

One of those friends was Jin Tao, in the next room.

Sophie rocked in her chair. Even though she didn't publicise it, Helen's disappearance was hardly private information. The story had been splashed around the media for years until even the newspaper editors realised it had run cold. If the sender meant to threaten to dig up Sophie's past he or she didn't have much to work with. There was nothing in the files that wasn't already on the public record.

She reached across the desk for her mouse and clicked the file closed. Beneath it sat the folder labelled 二. Sophie guessed what it might contain. In the corner of the room, the shrine to David sat now in darkness. She moved to it, dusted off the ash and lit a new candle. The walls immediately took on an apricot bloom. Gentle shadows played across the photo in the silver frame. Sophie picked up the photo and stared into it. The little boy watched her.

鬼

A PARK in Beijing in autumn. Sophie and David slouching, gloved hand in gloved hand, through browned and blushing leaves, the air cold and apple-crisp. David, interested in the world below him, bent low to examine the ground. On his head a winter beanie, green as the bush and round like a gumnut. Sophie turned her head to the clouds and the trees. Kites: she counted six of them flying high and bright above, their tails snaking sharply through the grey as their frames dipped and waved.

'Da Wei!' She gave his young shoulder a prod and pointed a gloved finger at the sky. 'Look down at your feet and you'll miss all this,' she said, her simple Mandarin earning her stares and nods from passers-by.

But David wasn't interested. He squatted at her feet. 'Boring,' he complained. 'Just for kids.'

She looked at her young charge, only a child himself, his gloves removed, fingers clawing at the rocky earth. 'And what's so interesting down there?' she asked, bending down to his level.

'The ground, Ayi. The earth. It's ancient.'

Sophie stared at David's pale face. So young and already so bright. Li Hua's son was destined for great things, but right now he needed to learn how to be a child.

'You need a little exercise,' she whispered with a wink. 'Come on, let's run together to the playground.'

David pulled his hands from the dirt, picked up his gloves and shoved them in the pocket of his jacket. Then, on Sophie's word, he broke into a gentle trot. She ran with him, purposefully falling back and surging forwards in an effort to inject some energy into his pace. The boy ran in spurts, pumping his arms, heaving out breath with the effort. He didn't look back or to the side to check on his competitor, but kept his head straight and his eyes focused on the crooked shapes of the equipment as the playground came into view around the bend. She had given him a task and he would accomplish it with minimal fuss and minimal pleasure. He would not try to race her, to interact with her or to have fun. He would simply do as he was told, run towards the play equipment, and there he would stop. Not for the first time, Sophie wondered how Li Hua, who was so open and so interested in people and community and friends, had managed to produce such an introverted child. She would've liked to have known his father. Perhaps that would have shed some light.

As he barrelled down the straight and the playground emerged from the shadow of the trees, David came to a sudden and brutal stop. Children swung and leapt about the pieces of peeling equipment, their laughter mixing with the melodic whine of an erhu, played by an elderly man who sat beneath a tree. David stood on short, tracksuited legs, catching his breath.

Sophie jogged up beside him and gave him a gentle push. 'What are you waiting for?'

David didn't respond. He looked miserably up at Sophie, his face now glowing a dusty red. Sophie pointed at the other children and did her best to sound encouraging. 'Go over there,' she said. 'Find some young friends.' The five-year-old studied the other children carefully, his gaze flitting from one group to the other as though trying to decide which would be his safest bet. Sophie knew he was fearful of their rowdiness, and that he felt shy and insecure. He would much prefer to play in the dirt on his own.

'Go on,' said Sophie. 'I'll wait here. Go find some friends.' She stepped away from him, nodding encouragement as she backed into the small crowd of people gathered around the erhu. David kept his eyes on her, holding her gaze as though it were a safety rope. She gave a last impatient gesture before turning purposefully away, an act she hoped would encourage the boy to take some social steps on his own. She spent some minutes absorbed in the music. When she peeked again, she saw David taking slow steps towards the other children.

David spent too much time alone. She worried for him. No siblings, no friends, a young life already spent mostly in the company of adults. No wonder he had no interest in kites. Li Hua had nodded her head in agreement when Sophie had raised her concerns. 'I blame myself,' she'd said, and Sophie hadn't understood what she meant. 'This is no country for more children. What kind of life can he have? No brother or sister, no father and so much competition, so many people. He must work so hard just to have an ordinary life.'

Li Hua had leaned close to Sophie. 'In truth,' she whispered, 'I had him only because I am so selfish.'

'Selfish?' asked Sophie.

Li Hua nodded and when she spoke again it was very matter-of-fact. 'I wanted a child. I knew my husband was dying and I did not want to be alone. But if I'd been less selfish, I would have had an operation, made sure I could never have a kid. It is no good, it is no good for him.'

Sophie hadn't known how to handle such a confession, had never encountered such brutal honesty. 'You can't blame yourself for wanting something so natural,' she'd stammered.

But Li Hua hadn't been convinced. 'It is not natural to have a country so crowded. I am selfish and his life will be difficult. That is why I really owe him. I will dedicate myself to him.'

Li Hua already spent so much time on David. Just reading through his schedule exhausted Sophie. Piano lessons. An English tutor. Ice-skating. A swimming coach. Trips to Hainan Island. Only the best organic foods. All this at only five. Yet David had had few experiences with other kids.

Sophie watched him tentatively join the line for the monkey bars. The others laughed and chattered but David stood alone and looked miserable. A group of older boys swamped him as they shouted and ducked and fought. *He'll start school soon*, Sophie thought. *That will sort him out.*

The erhu player began another piece. The sad tones soared and drifted, reminding Sophie of how far she'd come and how far away she now was from the hurt she'd endured. She'd run to Beijing for solace. She knew no one when she'd arrived and yet she'd somehow felt at home. She found small reminders of her mother in the gentle movements of the fan dancers and the couples waltzing to tinny music in the parks. She'd realised she fit in, could remove fish bones from her mouth with chopsticks and tolerate cubes of pig blood in her soup. She made friends, drank and danced with abandon and laughed long, hard and openly without fear.

She let go and started to figure out who she was.

Sophie returned her eyes to the playground. The monkey bars were empty. A group of children screamed in chorus from the flat surface of a roundabout as the older boys spun it from the safety of the ground. Sophie smiled. David would be terrified. Perhaps it would do him some good to experience those mixed playground emotions of pleasure and fear: that confronting rush of adrenaline and joy, the communal hysterics and comfort brought by sharing emotions and experiences with children around him. The roundabout slowed and so did the shrieking. Sophie strode towards the playground, ready to take David into her arms with a hug. But as the spinning disc slowed to a gentle twirl and the children jumped to the ground with giggles and shouts, Sophie saw that they were all girls. She glanced from the roundabout to the slide, the cubbyhouse, the se-saw and the parallel bars. There were children everywhere, but she couldn't see David. Fear spiked through her like electricity. She broke into a run.

'Da Wei!' she called, willing the little boy to emerge from behind a tree, his hands and face covered with dirt. She wound her way around the playground, roughly shaking children by the shoulders, checking faces and calling David's name.

A boy in a red beanie approached her.

'Excuse me, I have a little boy, Da Wei, you were with him over there.' She pointed to the monkey bars. 'Have you seen him?' The panic made her words spurt out in short gasps.

'Who are you, the maid?' he asked, suspicion in his voice.

Sophie bit down on the inside of her cheek. 'I'm his friend,' she said. 'Have you seen him?'

'Da Wei ...' The boy raised a bony fist to his mouth and called through it like a conch. 'Lu Cong!' Another boy ran over, skidding through the sand like a skater. The red beanie turned to him. 'You see a boy named Da Wei?'

Lu Cong grinned a toothy smile. 'I dunno.'

The red beanie turned back to Sophie. 'We don't know.'

Tears threatened. She raised a hand to her chest to quiet its heaving.

'Sorry, Ayi,' the red beanie said. 'How old is the kid?'

Sophie held out her fingers in the hand signal for five. 'He's five. He's this tall.' She stretched her hand out level with her thigh.

'I think maybe I saw him,' the second boy said.

A flicker of hope.

'His coat, what colour is it?'

That was easy, she had bought it for him herself. 'It's red.'

'Then everything's okay,' Lu Cong said, his words bringing Sophie sweet relief. 'He was picked up five minutes ago. He went away with his dad.'

Sophie tasted bile. 'Da Wei doesn't have a dad.'

She pushed past the boys, rushing to the edge of the playground, scouring the trees for a glimpse of David. She spun on her heels to find the boys fast behind her, sensing danger or buzzed on her fear or high on a mixture of both.

'Where did they go? Which way?'

'That way.' Lu Cong pointed to a path cutting through the trees to the side gate.

Sophie rushed to it. Outside the serenity of the park, Beijing pushed by with a roar. Fumes mixed with the scent of duck fat and spice. The traffic bellowed, sent plumes of black into a quickly darkening sky. Sophie looked up and down the street, her eyes searching for a glimpse of red. But the footpaths to her left and right were empty. If David had been here, he was now gone.

And then she saw it. Something green in the gutter. In three quick strides she was there. With a sinking heart, she bent down and picked up David's winter hat, that perfect green cap, round as a gumnut. Tears streamed out of her eyes as she held it to her face.

女孩

SOPHIE CREPT back to the computer, picture frame in her hand. She stood it on the desk next to her MacBook, shook the screen awake. The folder marked 二 appeared before her. She placed the cursor over it and clicked it open.

The files were photos and images and newspaper articles relating to David's disappearance. Sophie recognised many of the articles: she'd looked them up at the library herself. But the collator had included many references she had not come across: articles from Chinese-language newspapers and clips from the Mandarin-language news. She scanned through the documents, blinking rapidly to keep tears at bay.

Whoever had compiled this had gone to considerable time and effort. The missing people in her life compartmentalised neatly before her as a series of newspaper articles.

And now it's happening again. I have missing people all around me.

Might the third folder contain the answer to Han Hong's disappearance?

Sophie took a deep breath as she allowed the cursor to come to rest upon the third file. With a double-click, she opened it. In the next moment she felt her hand hit her mouth. Sophie stared at images of herself, scarf taut around her neck, face turned to the lens. It felt like looking in a mirror. The photographs had been snapped outside United English and the street shone with rain.

She already knew Zhou was watching her. But even if he'd taken the photos, how had he known where she lived?

She considered the three files again, a new thought dawning. Clearly, the sender was taunting her, reminding her that no matter how far she ran, she could never escape her past. Mysteries and missing people scattered the framework of her life.

But the more she considered the order of the pictures, the more she felt drawn to something darker. The owner of the bullet had sent her a clear message.

Sophie bolted from her chair and grabbed her parka, finally certain of one thing.

If she didn't solve this quickly, the next person to go missing would be her.

TAE HUN removed the last soju bottle from the corner booth and used his cloth to wipe up some spilled kimchi. The group in the corner had arrived early, left late and created a great mess in the hours between. A bunch of Chinese students, trying out Korean food. They'd complained that it was too spicy and too sour and they'd lifted their silver rice bowls to their mouths like pigs. Tae Hun wiped the table clean and hummed his favourite pop song. He consoled himself with the thought of a cigarette and a glass of Johnny Walker. These small pleasures would be his in an hour, amid the darkness of a nightclub, in a corner booth, with some friends for company, some good music and a girl or two. He'd look out for a pretty one tonight and he'd ask her to sit on his lap.

Australian girls were so stuck up. In Australia, the girls spent their whole evening sneering. If you tried to talk to one of them, she'd brush you off before you got a chance to ask her name. No wonder the women here were all single and haggard.

In Korea, it was different. In Korea, women actually dressed to impress. A man could invite a lady to come and sit with him. Back home in the clubs, Tae Hun liked to order Johnny Walker, champagne, plates of food and sweets, expensive cigarettes. Then he'd scan the crowd for the best-looking woman and ask a friend to invite her over. The girl would take a look and, if she liked what she saw, she'd comply. In Korea, men were men and women were women. Life was not so complicated.

Tae Hun bit his lip as he felt the first stabbing pain of homesickness hit hard in his gut. He still had five months of study to complete, but he would be home by Christmas and away from all this. He now dearly regretted his conversation with the English teacher. He'd opened a box that perhaps couldn't be closed and he had a sneaking suspicion that this would have negative consequences. He wanted to forget about Wendy and Han Hong and the rest. Now he wanted only to finish his time here, and go home to Seoul.

He loaded the last of the dirty dishes into a plastic tub and hoisted the tub to his shoulder. But as he turned towards the kitchen, he became aware of a woman calling his name. He felt his stomach muscles tense as he recognised the voice.

鬼

SOPHIE WINKED at Tae Hun as he followed her approach with his eyes. He had the flushed look of someone very tired or very emotional and his eyes were encircled with dark. Sophie felt bad about what she was going to ask him to do – the boy looked in need of his bed.

'How's it going?' she asked, peeling gloves from her fingers.

Tae Hun pointed to the tub full of dirty dishes, annoyance clear on his face. 'I'm kind of busy, Sophie. You? You want something to eat?'

Sophie shook her head. 'I need you to help me, Tae Hun. I need you to take me to that club.'

The boy's skin turned pale. The capillaries in his cheeks became visible under the fluorescent light.

'Which club?'

'The one you told me about. The place where you saw Han Hong.'

He picked up the tub. 'I can't, Sophie,' he mumbled. 'Sorry. I have to work.' He began to move away, his eyes fixed to the floor.

Sophie moved quickly around the table and placed herself in his path. 'Please, Tae Hun. You asked me to help you and I'm trying to. But I need to see that club for myself.'

Tae Hun looked up, shaking his head. 'Don't ask me to, Sophie, the club is illegal.'

'It doesn't matter.'

He tried to step around her. Then he lowered the tub. 'It might not be there any more,' he said. 'The illegal clubs, they move location.'

Sophie studied him. She guessed from the fear on his face, and his refusal to meet her eye, that the boy was lying. The deception made her more determined.

'I need to see it, Tae Hun.' The emotion welled in her throat. She noted that Tae Hun had flinched when he heard her voice break.

'I'm not sure if I remember how to get there,' he whispered.

Sophie pulled out her phone and retrieved the photo of Han Hong. She held the image out. 'She was your classmate and now you think something may have happened to her. You didn't want to go to the police so you came to me. I'm asking you to help me find her.'

Tae Hun stared at the photo of Han Hong and didn't speak.

Sophie shoved the phone back into her pocket. She'd go by herself. 'Just drop me there in a cab. You don't have to come in.'

He managed a defeated smile. 'I can't let you go there alone, either.' He pointed to a nearby table. 'Sit down, have a drink. I finish at midnight, we can go then.'

女孩

THEY WERE out west, somewhere near Ashfield. Sophie had watched suburban Sydney turn to Asia through the windows of the cab. Chinese characters advertising everything from dumplings to electronics to traditional medicine flashed by in hues of yellow and red. But, unlike Asia, the streets were empty. Sophie squinted at her watch. It was close to one.

They pulled up in a quiet suburban street. Sophie had imagined a club somewhere in the bowels of Chinatown or above a sex shop in the Cross. Not this. Not the suburbs where kids rode bikes over uneven concrete footpaths and mothers rolled prams to parks. It somehow made the idea seedier. What type of people would come looking for sex here?

Tae Hun mooched down the darkened street, pulling his tracksuit top to his chest to block out the cold. Then they were turning into the driveway of a darkened weatherboard home. It was a large block and the house, to the left of the driveway, was set back from the road. A high wooden fence protected the property from nosy neighbours and street-side eyes. Ugly metal bars protected the property's windows at the front and side. Sophie couldn't see any light coming from the home, and the darkness combined with the night's chill and silence gave her the creeps.

'Is this the right spot?' she whispered, pressing into Tae Hun's back.

He grabbed her hand. 'Come with me.'

They slid through an unlocked iron gate and walked hand in hand around to the back. There, the bright welcome of a sensor light announced their presence. The backyard spewed overgrown grass and several large mounds of dirt. To the left of the yard sat a windowless concrete garage. It stretched long and narrow, the length of the yard, its flat roof home to the shadowy outline of an old lounge set. Sophie followed Tae Hun but stopped in her tracks when the door opened and a man with some serious metal in his face stepped out.

The smash of house music escaped from the shed and into the night. Then quiet again, as the man closed the door behind him. He leaned against it to light a cigarette.

Tae Hun extended his hand. The man stuck his cigarette between two rubbery lips and reached out for Tae Hun's wrist. In a single manoeuvre he whipped Tae Hun's arm around behind his head and twisted his torso to place him in an uncompromising headlock. Tae Hun gave a startled whimper and Sophie felt her own hand slam against her mouth. Through the shock, Sophie registered irritation. This was how people felt when they realised too late that they'd placed themselves in the shit.

The man in the baseball shirt let out a laugh and released Tae Hun from his grip. Relief replaced tension. Tae Hun's giggle, high-pitched, rang out next to the deep guffaw of his captor. Sophie watched, sensing the screw in her belly loosen its grip. But something in Tae Hun's expression suggested a quiet unease. Sophie guessed that perhaps he knew there was an equally serious side to the joke.

'This is Cho,' Tae Hun said. 'I told him you were curious.'

Cho smiled at Sophie. Even in the dull light provided by the sensor, Sophie could see the nicotine stains on his teeth.

'Hi,' she said.

Cho responded by sending his gaze down Sophie's body and back again, coming to rest at her chest. She pulled the zipper on her parka straight up to her throat, dragging with it Cho's greasy-eyed stare and his smirk. They eyeballed each other. Cho maintained eye contact as he leaned across to Tae

Hun and spoke a few words that Sophie could not understand.

She looked over her shoulder at the house. It lay in darkness, blocking access to the relative safety of the road. The only way back to the street was through the gate at the head of the driveway. Sophie wondered whether it would be locked when she next tried to pass through.

And then Tae Hun addressed her: 'C'mon, Sophie, let's go.'

Cho opened the door to the shed and pulsing electronica exploded into the early morning quiet. Sophie followed Tae Hun inside, jumping away from the touch of Cho's hand on her back. The door closed swiftly behind her. Sophie leaned against it, felt a gentle resistance. Insulation.

She breathed shallowly through her nostrils, willing herself to tolerate the scents of tobacco smoke and cheap, sweet deodoriser. Dim lighting and a smoky haze made it difficult to see. The room was carpeted and contained a mix of odd furniture. A DJ in a basketball cap mixed beats in one corner. Along the opposite wall, a trestle table housed a multitude of different bottles and plastic cups. The patrons numbered about twenty: a couple of younger guys mixed in with men of middle age, nursing drinks and smoking heavily. They sprawled across the couches and chairs, some in groups and others quite obviously alone.

And that was it.

Except for the girls.

There were six of them. Tall, slender, Asian and mostly naked. They wore high heels and little else. One girl complemented silver shoes with a silver ring piercing her nipple. The ring had a tassel attached to the end and it twinkled as she turned. Another girl matched red stilettos with a pink plastic belt secured loosely around her hips while a third wore only a dog collar. The collared girl walked freely between the couches, but

Sophie noticed a chain swinging from the leather at her neck. She searched the faces of the women. Blank canvasses stained cherry red at the lips. Is this what had become of Han Hong?

'Come on, sit down. You're the only girl in here,' Tae Hun said. 'Besides them.'

He sat in a chair parked close to the door, another chair opposite, a small table in front. Sophie took a seat. She looked up at the door. Above it she saw the green letters of the exit sign. Something so banal and ordinary reassured her. Perhaps this wasn't a creepy house of horrors. This was a sex club, an illegal one, but nothing more. Maybe it was better to serve sex straight up on a platter, like this, than to hide it in the marketing mechanisms of mainstream pop music or reality TV. She allowed herself to relax.

'Who is that guy – Cho?'

Tae Hun lit a cigarette and took a deep drag. 'He's the doorman.'

'You guys were talking about me.'

'I told him you were my girl.'

Sophie leaned forwards in her seat. 'And what did Cho say to that?'

'Nothing.'

'Tell me.'

He shifted uncomfortably. 'He wanted to know if Aussie girls are a good fuck.'

Sophie looked away.

'You forced me to say,' Tae Hun said. 'And anyway, we're here.' He took his packet of cigarettes from his pocket and lit another for himself. 'Are you okay?'

Sophie leaned back into the chair. 'It's strange,' she said.

'What?'

'This. I mean it's ultimately just a strip club with naked

girls serving drunk men more drinks.' She looked around. You'd never know they were in somebody's backyard. They could have been in any seedy bar in the country. 'I mean, I don't understand the need for this. How is this any different from a legal club?'

Tae Hun exhaled smoke from his nostrils. 'There's more to it,' he said.

And then Sophie heard a cry. She jerked her head in the direction of the sound. The woman in the dog collar stood chained to a hook on the wall at the back of the room. A middle-aged man in a suit held her hair in one hand and her throat with the other.

Sophie shuddered. She turned back to Tae Hun. 'What's going on?'

'I guess the difference is, in a place like this, there aren't any rules.' Tae Hun stared at the table and flipped the cigarette packet nervously between his hands. He looked up at Sophie, a mix of fear and embarrassment etched on his face. 'I did try to warn you.'

ZHOU LOWERED the basket of chillis onto the wooden bench at the bottom of the stairs. Several other similarly laden wicker baskets sat nearby. Behind the wall the restaurant buzzed with the sounds of late-night diners hoeing in to steaming bowls of Sichuan chilli chicken, double-fried pork and hot boiled dumplings. The restaurant smells of sesame oil and Sichuan pepper filtered in to mingle with the storeroom's dry, garlicky air.

He wiped his hands on his whites and surveyed the storage space. The storeroom housed barrels of cooking oil, bottles of rice wine, jars of soybean paste, packets of Sichuan pepper, dried chilli, star anise and cinnamon – all the trappings of a typical Sichuan restaurant. But what had once been an ordered storeroom had recently become a jumble. Zhou couldn't move an inch without stepping on a bundle of something. The visible segments of linoleum flooring were covered in a layer of dust and oil and chilli flakes. Even the ceiling rafters seemed to groan from the weight of hanging garlic nets. It wouldn't be long until he'd be begging favours from the Uyghurs next door.

Zhou reached out and tested the weight of the shelves on the left side of the room. They were stacked high with bottles of soy and vinegar. He moved around to the end of the heavy wooden shelving structure and tentatively rocked it from side to side. When that didn't yield results, he turned around and placed his buttocks on the flat side surface. He pushed hard, straining to hear sounds of movement. But there was nothing. Zhou stepped back, counted the bottles lining the shelves and calculated it would take a morning to unload. On the wall beside the far edge of the shelving structure, the hinges of an unframed door were visible. The doorway led to the storeroom of the adjoining Uyghur restaurant. The two restaurants had once belonged to the same family before being sold off as separate businesses some fifteen years ago. Zhou knew the space on the other side of that door hosted a storeroom the same size as his or larger. He figured it might again be time to put pressure on the neighbours, open that door for business.

Zhou felt the tingling sensation of his mobile phone vibrating against his leg. He fished the phone out of his pocket and answered without bothering to check the caller ID. There was only one person who liked to call him this time of night.

'*Wei?*'

'We've got a spicy one over here.' The voice had a smothered quality, buried as it was beneath the chaos of electronic beats. But Zhou had heard enough to forget about his storage issues. The teacher hadn't heeded his warning.

It was time to pay a visit out west.

THE GIRL in the purple G-string returned with their drinks. She cupped each glass in a curled, slim-fingered hand and Sophie noticed that her long fingernails were painted orange. As the girl placed the drinks on the table, Sophie reached over and stroked her wrist. The girl flinched and eyeballed Sophie, her jaw set in resignation.

'You want? Then you pay,' she spat. Her bright lips slashed open like a brilliant red wound. Sophie pulled a fifty-dollar note out of her pocket and placed it on the table. The woman flicked a glance at it and pierced Sophie with her defiant stare.

'I'm looking for someone named Han Hong,' Sophie said, the words tumbling out in a rush.

The girl grimaced. 'You want to talk,' she said, 'you slap my face.'

Sophie sat back in the chair. 'What?'

'I can't talk to you unless you do it.'

They watched each other, eyes locked. Sophie saw sadness and fear, an unfitting confidence and a challenge in this woman's eyes. She wondered what was visible in hers.

The woman raised a pointed chin and tilted her cheek towards the ceiling.

But Sophie couldn't mark that taut white skin. Had the

woman been a monster, the revulsion would have been the same.

'I can't hurt you,' she said. 'I'm sorry. I'm looking for Han Hong.'

The woman rocked back on her heels, raised a slim wrist and pressed a painted fingernail to her lips. She smiled. 'Sorry. I can't help you. We don't go by our real names.'

'But she could be here?'

The woman shrugged. 'Lots of girls work here,' she said. 'We do it for the money and we don't need rescuing.'

'So you're working here of your own free will?'

The woman nodded. 'Otherwise I couldn't have what I want,' she said. She stood up and walked back into the middle of the room.

Sophie watched her go. When she turned back to Tae Hun, he was gone.

The glass warmed in her hand as she waited for him. She checked her watch. Quarter past two. While the green glow of the exit sign above the door still worked to settle Sophie's nerves, Tae Hun's absence worried her. What was this, some kind of trap?

The weight of a hand on her shoulder. 'Where did you go?' she asked.

Zhou took a seat in the chair previously occupied by Tae Hun. His dirty whites replaced by a pair of skinny jeans and a black leather jacket, he looked every bit the movie star. He stretched one long leg over the other and lit a cigarette from the silver zippo in his hand. He inhaled deeply and exhaled smoke from two wide nostrils.

Sophie sank deeper into her chair. The disgust and despair of the night receded from her senses as she realised this moment could mark the beginning of her end. She wondered what would happen if she were to pull herself up and make for the door. But her legs felt gelatinous; she didn't know if they would carry her weight.

'I told you to stay away.' The words shot out of his mouth and into Sophie's heart.

Her world slowed. It felt as if this were happening to someone else and in slow, underwater motion. She melted backwards, folding herself into the upholstery. Her hands found their way south, around her thighs and under the protective layers of her buttocks. She became aware of sticky leather softening into the crevices of her palms and mixing with the sweat there, shortening her life lines. The blood that pulsed through her veins to her brain felt heavy and slow and thick.

'It's the drug in your drink that's making you feel like this,' Zhou said, relaxed and cool. He smiled with something like reassurance. 'Some girls love it. Numbs the pain a bit. Don't worry, it will wear off.'

A surge of panic fought to make itself known on the surface of Sophie's consciousness but the drug in her system succeeded in holding it down. She was aware of a struggle somewhere deep within her, a need to express her fear, to scream, to pull herself out of this chair and crash out the door into the night. But more powerful was this thickening feeling, the warmth, a slight queasiness, a heavy weight in her muscles, a strong urge to close her eyes and sleep.

'I know you're tired, Sophie, but you need to listen.' Zhou was talking to her. His lips were moving and forming words that floated through the space between them, not quite settling in Sophie's ears.

'Hey.' A stinging slap to her cheek. She saw Zhou's black eyes hovering dangerously close to her own. She became aware of his breath tickling the small hairs on her upper lip. 'You pay attention,' he said, pointing a thin finger. He shook the tension from his hand and lit another cigarette. 'I don't know what you're doing here, but you need to stop now. This is not your business.'

Sophie fought to make sense of the words coming to her in warped and echoing tones. She fought the heavy pull of her eyelids and the nausea surfing her stomach in increasingly buoyant waves. She would try to answer. She needed to tell him what she wanted.

'I'm looking for a girl,' she mumbled.

'Aren't we all,' said Zhou.

'Her name's Han Hong.'

Through the haze, Sophie saw Zhou's eyes roll and his mouth break into a grin. He leaned forwards and waved his finger in front of Sophie's face.

'You think I'm going to talk to you about any of these girls,' he mocked. 'I told you. This is none of your business.'

Sophie wondered how he would react if she vomited. Here. Now. Onto that finger and into his face.

'I don't care about your business,' she managed. 'I just want to find Han Hong.'

'Why?' he said with a smirk. 'You want to fuck her or something?'

The words repeated themselves in Sophie's head, the blunt devastation of their meaning softened only by the chemicals in her blood.

Zhou regarded Sophie with a smile sprayed flat to his face.

'I knew a Han Hong,' he said finally. 'And she went back to China.' He stubbed his cigarette out on the table leg. 'Too bad for you.' He propelled himself out of his chair and scooped Sophie under the armpits. 'It's time to go.'

'I'm waiting for a friend,' she slurred as Zhou dragged her to the door.

'I think you mean your friend is waiting for you,' he said.

With the opening of the door came an icy blast of night air. It stung Sophie's face with its sharpness.

And then she was against the outside wall of the bunker, her face meeting the wall with a bash. Zhou spun her around. His hand was at her neck and the metallic ice of the night air was replaced with the cool of a knife, its smooth blade resting flat against her cheek. Zhou's breath was on her lips. The scraping of metal across the surface of her skin. Stale cigarette smoke. A distant moan. A faint pounding in her head. Garlic. These were what Sophie would remember this moment by.

'You are pretty.' Zhou's voice was a whisper. 'I gut pretty things for a living. And do you know what I do with them?'

The blade pressed into Sophie's cheek and she felt a burning sensation as her nerves prepared for her flesh to part. Zhou squeezed her neck with his left hand and scraped his knife along her skin with the other. His eyes bore into Sophie's, a slight curl to his lip.

'I turn pretty things into delicacies,' he said. And then the pressure on Sophie's skin released and Zhou shoved the knife into the back pocket of his jeans. He released his grip enough for her to gasp at the air in a great moan and pull it hungrily down into her lungs.

'It would be wonderful to see you bleed,' Zhou said. 'If you ever come back here, I guarantee that will happen. I will open you up and turn you out. I'll make you look like a beautiful kidney flower.'

Zhou pinched the skin on Sophie's neck as his hand made its retreat. Her legs slid out. Her parka scratched a rough tune into the night as it skidded down the brick wall with her body. Collapsed among the dewy weeds, Sophie watched Zhou's leather shoe rise out of the grass and swing backwards in a slow arc. It slammed, with a thud and a burning rush, into her chest.

鬼

SOPHIE DIDN'T know how much time had passed before she felt she could breathe properly. She'd heard Zhou move away from her some minutes after the brutal kick that had knocked the air out of her lungs and sent all her pain receptors shrieking in her chest. She'd heard the rush of club music escape from the shed as the door opened and she'd jumped with the slam of the door as it sealed again, cutting the outside world off from the horrors within.

Sophie pressed her palm to the ground and spread her fingers into the earth. Suction-cup fingers, an old yoga teacher had liked to call them. She used what strength she had left to push herself up from her foetal position so that she could sit and rest for a moment, her back to the wall. Around her, the empty yard stretched long and dark. The sensor light had extinguished itself, fooled by Sophie's crumpled and unmoving body in the grass. Sophie guessed that upon her movement the yard would once again become illuminated. She wondered whether she would be pursued, whether the side gate would open; whether Tae Hun was still alive.

And it was this last thought that made Sophie creak to her feet and break into a run. She hurtled wildly through the film of yellow sensor light, around the corner of the house and down the concrete path to the gate. The black grille swung open like a flap. Sophie clambered through it and sped down to the footpath of the street beyond.

She emerged onto the street heaving. Her gasps broke the night like sobs. She bent to her knees and clasped them to catch her breath, then lifted a hand to her mouth and bit hard on her knuckles, diffusing the pain, quieting her rushing mind. Calmer, she lifted her head and looked straight at a darkened mound of a figure huddled deep in the overgrown grass of the nature strip. Tae Hun.

Sophie moved gently to him and pushed his shoulder with her palm. Tae Hun groaned and rolled onto his back, exposing his face to the night.

'Tae Hun? What did they do to you?'

His left cheek had swollen to the size of a grapefruit and his left eye had disappeared into his head. Blood trickled from both sides of his mouth. His shirt had rustled itself above his waist and even in the dusty light from the moon, Sophie could see his torso was bruised black and red.

'They bashed me for bringing you in,' he said in a voice that came out like a rasp. 'I think they wanted me dead.'

Sophie fell to her knees and reached her arm out to him. He rolled onto her knees and threw his arms around her legs with a heave.

'I thought you were gone,' he whispered. 'I thought I lost you here.'

Lost you.

Sophie pushed her fingers through his matted hair. She knew what it felt like to be responsible for someone, to lose them, to wonder what pain they had been forced to endure because of your neglect.

'Come on, little brother,' she whispered. 'Walk with me and we'll make it back down to Burwood Road.' She threw her right arm around his waist and pulled his left arm up over her shoulder.

'Sophie?' Tae Hun said when they neared the glow of the main road.

'Yeah?'

'What do we do now?'

Sophie looked across at his weeping face. Dried blood had caked itself to his chin, eyes and cheeks, and the swollen left side of his face was a tie-dye pattern of pink. For the first time since Wendy's suicide, the desire to pursue unanswered questions subsided.

I'm not my father's daughter any more. I don't want to disappear. Fuck this.

'We take you home and clean you up,' she said. 'Then tomorrow we go to the police.'

女孩

SOPHIE'S EXPECTATIONS were low. She only knew that Tae Hun had lain beside her in her bed and moaned while he slept. This morning when they woke, his pillowcase was stained brown from his blood.

'Leave it, Sophie,' he'd said as she dressed the wound above his eye. 'These people, they don't answer to the police.'

'You think I don't know that?' And she'd been surprised by the accusation in her voice.

Tae Hun had regarded her, scorn shining through his bruises.

He was right, she knew that. When had the police ever helped her? In Australia they'd failed to find her mother and in China they'd failed to find Da Wei. She doubted anyone in uniform would ever find out what had happened to Han Hong.

But this was too big for her to go alone. She'd tried, and Tae

Hun could barely see as a result. She couldn't risk placing him in danger again.

'That man threatened my life and yours,' she'd said, doing her best to sound convincing. 'I am not going to sit on it.'

And so they were here. The cop at the counter was all protocol and no emotion. With a freckled finger he pushed a sheet of paper from his side of the counter to theirs. 'Fill in the form,' he said. 'And we'll lodge your report.'

'Don't you want to hear what we have to say?'

He looked up from the counter. 'I can't help you until you fill in the form.'

'Have you seen his head?'

The constable nodded slowly. With a helpless shrug of the shoulders, he pointed to a row of chairs positioned along one wall. 'He might feel more comfortable with a seat.'

Sophie helped Tae Hun to a chair. The cop stared as though he knew her.

'I think we've met before,' he said, when she returned to the counter.

Sophie pulled the form towards herself and picked up a pen.

'The jumper,' said the cop. 'Outside the language school. You were there.'

Sophie looked at him, remembered the young cop with the face full of disdain. He'd disliked her then and given her a guilt trip for hanging around. And now here he was, pedantic about paperwork and ignoring the real story in front of him.

'It's always the same,' she said, shoving her hands in her pockets, a finger touching cardboard.

'I beg your pardon?'

'Forms, protocol, administration. Does anything ever get done?'

'It's all about numbers here. If you and your boyfriend are

having domestic issues, it might take the investigators a while to get onto looking into them.'

Sophie fingered the cardboard in her pocket. She pulled it out, turned it over: the business card from the PI, Damian Sommers.

Always do everything for yourself, Seamus had said. *But never be afraid to ask for advice.*

Sophie made a decision. 'Forget it,' she said. 'I've changed my mind.'

She took satisfaction in the cop's quizzical look as she backed away from the bench.

Tae Hun stood up as she approached. 'What do we do now?'

Sophie pulled her phone from her bag. 'You go home,' she said, keying in Damian's number. 'I'm going to talk to a PI.'

鬼

THEY MET at a grungy Surry Hills coffee shop. Damian wore jeans, a T-shirt and a pair of brightly coloured high-tops.

'No suit today?' asked Sophie when he sat down.

'I call this my down time,' he said, flashing a smile.

'Your day off?'

He nodded. 'Most of my sneaking around is done Friday night till Sunday, cheating lovers and all that,' he said. 'I only wear the suit to blend in with the five o'clock crowd anyway. Makes it look like I'm working a real job.'

'You don't consider private investigation a real job?'

'It pays okay but there's a lot of running around, sorting through other people's rubbish, crawling through confined spaces, checking pipes for foreign objects. Stuff better suited to overalls.'

She couldn't resist a jab. 'So the suit helps you pick up chicks?'

Damian smiled. 'Something like that.'

The coffees arrived, a cappuccino and a long black. Damian sipped his coffee straight through the foamy top.

'The coffee here is the best,' he said, wiping milk from his lip with a napkin. 'Almost as good as Melbourne.'

'My hometown.'

'Yeah, I can kind of tell.'

Sophie laughed. 'Oh yeah?'

He nodded. 'Must be the bruises. You're a rough lot down south.'

He'd got that one right. Rough as guts. Time to change the subject.

'Do you want to hear my story?'

Damian took out a notepad and a pen. 'I do,' he said, all serious.

She studied him. He had the lean, jowl-less look of a man not yet thirty. He should be throwing back beers at the pub or taking his board out for a surf. What was he doing here in this grungy cafe taking an interest in the problems of a woman he'd only just met? Would he be hitting her up for big money?

'And what are you going to do with the information?' she asked.

Damian considered her. 'I don't know yet,' he said slowly.

'Because I'm not going to pay you.'

A faint smile played on his lips. 'Then why did you contact me?'

'I had a feeling.'

'About what?'

'That you'd give a shit.'

He sat back in his chair, hands folded across the back of his head. 'You're right on that one,' he said. 'I give a shit about what happened to you and I want to find the person who damaged your gorgeous face.'

女孩

SOPHIE RETURNED home to find a note on the fridge.

Are we still on for the trip? Call me.

The trip. She and Jin Tao had made plans to skip town and head west to the Blue Mountains. They'd organised a bluestone cottage and planned to build a log fire, make Chinese corn cakes and wild mushroom ragu, drink tea, read trashy magazines and sleep. They'd made the booking weeks ago and planned to leave today. Sophie hadn't thought of it since.

She went into the bathroom and considered her face in the mirror. The bruise on her cheek bloomed a blotchy purple and the whites of her eyes were streaked with red. The skin on her lips had cracked and started to peel. She could definitely do with a break.

She needed to collect some supplies. In the kitchen she sorted through the resuable shopping bags, selecting the one containing the least number of useless receipts. Then she picked up the phone.

Jin Tao answered on the first ring. 'Okay, spill the goss. You could have just told me you were seeing someone.'

'Huh?'

'Someone stayed over last night.'

Sophie fingered the bruise. Jin Tao had it all wrong but how she wished he were right. She wished last night hadn't happened, that she hadn't chased down Tae Hun and gone out to the house in Ashfield. She wished she'd simply gone out to a club, had too many drinks, pashed a strange man and brought him home.

'That was just a friend,' she said.

'I don't get to share your bed, Sophie,' said Jin Tao.

There was no point delaying it.

'You remember that guy, Tae Hun?'

She caught a sharp intake of breath on the end of the line.

'What are you doing, Soph?' Jin Tao had lowered his voice but she detected the steel in his tone.

'I was with him last night,' she said, hoping to sound light.

'And what did you guys get up to?'

'I'll tell you on our way to the mountains.'

'I'm only going to say this once,' said Jin Tao after a pause. 'Your dad was a PI and look what happened to your family. You chose not to become a detective, Soph. I wish you'd try to remember that.'

It's in my blood.

'No need when I've got you to remind me,' she said. 'I'll catch you soon.' A wave of disappointment washed her insides. She'd forgive Jin Tao for bringing up her father but she imagined she would have a battle convincing him that she'd done anything right last night. It was true, she was lucky to have escaped with little more than some bruising and a scare. Damian had agreed. And then he'd quoted a whole bunch of terrifying statistics about the number of illegal brothels operating in Sydney and the things that happened to the women who worked in them.

'But something about what you've told me is different,' Damian had said.

'What?'

'The violence,' he'd said. 'Illegal brothels are usually exactly that. The men who visit them get off on knowing the women are desperate and exploited. They also like the fact that there are no rules and no chance the proprietors will call the police if they do something off. But brothels specifically set up for violence, that's something different.'

Sophie slung the shopping bag over her shoulder. The weekend away would give her a good opportunity to clear her head. Next week she would contact Damian and see what he had turned up.

鬼

BY THE time she arrived at the restaurant, Sophie no longer felt cold. The wind, brutal when she'd started out, now refreshed her; the skin beneath her many layers felt clammy with sweat. She looked at her watch. Seven minutes early. She'd completed the walk from home to Blue Lotus in near record time.

Jin Tao's Audi was parked against the paling fence opposite the door. Sophie dumped her backpack beside the wheel and leaned against the car to drink from a bottle of water. She'd seen Jin Tao through the dining room window on her way around. He'd appeared deep in conversation with a delivery guy. She noticed he'd dressed in his favourite old flannelette shirt, a piece of clothing he reserved for bumming around on the couch and doing nothing much at all. That was what they both needed, a weekend to unwind and do nothing but share each other's company. Who knew what clarity such space might bring?

She drained the remnants of the water and lobbed the bottle over to the open recycling bin. It hit the corner and bounced off onto the cobblestones, the clatter making the alley cat jump. Sophie collected the bottle. She dropped it into the bin as the kitchen door opened and Jin Tao popped his shiny head out into the lane.

'You going to hang out in the freezing cold all day, or are you going to come in?'

'Hello to you too.'

Jin Tao pushed the door open wider. 'Jesus,' he said. 'What happened to your face?'

Sophie touched the bruise, turned her head.

He softened. 'Come in, why don't you,' he said. 'I'll put the kettle on.'

Sophie raised a hand. 'We'll be here all day. The idea is to get you away from your work.' She took another glance at her watch. 'I'm early and you've got another two minutes to be on time.'

Jin Tao grinned. 'I can do better than that. I'll be out in one.' He disappeared into the kitchen, the door banging loudly. The vibration caused the lid of the recycling bin to clang shut, revealing a cardboard fruit box, rammed with newspapers and paperwork, wedged against the wall. The yellow highlight against the text of a bill caught Sophie's eye.

She stepped closer. A payment order for meat. The payment was made by Jin Tao on behalf of Blue Lotus. The supplier's name, printed clearly in black felt-tip beneath it, was Jonnie Zhou. Sophie picked the bill out of the bin with pincer fingers. She spread its double page wide, stared at the black and white text and Jin Tao's signature, his familiar scrawl.

Zhou: the surname was one of the most common in China. There'd be hundreds of Zhous in Sydney alone. Recent memories flashed before her like the frames of a film. Jin Tao's absences from the restaurant. The scratches on his face. The sighting of Zhou in the Cross near Blue Lotus. Li Hua would say these were more than coincidences.

Everything's connected. How had Zhou known where she lived?

The door banged shut again. Jin Tao stood with his back to her, a duffel bag over his shoulder, fiddling with the deadbolt. Beside him on the ground sat a lidded box and a long-handled shovel.

Always pay attention to the details.

Sophie stuffed the invoice back into the box with the

newspapers. She moved quietly to the car, her mind aflame.

The name had to be a coincidence, she *needed* it to be a coincidence.

Her thoughts jumped to Seamus and his large, imperfect heart. As a girl she'd viewed him as a hero; her mother's great rescuer from a life that had been frightening and dangerous and soiled by crime. She'd thought her father to be one of the good guys. And he was. He'd saved her mother from certain execution: people didn't witness murders inside the Walled City and live to tell about them.

But even good guys get it wrong. *Or go wrong.*

And crims need PIs too.

Seamus had been bent, in with the wrong people. Sophie had learned this long after Helen disappeared, when Seamus, his eyes red from crying and his face ruddy from wine, told her everything. It was his fault Helen had disappeared. Seamus had saved Helen once, and brought her to Australia, where he'd loved and protected her. But his shady dealings had finally caught up with him. Helen had become payback.

Already exhausted from her own fear and grief, Sophie had wanted to vomit. In the den that night, it had felt like her whole world tilted; she knew that her axis would never be the same. Her father was a crook and she had lost her beautiful mother because of it.

She had run out of the den and out of her family home. She'd never seen Seamus again.

'Cat got your tongue?'

Jin Tao's voice jerked Sophie alert. He stood behind the car, loading gear into the boot.

'What's that for?' Sophie asked, pointing to the shovel.

Jin Tao grinned and slid it into the car on an angle. 'A little project I've got for us in the mountains,' he said. 'It's a surprise. You'll find out when we get there.'

女孩

IT WAS colder in Katoomba. The air had the kind of bite to it that Sydney rarely managed. The sky stretched high and wide, like the beginnings of an embrace.

Not that Sophie could see the sky now, enclosed as she was in a tunnel of ghostly blue gums. She found herself puffing as she hurried to keep up with Jin Tao on their hike through the bush.

'Let's go for a walk,' he'd said when he pulled up at the side of the road.

'Now?' They hadn't rolled into town yet. 'You don't want to check-in first, dump our stuff?'

Jin Tao had pushed open his door. 'I need a leak for starters,' he'd said. 'Wait here and I'll be right back.'

Sophie had leaned into the leather, pulling her coat closer to block out the cold. She'd looked out at the eucalypts – grey leaves, white trunks glowing like bones.

The passenger door had jerked open and Jin Tao had offered his hand. 'C'mon,' he'd said. 'I've a surprise for you. Something you need to do.'

She'd unfastened her belt, jumped onto the gravel. Jin Tao had collected the shovel and the box from the boot. 'I can't carry them both,' he'd said, offering the box to her. 'Promise not to peek inside or you'll ruin my plans.'

Sophie had reached for the shovel instead.

He'd shrugged. 'This is lighter, but whatever.' He'd turned, raising the box to his shoulder, and begun stomping through long grass towards the trees. 'There's a track here. I used to walk it with my *yeye* as a kid.'

She'd followed him through the grass, eyes peeled for snakes.

Now, with sheets of trees on either side, the unease she'd felt in the laneway behind the restaurant gnawed. She could only think of a sinister reason someone would take a shovel into deserted bushland; she felt strangely comforted by the fact she was the one holding it.

'Here.' Jin Tao stopped just ahead of her and placed the box on the ground. 'I know you're into ritual and I thought we could make one of our own,' he said. He toed his boot at the earth. 'I reckon this is a good spot to dig.'

Sophie looked about. Walls of gums glowed white around the small clearing. She gripped the shovel tight.

'What is this, some kind of treasure hunt?' she said, trying to make the question sound like a joke.

Jin Tao studied her for a long time. 'I think it's time to say goodbye to the past,' he said. He knelt and began peeling the tape from the box.

Sophie looked from him to the ground, moist from rain, a patchwork of black earth, green grass and decaying leaves. Who had she told about her weekend away? And what the fuck was in that box? Her mind conjured predictions.

She tightened her grip on the shovel.

Out of the box, Jin Tao took a sapling. A plant in a black pot.

'What's that for?' Sophie heard her voice ask the question, but her mind had raced a hundred beats ahead. He didn't have a weapon. He hadn't planned to harm her.

'It's a blue gum, like the rest of these,' Jin Tao said, motioning to the bush around them. 'Some people call them ghosts, because of the white trunks. It's for you. To plant here for David.'

Sophie stared at the tree. 'I don't understand.'

'He's your ghost, Sophie. He's haunting you and colouring your view of everything around you. That shrine in your room, your obsession with these missing students, it's all related. It's consuming you and putting you in danger. It's unhealthy and unsafe.'

'And how's a tree going to help with that?' Sophie hoped the dryness in her voice distracted Jin Tao from the moisture forming in her eyes.

'You plant this gum and you watch it grow. You come here when you want to talk to David. You go home and you stop with the shrine and the incense and the obsessing. You move on with your life. You forgive yourself.'

The tears were running now, hot and wet against her cheeks. Sophie swiped at her face with the back of her sleeve, embarrassment and relief and thankfulness clambering over each other.

Jin Tao stood and moved towards her, his arms open. Sophie allowed herself to step into them.

THE IRON gates opened to let out the flood. A sea of royal blue, the colour of prize ribbons, surged forwards. Justin stepped up onto the nature strip. The girls wore their hair in high ponytails and short, shaggy bobs. They flowed through the school gates and down the footpath in a huge, seething, cackling mass. Justin watched them with wonder, amazed at the volume of their taunts, shrieks and laughter and stunned at the happy confidence on their faces, in their straight-backed postures and in the quick flicks of their heads. He didn't remember childhood like this.

Justin's childhood had been one of shy slinking away from things: first from his father's hand and then from his mother's sweet, fermenting alcoholic breath. At school he had hidden from the bullies with his head down and shoulders scrunched together. He'd walked along walls and slid around corners, spent lunchtimes in graffitied library carrels and free periods locked in toilet cubicles. There, in the light, quiet space of the toilet, with only the drip of the urinal and the occasional hiss of a student taking a piss to disturb him, he'd taught himself to release.

Justin had known that most boys learned to masturbate in their beds. But for Justin, his bed had seemed inappropriate. His bed had been his sanctuary, the place where he felt warm and safe and hidden. He retreated there when the fighting between his parents started to suffocate him. He lay on his bed with his pillow over his head and almost succeeded in drowning out the screaming and the crashing and the sobs. Warm and safe, Justin would be comforted by the knowledge that no one would come for him here, that soon he would be sleeping and so would they. In the morning, the night before would be forgotten and everything would be all right. So although the thought of masturbating in his bed did occur to him, he never acted on the impulse until he'd moved away. He hadn't wanted a soundtrack of screaming to interrupt his pleasure. For the teenage Justin, bed was a place for sleep or for comfort and it was only in the toilet cubicle where, bored and lonely, Justin would take his cock in his hands and rub it.

To Justin's horror and surprise, later, when he'd moved away from his parents and their shouting, he realised that, perversely, he missed the fear and the screams. And later still, when the joy of sex had faded and the act had become perfunctory, Justin realised he found the sounds, sights and imaginings of violent goings-on helped arouse him and helped him to climax. Justin didn't understand it but he accepted it and, in time, came to embrace the fact that this was who he was.

Once the flood had thinned down to a trickle, Justin's attention snapped back to the gate. His daughter would dawdle her way out soon enough, and he would take her bag or her instrument and they would walk to the car and catch up. Today there was an audition to attend, and with her mother held up at the office, Justin had offered to help out. It was the least he could do, he felt, his conscience eating away at him as it always did when he thought of his wife and child and the shame they would feel if they knew what he watched to turn himself on. Not that he was causing any harm, another part of him reasoned.

There couldn't be a man on the planet who didn't watch some kind of porn. It was fantasy, not reality. Justin hadn't followed in the footsteps of his father; he had never lifted a finger to his wife and the very thought of her in pain made his stomach turn. Justin knew the girls in the movies were real, that their screams emanated from a dark place within them, that the blood and the bruises and the welts were real marks on real skin. But these girls were foreign, from a place far away, doomed perhaps, but not because of him, not because of anything he had done. With or without his patronage, these films would still be made, these girls still injured, their screams still released. There was nothing he could do. And he deserved some pleasure.

'Dad!'

Justin snapped his head up and saw Isobel emerge from a side gate further along the street. Justin smiled at her. Her cello case scraped against the pavement as she dragged it behind her.

'Hi, sweetie,' he said, taking the cello strap from her hand. 'Ready to play your best?'

Isobel nodded, and looked behind her. 'Joy Lin,' she said, a puzzled expression on her face. 'She was just behind me.'

Justin followed Isobel's gaze up the street. 'Who's Joy Lin?'

'She's coming with us to the audition,' said Isobel. 'I'm guessing Mum didn't say.'

No, thought Justin, *Mum didn't say*. He supposed this meant he would have to take Joy Lin home as well.

'There she is.'

Justin's heart skipped several beats. A slender girl walking tall on long legs approached them. She wore a short skirt and high socks and a slip of thigh, between hem and cuff, shone creamy and inviting. Long black hair hung in a loose ponytail slung carelessly over one shoulder. The girl's face, blooming with good health, hosted large brown eyes, broad cheeks, wide apricot lips, a shy smile. Beneath the dark tresses, Justin glimpsed a flash of red. She wore tiny earrings, like rosebuds, in her ears. Justin's emotions converged in a heap. At the same time that his heart fluttered, his cock stirred. A wave of revulsion washed through him, making him want to claw out his eyes.

The young girl walking towards him looked just like one of them. One of the screamers.

'Sweetie,' Justin whispered, nudging Isobel's shoulder. 'You didn't tell me you had a Chinese friend.'

Isobel rolled her eyes and groaned. 'Don't be so old-school, Dad, she's *Australian*.'

Joy Lin's shy smile extended into confidence. She unfurled an arm and offered a hand. 'Hi, Isobel's dad, it's good to meet you,' she said in a voice so light and youthful that again Justin felt he was about to be sick. 'My parents are from Malaysia, but our ethnicity is Chinese.'

'You okay, Dad?' Isobel put a hand on his arm and looked up at him, her bright eyes narrow with concern.

Justin forced himself to push away the thoughts of screams and pain and the sudden realisation of the youth of these girls and their innocence – *just like my daughter*. It was like he'd experienced an amphetamine shot to the heart. The girls in the films he watched were real and not much older than children. They were flesh and blood and shy smiles and brown eyes. Some of those girls might even have once played the violin. How could they have ever envisaged what would become of them?

'Nice to meet you, Joy Lin.' He heard the strain in his voice. 'Here, let me take your bag.'

'That's okay, Mr Holmes, it balances me out,' the girl said, indicating the violin case in her other hand. Hoisting her bag higher on her shoulder and slipping into step with Isobel, she flashed him a grin. 'Thanks very much for the lift.'

The two girls walked ahead, giggling, as the three of them made their way to the car. Justin trailed behind, lugging Isobel's cello and fighting a sudden desire to cry. He found himself slinking into the shadow of the high school's wall, allowing the sleeve and shoulder of his jacket to scrape gently against the concrete. For the first time in years, he found himself craving the comfort of his childhood bed, where he could hide his head until morning when everything would be all right again.

SOPHIE SQUATTED, feet flat, on the stone bench under the cherry blossom in the garden. She warmed her hands around a mug of oolong, breath disappearing into the vapours of the day. The world out here smelled of wood fire. If she tilted her head, she could see the smoke wafting from the chimney of their stone cottage. It followed the drift rising from a neighbour's home, spiriting away into the sky.

They had visited this cottage three times, always in winter. Sophie had never seen the tree in bloom. She imagined, with the flowers unfurled and the world green and fresh and new, this place would have a different feel. But she liked it now, bare, cold and harsh: the smells of eucalypt, earth, smoke and baking bread soaking into her pores, the chill in the air making her throat sing and her cheeks glow. She found complex beauty in the ragged branches, dripping eucalypts and haunted, scraggy piles of wood. A bush winter gave her a sense of calm and comfort.

'Want a top-up?' Jin Tao stood beside her in his muddy hiking boots, a thermos of hot water in his hand. Sophie placed her mug on the bench. He filled it carefully with water and then slowly filled his own cup. He leapt up onto the bench next to her and folded himself into a squat.

'Do you know where the first tea plant came from?'

The question sounded more like a statement. Sophie picked up her cup and blew gentle ripples onto the surface of the dark amber brew. She took a sip, felt the liquid soak into her tongue. Her mind drew images of curled leaves, broken twigs, a camp fire. The tea washed her mouth and coated her throat. She felt it warming her insides, bringing with it a sense of peace, distance from her physical presence and a separation from the events of the day before. Its comforting embrace dulled Sophie's angst. It even eased the throbbing of her face.

Jin Tao took a sip and again examined his cup. 'This is a Buddhist tale,' he said. His voice blended smoothly with the textures of the day, interrupting Sophie's sense of inwardness no more than breath or the whir of wind passing through leaves. She allowed her eyelids to drop a little. She viewed the brown and grey winter world through neat slits and out of focus.

'There was this monk. I can't remember his name. He set out on a nine-year meditation. He meditated night and day without sleeping until one time, and only once, he allowed himself to fall asleep.'

Sophie exhaled, bringing with her breath a slight nod of her head.

'And when the monk awoke, he felt disgusted with himself,' said Jin Tao. 'He was so disgusted that he cut off his own eyelids.'

Sophie's eye's snapped wide. All the fear and revulsion from the night before stormed into her veins. She lurched backwards as her feet slid out from under her, throwing the curve of her lower back against the stone of the bench and her bottom to the ground. The green mug fell from her hands and smashed against the ground, its contents splashing into Sophie's jeans, where it soaked and burned.

'Shit, Soph!' Jin Tao scrambled to his knees and stretched

his hands down to Sophie's armpits. Using one leg as a lever, he hauled her up.

Sophie clutched at her thigh, which the tea had stained dark. 'I'm all right,' she said. She looked down at the smashed pieces of porcelain splayed like chunky confetti. She focused on the edges of the shattered pieces, studying their jagged shapes, urging her mind to settle and return to its state of calm.

But the meditative peace of the moments before had gone. Emotions flooded Sophie's system, thick and heavy and stifling. Now she saw danger in the crooked curves of the branches, spread out like bony fingers, their thin twigs a thorny web hanging over her, and suffocation in the wet piles of autumn leaves lining the back fence.

Jin Tao placed a firm hand on her shoulder. 'You'd better change,' he said, his voice laced with concern. 'Come inside where it's warm.'

Sophie wiped a sleeve across her face, took Jin Tao's hand and allowed him to lead her in.

鬼

LATER, BY the fire, Sophie stared at flames that licked and leapt.

'You were telling me something about tea,' she said.

Jin Tao had his back to the couch, his legs stretched out to the fire. Sophie noticed he wore socks with individual toes sewn into them. She pinched Jin Tao's big toe between thumb and forefinger. 'I never knew you were such a dag,' she said. He flicked her hand away with a flinch of the foot. 'Finish the story about the tea. We got up to the bit about the eyelids.'

Jin Tao studied her. 'You seemed like you were reflecting out there,' he said. 'And you were drinking tea. The thing about the eyelids is that when the monk cut them off they fell to the ground and from there arose the first tea plant in China. Or so they say.'

'Gross.'

Jin Tao smiled. 'So, ever since that time, meditating monks have used tea to keep awake and mindful.'

'And you're telling me this why?'

'You're dealing with something bigger than you,' he said. 'I've been dismissive, not mindful. If you want to talk, we can sit here, drink tea, talk all day.'

Sophie reached over and rubbed Jin Tao's leg through his tracksuit. 'Thanks.'

'Tell me what you know.'

Sophie talked and Jin Tao listened, only interrupting to top up her teacup, put more wood on the fire and fill the thermos with fresh water. When she finished it was dark outside and a long time before Jin Tao spoke. He ran a hand across his shiny head.

'So we know these things,' he said finally. 'A couple of students at the city language schools have gone missing. These students are female and Asian. The missing students have gone unnoticed because they are only a few among many and because other women are attending classes under their names. Wendy was perhaps one of these substitutes.'

Sophie nodded.

'Next, we have Tae Hun's friend, Han Hong. She's missing and a substitute is attending classes on her behalf. But Tae Hun saw her at an illegal S&M club and took her photo.'

'Which I have on my phone,' Sophie said.

'Right,' said Jin Tao. 'But we don't know where she is now. We also know your student, Su Yuan, is missing and a girl pretending to be her is taking her place. This has only just happened.'

'Correct,' said Sophie.

'This girl told you everything was cool, that the whole visa scam substitution thing goes on all the time, that everyone knows about random girls earning cash in their spare time by delivering drinks semi-naked to boozed-up stockbrokers.'

'Something like that.'

'And you want to go ruin their party?' Jin Tao had a curious smile on his face.

Sophie stared. Had she become the nagging school ma'am, ruining the midnight feast? Did it really matter if a few consenting women played the system in order to make money on the side? What was she, the morality police?

'Like I said, this visa-fraud stuff goes on in the cooking schools, too,' Jin Tao said. 'But for it to work, there's got to be someone on the inside.'

Sophie's mind sorted through a jumble of images – Maria eating banana bread; the receptionist from Central English stinking of tuna; Pete in his fire warden's helmet, insipid and weak and anything but a people person.

'The weird bit is the guy at the market,' said Jin Tao. He flexed his toes. 'He wouldn't have attacked you if he didn't have something to hide.'

Exactly. If everything was as cool as the substitute said, if all the women were happy and working of their own accord, then they hardly needed shadowy figures like Zhou operating as their own personal minders. He obviously had a secret he didn't want to share, and, judging from the way he'd roughed her up, it was something pretty dark.

She turned to Jin Tao. 'So what have we got?'

He smiled gently. 'Mindfulness means patience, analysing what you've got, turning it over slowly.'

'I thought you were going to figure it all out for me.' She

was serious. Every inch of her physical and emotional body resisted the idea that this mystery was hers to solve.

Jin Tao sighed. 'All right, these illegal clubs exist, but everyone knows that. You didn't see Han Hong or Su Yuan there, you didn't know any of the girls there, and there's nothing to suggest they are not there of their own volition and that they are not being paid extremely well. In fact, the girl you spoke to said as much herself. Han Hong may have made her money and now be paying for an expensive business degree at Sydney University. Or she might have gone back to China, like Zhou said.'

'And as for Zhou?'

'You don't know any more about him other than that he's violent,' Jin Tao said. 'But so are a lot of men when it comes to protecting their business ventures, illegal or otherwise.'

'So we've got nothing, is that what you're saying?' asked Sophie, her heart sinking.

'I'm saying you need more information.' He poured more steaming water into Sophie's cup. 'Drink tea, be mindful and patient, think outside the box.'

Sophie took a sip of her tea. 'There is something else,' she said.

'What?'

'That Zhou guy. When he grabbed me in the market, he was wearing chef's whites. I guess that's why I didn't put two and two together about his business. I didn't know what business he was referring to.'

Jin Tao looked up, interested.

Sophie continued, 'And then when he grabbed me in Ashfield, he said he guts things for a living ...'

She stopped. Jin Tao was staring at her.

'What?' she asked.

'Chef's whites?' he said, frowning. 'Are you fucking with me or are you serious?'

'Not fucking with you. He was wearing whites, dirty ones, too. Like he was in the middle of gutting something. I guess that makes sense, if he's a chef.'

'Or a butcher,' said Jin Tao.

'He said he guts pretty things for a living.'

'Ask a butcher for a definition of pretty and he'll say a butterflied lamb,' said Jin Tao, absorbed in thought.

'Right.'

'The thing is,' he said slowly, 'I know a butcher named Zhou.'

Sophie sat up straight. The bill in the rubbish bin. The sighting of Zhou in the Cross.

'Zhou's a fairly common Chinese surname,' Jin Tao continued. 'I didn't make the connection before …'

Sophie waited.

'The guy I know works down in Chinatown,' he said. 'I get my meat from him. I take it from the kitchen door myself.'

'So you know the address of the shop?'

Jin Tao nodded.

'I'll tell Damian.'

'Who's Damian?'

Sophie hesitated. 'A private investigator.'

She watched his face darken as he took her words in.

'You really want to go back there, Soph?'

It was a fair question. But one she just couldn't answer.

JUSTIN LAY alone in sheets sticky with his sweat. He hadn't moved from bed since the morning when he'd hobbled to the ensuite, complaining of stomach cramps and nausea. He had lied, of course, and Veronica, in her usual flurry, had bought it. She'd put a jug of water by the bed and left. But this time was different. Today, Justin decided, he was at war with himself. Today was his time to reflect and reprogram and shoot down the demon in his head. Today was a day for new beginnings and, if he was successful, then tonight he might find rest. Next week he would return to his work, ignoring the temptations of the alleyway, and hold his head high. This was called quitting – cold-turkey style.

Justin's phone vibrated and he ignored it. Veronica had called him twice already and the concerned throb of the mobile had sickened him further and made him want to weep. He didn't deserve her and he didn't deserve his daughter or this large warm house and this comfortable suburban life. He twisted unhappily in his bed. The confusing part, he thought, was that he still desperately wanted to look.

It had been twenty-four hours since the audition, since Justin had stolen glances at Joy Lin as she sat chatting cheerily in the back seat. Twenty-four hours since the shattering realisation that the girls in his videos were little older than kids. It had been the tedium of the schoolgirls' chatter that did it; the conversation had charted petty waters, from the pattern on their geography teacher's dress to the latest evictee from a reality television show and the number of kittens born to Joy Lin's favourite pet cat. Joy Lin had laughed when he'd suggested they spend their energy preparing for the audition at hand. 'Mr Holmes, we can't be that serious,' she'd giggled. 'We're teenagers!'

And the word had struck him in the heart like a knife. What kind of man hides away from his family to watch teenagers getting hurt? He had vowed to stop.

Justin had climaxed three times since the morning. He'd craved the short burst of calm that flooded his body with each orgasm. For a few precious seconds, his body bathed in warmth, Justin had relaxed and almost found sleep. And then the guilt had come creeping back and his wrist had started throbbing and the nagging pull of the DVD player again made itself known in his head.

'Fuck off!' Justin groaned the words into the room as he yanked his pillow out from under his head and pulled it over his face. 'Fuck off, fuck off, fuck off, fuck off.' Tears soaked into the cotton, creating wet patches in places where there were none. He knew he should get out of the house, go walking, go to the park, go to the shops. Why didn't he go? Why would he risk staying here?

Thirsty. He was thirsty. The jug stood on the bedside table filled to the brim with water and slices of lime. Thanks to Veronica. As Justin tossed the sheets away from his body and slid into his slippers, he remembered the earlier conversation he'd had with his wife. She'd been concerned for him, suspected something was up at work and had even mentioned the D word.

'I'm not depressed, babe,' he'd said, smiling with what he hoped was a show of strength. 'I'm just tired and crampy.'

She'd laughed. 'Like a woman on her cycle.'

'Except with more wind.'

Justin ignored the water jug and padded down the hallway to the kitchen. The walk took him past the lounge where the television and DVD player glistened. He forced himself to walk directly to the kitchen. And there, as he poured himself an orange juice, he heard the clock in the hallway strike eleven. Justin drank steadily, his eyes fixed on the glass at his mouth, knowing that on finishing its contents he should return to his room and his bed and knowing, at the same time, that on finishing its contents he would lose his morning's battle and he would make his excuse. If he called now he would have time to receive a delivery and watch it before the girls returned. If he called now he could settle in for the day. He would have something to do. Justin flicked a glance at the TV in the lounge room and another at the low-hanging sky outside. It was warm and comforting here and he needed to relax.

Justin returned to the bedroom and slid open the bedside drawer. He unrolled a pair of socks and shook out the red earrings. Joy Lin had taken them off in the car, claiming that her lobes hurt. He'd pocketed them quietly and taken them home as a reminder. It was okay, he thought, as he thumbed them over in his palm. It was all right, he could do this and nobody would know. This would continue to be his secret indulgence, a reward for the long hours he put in at the bank and an escape from the stresses and ordinariness of his life. He didn't drink to excess, he didn't smoke, he didn't cheat, he had no other vice. As for the girls, they were foreign, from another world, another place. They were women, they were old enough, their fate had been sealed by their own choices.

They were not like his daughter and they were not like Joy Lin.

Justin smiled with relief as he felt the resignation flood through his body, relaxing his muscles and his fear. He would stop but the time to stop wasn't now. The torture in his bed this morning had been part of his process and maybe if he'd stayed, he would have made it through the day. But he'd been thirsty, not his fault. He'd gone to the kitchen and he'd heard the clock strike. And that had given him the idea. Next time he'd be stronger, but next time was not today. Today he would forgive himself and he would start again tomorrow. Justin took out his wallet. His cock tingling with excitement, he flipped out the card with the number, picked up his mobile and dialled.

女孩

CHO RECOGNISED the voice on the other end of the phone.

It was the suit from the suburbs, the guy who kidded himself that he had his addiction under control.

Cho used to find it amusing to watch Mr Holmes peruse the hardcore film selection on offer at the shop. The man could barely keep the sneer of distaste from his face. It was as though he thought he was different from the other men who rented films and bought sex paraphernalia – as though his expensive suit made him somehow less perverted.

'I'm after an order,' the voice said softly over the phone line.

'What are you after?'

The man on the end of the line hesitated. Cho heard a scraping sound, like fingernails against stubble. Then, 'The usual.'

But the pause told Cho he could put another offer on the table. 'You ready for something a little different?'

'Different how?'

'We organise private appointments if you feel like something a little more ... personal.'

Another pause as Cho let Justin digest the suggestion. 'I'm not interested in ordinary sex with a prostitute.'

'Who said anything about sex?'

Cho listened again as the man took this in. Men who were into violence and sadism rarely actually wanted to have sex. But present an opportunity for them to play rough and dirty without the threat of assault charges and it was a different story.

'How do I organise an appointment?'

Cho smiled. 'You don't organise anything,' he said, keying Justin's address into his mobile. 'You sit tight and we'll do the rest.'

鬼

THERE WEREN'T any seatbelts in the back of the van. There weren't even any seats. Justin looped his hand through a leather strap hanging from the ceiling and held on tight as the vehicle lurched its way through the stop-start afternoon traffic. There were no windows. He hoped the driver intended to deliver him to the agreed destination and was not instead taking him somewhere remote to place a bullet in his head.

The van lurched and so did Justin's stomach. The van reeked like the blood and bone his wife liked to use in the garden. It smelled like something had died in it.

Justin ran through his plan again in his mind. He'd decided this would be the last time for all of this. After disconnecting the phone call he'd destroyed the magazines he kept stashed in the ceiling at home, thrown them on the coals of the Weber and filled the backyard with acrid black smoke. He'd chucked the remaining films in the glove box. He planned to dispose of them in a city dumpster. He would rid himself of this obsession because he had no choice, because he loved his daughter, and if she ever learned of his secret life it would destroy him. So this would be his last time. A celebration, a final climax. After this he would no longer need the images. He would have the memory of his own experience, his own participation. It was not so much more terrible, he reasoned. It was simply a means to an end.

'You ready, boss?' The driver stared at him through the rear-vision mirror and Justin felt his stomach heave, this time with excitement.

'We're here?'

The driver nodded. 'You pay me now.'

Justin felt in his pocket for his wallet. Fuck! His wallet! On the floor. Justin grabbed at the black square of leather and his fingers touched something sticky. He brought them to his face and examined them. The substance was dark. Like old blood.

The door slid open and Justin saw the footpath shiny with rain. An open doorway stood opposite the van, a set of concrete stairs leading to the floor above. Justin followed the driver up the stairs to a landing and left to a door marked with the number 14. The driver unlocked the door with a key attached to a chain around his neck. 'You have one hour,' he said with a grin. 'No rules.'

Justin stared back at the man. How hardcore did this organisation think he was? Hardcore enough to watch their recorded material, he reasoned. But watching someone in fear was different from inflicting pain and suffering himself. He didn't plan to seriously hurt the woman behind that door. He planned to slap her around a bit, do some things he could never do with his wife, fill his brain with fantasy material for the boring months and years left of his marriage, and then leave. He'd put all this revolting stuff behind him.

The driver was still talking as he pushed open the door. 'Have a good time, get your money's worth.'

And then Justin was in the room.

A Persian rug in shades of blue and red reached almost to the walls, exposing centimetres of unpolished floorboards at each side. Grey foam sheeting, rippled to resemble giant cardboard egg containers, covered the walls instead of wallpaper, soundproofing the room from the street below. The girl sat in one corner, dressed in cut-off denim shorts and a black singlet, knees bunched towards her chest, arms behind her, hair cascading down either side of a perfectly proportioned face. She regarded Justin purposefully. Justin felt her eyes on him as he took in the faded green armchair against one wall and the plastic-covered mattress on the floor opposite the door.

Justin moved to the armchair and perched tentatively on the edge. He sat silently, watching the girl watch him. He admired the fact that she, the captive, had the courage to stare him directly in the eye. It seemed she wasn't afraid of him and he wasn't sure why. He wasn't sure how this made him feel, but he certainly didn't feel turned on.

'What's your name?' It seemed an obvious place to start and Justin tried to ignore the insipid tone of his voice.

She said nothing, the faint trace of a smile on her lips.

He shifted uncomfortably on the edge of the chair. He knew this was not how it was supposed to go. He'd entered the room with a licence to everything, and here he was, attempting to make conversation. He should get up and move on her now, pummel her a bit with his fists, flip her face into the plastic sheeting, pull off those denims and take her from behind. This was his fantasy and what he had seen happen a hundred times before on screen. This was his opportunity. What had happened to his balls?

'You have a name?' he tried again, desperate to close the silence between them.

'What does it matter?' Her voice contained an accent but also a giggle, as though she thought the whole thing a joke. She was right, he reasoned. In this room, names didn't matter. Knowing her name would make the whole thing harder, it would make her seem real, give her an identity. That was the last way he needed to see her if he was going to go through with this.

Justin examined the girl closer. She stared right back at him and stretched out her bare legs, crossing one foot over the other. Her skin was flawless, the creamy colour of a weak latte, her lips wide and pink. She had short, muscular legs but a long torso. Small breasts, each one just a handful. He admired her toned arms, the soft arc of her muscles.

'Let's call you Joy Lin.' The words were out of his mouth before his brain caught up. Where did that come from? Revulsion washed through him. So he had a thing for young girls then. Girls like his daughter's friend. Girls like his daughter. This would not do at all. What the fuck had happened to him?

'You're not fat like the others.'

Justin looked up. The girl had spoken in a strong, clear voice. No fear there.

'What?'

'You're not fat like the other men. And you're not old and you're not ugly.'

Justin turned her words over in his head. 'Are you trying to pay me a compliment?'

The girl shook her head. 'I'm wondering why you're here.'

'You know why.' He should stop this now. Get up and get down to business. See how much she had to say then. It was very different, here in this dingy room in this rotting building at the rear end of the city. The idea of the plastic mattress cover revolted him and, as for the girl, who knew how many men she'd been with and what kind of diseases she'd picked up.

'What about your wife?'

There was that too. The girl was staring at Justin's hands. His wedding ring. It was different also, actually doing it. Different from watching DVDs at home in bed with a homemade lunch beside him. Justin had never actually cheated on Veronica in seventeen years. Now, he wasn't sure if he wanted to.

'I guess you have a wife and maybe some children. You have a family.'

'I don't have time for this.' She'd hit close to the bone this time. He needed to show her who was boss. Justin pushed himself off the chair and moved towards her. She flinched back into the corner as Justin's hand brushed her leg and his fist closed around her ankle. But in the next moment she had collected herself and Justin felt her leg slacken beneath his grip.

'I'm looking for my sister,' she said.

Justin released her ankle, as much from surprise as from anything else.

'There's a photo in the pocket of my shorts,' she said. 'Take it.'

Justin recoiled.

'I'm here because of my sister,' the girl said, thrusting a hip forwards so that Justin could see the pocket. 'Please take the photo and have a look.'

Fuck it. Justin leaned towards the girl, slipped two fingers into the front pocket of her shorts. He pulled out a grimy photo, laminated, passport size. This wasn't the deal, this wasn't what he'd paid for. He didn't want to know this girl's personal story, he didn't want to hear about her sister and he certainly didn't want to look at the girl in the picture.

But the woman in front of him was persistent. 'She came out here and she did this job,' she said. 'If you have been with other women then maybe you've met her, maybe you know something about whether she's all right.'

Justin shook his head, pleased to realise he had an easy escape route. 'I haven't been with other women.'

The girl smiled as though she didn't believe him. 'So I am the first one?'

Justin hoped the blush he felt spreading to his cheeks didn't show. 'I don't know your sister,' he said, desperate to shut the conversation down.

'Just take a look.'

Justin sighed and looked down at the photo. Anything to shut her up.

The passport-sized face smiling back at him belonged to a teenager. She was pretty, the way they all were, with black hair hanging down to her shoulders and large eyes. She looked vaguely familiar, but he guessed that was probably due to the similarity she bore to the girl in the room beside him.

Then he noticed the gap between the girl's front teeth.

He fought hard against vomit.

He did know this girl. He knew her intimately. He had watched her last moments because they were recorded on digital video.

He'd watched this girl die in a snuff film.

THE RAIN that had begun to fall in Katoomba accompanied them all the way home. Jin Tao's wipers worked at full throttle as he turned into Hopetoun Street. Sophie stared out the side window and admired the sheen on her suburb as it soaked in the afternoon wet. Then, out of the grey, a flash of colour.

'Stop!' Sophie's voice rang out just as Jin Tao slammed his foot on the brakes.

'Shit!'

Sophie lurched forwards, her seatbelt jamming taut against her belly. The car screeched and came to a jolting stop in front of a man in a hooded orange anorak. He stood in front of them, arms raised as though he'd hoped to stop the moving vehicle with his fingers.

Sophie recognised him immediately. She rammed open the door, her heart in her throat. Brad.

'What the fuck, man?' Jin Tao reached him first. 'Did you even look where you were going or do you have some kind of death wish?'

'Are you all right?' Sophie had her arm on Brad's shoulder.

He spun to face her. 'Sophie.' His voice was little more than a whisper.

'Are you all right?' she repeated.

Brad took a deep breath and nodded. Yes. Then, with a smile and a gentle shake of the head, he said, 'What's your friend trying to do, kill me?'

Sophie threw a look at Jin Tao. He had his head bent low, examining the front of the car.

'We didn't see you. I yelled for him to stop.'

'Then I think I probably owe you my life.'

'Did we hit you?'

Brad held his thumb and forefinger an inch apart. 'This close,' he said, more to Jin Tao. From the set of his jaw, Sophie could tell Jin Tao was seething. She had only one task now – to calm the situation before Jin Tao turned irate. 'What are you doing here?'

'Oh, I remember.' Jin Tao's acid tone told Sophie that she was too late. He stepped closer to Brad, closing the space between them. 'You're Sophie's mate from the restaurant?'

Brad nodded. 'The tea guy.'

'The tea guy. Yeah.'

A small pause as the two men eyeballed each other. Jin Tao spoke first. 'Didn't anyone ever teach you to look both ways before crossing the road?'

Brad pointed to Jin Tao's car. 'Didn't anyone ever tell you to use your lights in the rain? Improves visibility.'

Jin Tao's face darkened. Sophie dropped her eyes. Brad had a point. How come Jin Tao hadn't seen him?

'What are you doing here?' she asked again, to cut the silence.

Brad turned to her, a smile on his face. 'Let's just say I was in the neighbourhood. Thought I'd drop by and say hi.'

In the neighbourhood? But you're never in my neighbourhood.

'So you're going to come in for a cup of tea?' asked Sophie, ignoring the groan from Jin Tao.

Brad shrugged. 'I'm on my way back to work. Got to defend my territory.'

'Meaning?'

Brad shrugged, 'Politics,' he said. 'Our storage room shares a door with the Sichuan place and so they think we should let them use it. Even in Australia I can't get a break from people taking over my space.' He turned to Jin Tao. 'No hard feelings, okay?'

Jin Tao rolled his eyes. 'Whatever, man.'

They watched Brad slouch off in the rain. Sophie couldn't help feeling that he'd let them off easy. They'd nearly knocked him flat.

'Maybe I should go after him? Make sure he's okay?'

Jin Tao shook his head. 'He said he was in the neighbourhood,' he said. 'Does he drop by often?'

Sophie watched the orange anorak reach the corner and disappear around it. 'Never,' she said, the question reverberating in her mind. Brad never popped around, and on the one time he had, it had nearly killed him. 'Pity we missed him,' was all she could mumble.

Jin Tao laughed, the tension from the afternoon rolling through his shoulders as he finally loosened up. 'Oh, so you wanted me to drive into him?' he asked, amusement in his eyes. 'Next time I'll aim better.'

'Not funny,' said Sophie as she slapped the car's boot with her palm. 'Open sesame.'

'I've got to park it.'

The accusatory tone in Jin Tao's voice made Sophie even more eager to get away. He didn't want to be on his own, she knew that. There were never any parking spots around their place unless you got one at six-thirty in the morning. He could be half an hour circling the block, and that would be on a good day. But after the close call with Brad, Sophie needed to be alone for a bit. Something was off and she had a need for her own defensive shield.

'You nearly ran into my friend and I just want to go home,' she said, keeping her voice steady. 'Pop the boot now and park the car on your own.'

Jin Tao held her stare for a beat. Sophie tried to imagine he looked bewildered. In fact, she decided, he looked pissed off. She couldn't really blame him. But at the same time she was pleased to have a reason to grab her baggage and head over to her balcony and out of the rain.

She took her rucksack from the boot and watched Jin Tao hoon to the end of the street and turn left. The tyre screech told her he'd made it without crashing into the terrace at the intersection. She slung the rucksack over her shoulder and sloshed her way through the rain.

At number 36 she lifted her head. She'd expected the iron fencing and the trimmed-back roses that marked her home, but not the man waiting for her on the doorstep. Damian.

'Hey,' he said. 'Thought we could check out the butcher shop together. Fancy a trip down to Chinatown?'

女孩

THEY FOUND the butcher shop easily enough. Closed.

'At least I know where to come back in the morning,' Damian said. 'How about we get a coffee and go over what we know?'

'Sure.' Sophie tried to hide her unease. Of course the butcher would be shut. It was a Sunday afternoon. She should have known it and Damian should have known it too.

They chose a place on Sussex Street. Sophie's bottom

jammed against the outside rims of a too-small leather stool, her elbows resting on a bench only wide enough for her coffee cup and its saucer. For a cafe in Chinatown, the place was unusual in that it sold tea by the bag. Sophie sipped on a long black that had arrived at a temperature close to boiling and which had ripped the skin from the roof of her mouth.

'You eating?' Damian pulled a stool across and sat down on the other side of the skinny bench. 'I've ordered raisin toasts. It's spelled in plural on the menu, so I guess that means there'll be enough to share.'

Sophie grinned and glanced at the blackboard menu positioned high on the wall behind her. The items were chalked neatly in colourful pastels and nearly every item listed contained a mistake.

'"Please take care of the grass with your gentle loving heart",' she said, fingering the jade necklace hanging at her throat.

Damian stared at her, bewildered. 'Beg pardon?'

'An English sign I saw on a lawn at a park in Beijing,' she said. 'The Chinese version said, "Please don't walk on the grass".'

Damian laughed. 'Can you imagine the mess we'd make if we had to translate all our signs into Chinese?' The waitress arrived with toast and coffee. 'If this bench were any narrower, I think my food would be on the floor right now,' he muttered as he arranged the plate of toast and the coffee cups around his elbows. He took a sip of his coffee and watched Sophie over the rim of his cup. 'I looked into your story,' he said finally.

She leaned towards him. Bruises from the other night still tingled when she brought her fingers to her skin. The memories of what had happened had pierced her dreams ever since.

'No known illegal brothels operating in the Ashfield region,' Damian said. 'I did a satellite search of the homes in the area you described and found three with substantial backyard sheds, similar to what you outlined.'

'You checked them out?'

Damian nodded. 'I invented warrants, faked like a cop. I told the owner-occupiers we were investigating suspected hydroponic labs in the area and informed them I had permission to inspect the sheds. The first two contained gardening equipment. The third a pool table, a beer fridge, a flat screen TV and a bunch of uni students hanging out on bean bags.' He stared at Sophie, unblinking. 'No disco balls.'

Sophie sat back on her stool, turning Damian's story over in her mind. 'And you haven't had a chance to check out the butcher shop.'

'You said that the night you went out there, Tae Hun had been drinking?'

'Sorry?'

Damian pushed a crumb around his plate with his finger. When he looked up he pierced Sophie with his gaze. 'Had you yourself consumed alcohol or drugs?'

A wave of indignation surged through Sophie's system. 'What happened to me was real, you saw the bruises.'

Damian nodded. 'I see them still,' he said quietly.

They sat in silence for a moment. Damian licked a finger and used it to collect the crumbs on his plate. When he'd picked it clean, he spoke again.

'I ran a search on your friend Tae Hun.'

'Yeah?' Sophie felt that wherever the conversation went now, it wouldn't go anywhere good. Her feathers had been irreversibly ruffled; a malaise had settled in.

'It seems he was one of several witnesses to a stabbing at World Square last March. You probably heard of that one. It was all over the news.'

'The fight that started in Hungry Jack's?' she asked, curiosity piqued.

Damian nodded. It had indeed saturated the news for the best part of a week. Two Korean students, one the son of a famous pop star in that country, had begun a dispute in a hamburger restaurant on George Street. On being told to take their noise outside, they did. And with them went a trail of onlookers, all yelling support and abuse and encouraging a fight. On the footpath, a knife was drawn and the pop star's son took off, pursued by the boy with the knife and the curious pack. He managed to cross Liverpool Street before he was overwhelmed by his attacker on the corner outside the World Square shopping and residential complex.

The boy was stabbed seven times, and when it was finished the attacker ran away and so did the mob, leaving the student alone on the street, choking to death as the blood flooded his lungs and drowned him.

Tae Hun had been there.

'I never knew he was involved in that,' Sophie said, exhaling a slow breath.

'He wasn't charged with anything,' Damian said quickly. 'In his statement he said he was already on the street when the fight started in the restaurant. He said he didn't know either of the students and he claimed he simply got caught up in the crowd. He saw the victim fall to the ground but he didn't see any blood and he didn't realise he'd been stabbed. He said that if he'd known, he would have done something to help.'

Damian brought his lips together. His face suggested he doubted Tae Hun's story. Sophie's own instinct was to believe it. But why hadn't Tae Hun mentioned it? The guy witnessed a murder and said nothing. He visited strip clubs and underground parties featuring sex and bondage and violence. What sort of man was he? Did he really want to help Han Hong or did he have another agenda? Had he been telling the truth?

'It seems your friend has a knack for locating violent situations,' said Damian, echoing Sophie's thoughts. 'You know him – do you feel you can trust him?'

Sophie twisted a sugar sachet between her fingers. 'I don't know him well,' she admitted. 'I suppose it's fair enough that he didn't tell me about the murder. That's pretty heavy shit to disclose.'

'It is.'

'But I felt he was genuine in his concern for Han Hong. She was his classmate. Tae Hun spoke of a camaraderie between foreign students, a sense of needing to band together and look out for one another. I think that was genuine and I don't know why he'd make it up.'

'This is just an idea that I'm going to put out there,' Damian said. 'Perhaps Tae Hun was using you.'

'Using me how?'

'Sometimes people who've been involved in a crime get actively involved in the hunt for a solution. They feel as though this makes them look innocent, and sometimes it assists in resolving a guilty conscience. There was a case a couple of years back, of a man who killed his wife and two-year-old son with a hammer. He disposed of their bodies at the rubbish tip and constructed a series of fake emails from the wife, so that it looked as though she'd run off on him and taken the kid with her. He went on the news to appeal for their whereabouts and to beg her to come home. He played the distraught husband trying to find his wife so well that the public were fooled, when he was the killer all along.'

'Are you saying that Tae Hun had something to do with Han Hong's disappearance?'

Damian levelled his gaze at her. 'I'm saying this club the two of you visited doesn't appear to exist any more. I'm saying Tae Hun is a guy with some dark things on his résumé. I'm saying it's ironic that he took you to a club where he claimed he was known, and yet you wound up getting beaten to a pulp.'

'As did he,' Sophie said.

'I'm saying if the police start to question your mate about the disappearance of his classmate, he very conveniently has the backing of a respected English teacher, who will say he expressed fears for the girl's safety and that he worried she was in danger.'

'I don't buy it.'

'Very often,' said Damian, 'the last person to see a disappeared victim is the first person police will interview. Do you know why?'

'Because statistically they are most likely to have had something to do with the disappearance.'

'That photo that Tae Hun gave you, is it dated?'

Sophie took her mobile from her leather satchel. She pulled up the picture of Han Hong.

Damian stared at the picture, as though for the first time. 'Your friend said he took this picture?'

Sophie nodded.

'What, just snapped it with his phone?' He looked at her, satisfaction softening his features. 'You might want to talk again to Tae Hun,' he said quietly.

'Why, what is it?'

Damian pointed to the phone's screen. 'I've only studied a little bit of photography but I know enough to see that this girl's backlit.'

Sophie examined the photo again before looking back to Damian. 'Meaning?'

'Meaning this is a professional photograph.'

'She's gone and turned model?'

'I don't know what's happened to her. But whatever Tae Hun told you about how he obtained this image, it wasn't the truth.'

Sophie returned to squinting at the image. Damned if she would have picked up the backlighting. She suppressed the surge of irritation that rippled through her and threatened to spill into her voice. 'You're sure about that?'

'About the truth bit, yes. About whether that image is a photograph ... nope.'

'What's that supposed to mean?'

'There's another possibility, too.'

'What's that?' Sophie asked, trying hard not to let her frustration play on her face.

'That image could be a photograph or it could be a still from a film.'

Sophie stared at the eyes peering out from the face on the mobile phone screen.

A still from a film.

The girl in the market had said some women made sex films for a living.

鬼

SOPHIE PULLED her mobile from the back pocket of her jeans as soon as Damian stopped outside her house.

'I'll check out your butcher shop first thing in the morning,' he said, as she got out of the car. 'If your butcher's there he might be able to shed some light on Han Hong's whereabouts. A police badge can sometimes make even hardened crims talk.'

'But you don't have a police badge.'

He flashed another grin. 'Like I said, I'm a good fake.'

'Call me if you find anything interesting.'

Damian saluted with mock seriousness. 'Same goes for you,' he said, shooting two fingers in her direction.

Sophie watched as he pulled out from the kerb. She ignored the rain that spattered over her head; it slipped in sneaky streams down her neck and back. She brought up Tae Hun's number.

He answered on the first ring. 'I don't think you should talk to me any more,' he said simply. That was it, no greeting, no small talk, no inquiry. His voice sounded flat, rehearsed, as though he'd been waiting for her. He'd been shaken by the other night's events. Or maybe Damian was right. Maybe Tae Hun was more involved in this than he'd let on and maybe he simply wanted to shake her.

'Hello to you too,' she said, working to sound casual.

'Please don't call me any more,' said the voice at the end of the phone.

'Okay,' she said, searching for the right tone and words that would keep him on the line. 'Tae Hun, I have a question.'

Silence. But he hadn't hung up, and that meant he was willing to listen. Whatever he may be involved in, whatever had happened in his past, Tae Hun had come to her genuinely for help, she felt sure of it.

'The image you showed me of Han Hong, you said you took the photo of her at an illegal club.'

'So?'

'I think you lied to me about the photo.'

Silence again. Then, 'What do you mean I lied?'

'You didn't take that picture. Or if you did, you didn't take it in the club like you said you did. I need to know where you got it and why you didn't tell me the truth.'

He was silent on the end of the line. Then, quietly, 'It's too dangerous.' He sounded scared.

'Are you involved in this somehow?' Sophie asked. 'Is that why you didn't want to go to the police?'

He sighed. 'I can't talk about this now,' he said. 'Not on a mobile.'

'Can you meet me one more time?'

Another sigh, more silence. Then, 'One more time. Tomorrow outside Central English at one.'

女孩

ALL SOPHIE wanted to do when she finally fell in the front door was strip her wet clothes from her body and crumple into the shower. In the hallway she kicked off her sneakers and peeled away her wet socks. She went into the living room, where Jin Tao's duffel bag rested against the couch. He would have dumped it there before hoofing it to the kitchen to sort out something for a late lunch. Sophie listened for sounds of movement in the kitchen, hating the knot of tension forming in her stomach. Should she attempt to make peace with her friend and join him there? Or should she skulk off to the bathroom and give them both some more time to cool off? She'd decided to bite the bullet on the former when she realised that, except for the sound of the rain on the roof, the house was quiet. Jin Tao had gone out. Relief coursing through her, Sophie made for the staircase, pulling her raincoat from her body. The carpet felt warm beneath the damp skin of her feet and she dug her toes deep into its pile.

At the top of the stairs she threw her raincoat over the banister before pushing open the door to her room. She stopped.

A thin rope of twine lay delicately in the centre of her bed. It had been knotted into the distinctive shape of a noose.

She was beside the bed in two steps. In one movement she pulled the noose off the bed and flicked it away, like a poisonous snake. She sat down on the bed, her heart hammering. The wet fabric clinging to her hips and shoulders clasped her body like a vice. She had to get it off. She clawed at her top with cold hands, her nails scratching at the damp skin of her back as she peeled the material up and over her shoulders.

A list of possible suspects flipped its way through Sophie's head. There had been the unusual encounter with Brad in the street and then there'd been Damian waiting for her on the doorstop. Sophie shivered as she unhooked her damp bra and let it fall to the floor.

But there was only one person she knew for sure had been in the house.

'You're here.' He was in the room before she had a chance to bring her hands to her breasts.

'Shit.' Jin Tao turned his head away, one arm raised to shield his eyes.

Sophie grabbed her pillow and brought it to her chest. 'Do you mind?'

'Your door was open,' he said softly. 'I didn't think to knock.'

'I didn't think you were home.'

'Yeah. In my room. Attending to some business.'

'So you just come into my room whenever my door's open?'

Jin Tao shrugged, still looking away. 'It usually means you're available to chat.'

'And what about when I'm not here?'

'Then you close your door.'

Sophie pulled on the T-shirt that she wore to bed and

pushed the pillow against the wall. 'Do you often come into my room when I'm not here?'

Jin Tao turned around to face her. 'What exactly are you getting at?'

'That.' She pointed to the twine curled around the wastepaper basket.

Jin Tao bent down and picked it up by one end. The noose dangled in the air.

'I found it on my bed when I got home.'

Jin Tao's hurt showed on his face. 'And you think I put it there?'

'I don't know,' she said. 'But who else has access to my room?'

He threw the twine onto the bed. 'I'm not sure what's going on here, Sophie, but it's starting to look pretty serious.'

'So you have no idea how it got here?'

Jin Tao sat down slowly on the bed, shaking his head. When he turned to face her, she saw sadness in his eyes and disappointment in the set of his jaw. 'How could you think I would do something like this to you?'

She didn't have words. In her heart she knew there was no way Jin Tao would torment her like this; she could trust him. She had to – she had no choice.

You've given him a part of your soul.

But when Jin Tao reached a hand out to stroke the top of hers, Sophie found herself shrinking away.

'You're really scared of me, aren't you?' he said, his voice dead.

Yes. No. I don't know.

'I'm sorry,' she said. 'But I'm not sure your tree-planting idea was much of a success.'

鬼

WHEN SOPHIE walked into the staffroom on Monday morning, Chuck hurried over to her with a hug.

'Honey, we were worried about you,' he whispered, his mouth close to Sophie's ear. 'You left on Wednesday and you never came back.'

Over Chuck's shoulder, Sophie watched her colleagues pretend to be busy. He'd probably told every staff member who would listen – and that was all of them when it came to gossip – how concerned he was for poor Sophie and her emotional reaction to Wendy's death. This was why Sophie now saw colleagues steal fleeting glances in her direction. The only person who seemed entirely uninterested was Lenny, sitting as he always did at the end of the room, hoeing into a breakfast of sushi rolls and tea. Good old reliable Lenny. Sophie extracted herself from Chuck's grasp.

'I can't think why you were worried, Chuck,' she said, loud enough for those closest to them to hear. 'I had some leave, went to the mountains. It was chilly.'

Chuck smiled tightly and took Sophie's hand in his own two. 'I haven't raised your concerns with Pete,' he said.

'Don't. I'm sure I overreacted.'

Chuck's grip relaxed. 'Good,' he said. 'But if you need to talk . . .'

Sophie said nothing. She removed her hand and wove her way to her desk. Amicable chatter and weekend anecdotes again filled the air.

'What a dickhead,' grumbled Lenny to Sophie as she sat down at her desk.

Sophie smiled. 'Nice weekend, Lenny?'

Lenny yawned. 'It was a weekend.' He looked at her. 'You

know Chuck was buzzing around here all last week stressing his little head out about you?'

'I guessed.'

'The man needs to make up his mind which team he bats for.'

'We had an upsetting conversation, that's all,' said Sophie.

'About the suicide chick?'

'Sort of.'

'Because you asked me if I knew her.'

'You said you didn't remember.'

'I know what I said.' Lenny bit into a fresh sushi roll. 'The thing is,' he said, wiping his mouth with a napkin, 'I remember.'

Sophie edged her chair forwards. He continued chewing, slowly, as though the conversation were closed.

'So?'

Lenny raised an eyebrow and swallowed. 'Patience, kid, let me finish my breakfast.'

Sophie turned back to her desk. She knew it was futile to push Lenny into anything. The man was stubborn and irritating and he seemed to enjoy the reputation. She tried to work on her class plan, urging her mind to switch on and get into gear. But each time she looked at her lesson plan, her thoughts turned to Wendy and Su Yuan and Han Hong and the butcher named Zhou. Eventually she gave up. Today she would have to wing it.

'It's not much, but you seem so cut up by all this I thought I may as well share it with you,' Lenny said finally. 'I taught her for a bit,' he said, trapping Sophie with his clear blue eyes. 'Funny girl, laughed a lot – when she wasn't nodding off. I remember her because she had this strange fixation with walls.'

Sophie frowned. 'Pardon?'

'You heard right,' said Lenny gruffly. 'Anyhow, she asked me several times how to describe the action of the walls *listening*.'

Sophie stared at him, a slip of recognition jangling somewhere at the edge of her consciousness.

'I thought it must have been some Chinese expression she was trying to translate into English. Maybe it was, I don't know.'

'She wanted to say that the walls were listening?'

Lenny shrugged. 'I know it sounds strange, but she asked me and I told her and that's about all I remember. Don't ask me anything else because that's all I have.' And with that, Lenny returned to being his usual curt self. He zipped his pencil case and picked up his books. 'See you after class.'

THE SCRATCHING of bolt against latch woke Han Hong from an uncomfortable sleep. They were back for more.

She focused on her sense of smell. Her nostrils flared against the rough hem of the blindfold as she fought to catch the scent of something savoury. But there was nothing. Only the familiar stale air of her prison, its silence now punctuated by the scrape of what she knew was a camera tripod and the shallow, ragged breathing of her captor.

Just how much more torment she could endure, Han Hong did not know.

What she did know was that the soup had stopped coming and she was growing weaker.

And this could only mean one thing.

They didn't intend to keep her alive for much longer.

She did not have many films left to make.

THE CUTS in the butcher shop window were like none Damian had ever seen. A pig's head stared at him through the finger-smudged glass. *Are you talking to me?* Damian pressed his forehead against the window. The pig stared back, its beady eyes glazed and shining. Inside the store, an elderly Chinese woman glared at him. The place was crowded, customers spewing out the door. Inside he could hear them barking orders in languages he couldn't understand to white-coated men who worked the counter and broke apart huge slabs of meat on round wooden chopping boards with blades ten centimetres wide.

He'd already fought the crowd once, to be told by the man doling out pigs' trotters that a butcher named Zhou did exist but that, no, he wasn't working today.

'You look at the restaurant. He works there too.'

'Which restaurant?' Damian had asked, his phone in hand, ready to take down the address.

'Firewater,' the butcher had said. 'Very spicy.'

Damian had punched the restaurant's name into his phone. The name sounded familiar but he couldn't quite place it. As the page loaded, he'd stepped back out onto the pavement and come face to face with the pig.

'Excuse me.' The elderly lady who'd frowned at him from

inside the butcher shop tugged on his arm. Her hair shone unnaturally black, contrasting sharply with the many deep furrows on the face that she turned up to him. She smiled a crowded mouthful of long and yellowing teeth and beckoned him to the side of the road.

'You looking for a girl?' she asked, her voice almost a whisper.

'Pardon?' Damian had to stoop to bring his ear level to her mouth. She wore a strong perfume but beneath that she smelled faintly of garlic.

'I said, are you looking for a girl?'

He heard her clearly this time, and, from the sparkle in her eye, Damian guessed the lady had mistaken him for someone else.

'Yes,' he said, deciding to play along.

'You at the wrong place,' she said, with a giggle. 'You go there.' She pointed to an open doorway next to the butcher shop. Inside, a steep set of stairs ascended into the main body of the building.

'What do you know about the girls?' he asked.

She smiled again. 'I been around,' she said. 'I see men like you for a long time.'

Damian tilted his head skywards to examine the building's facade. It was a pale pink Art Deco number, about six storeys high and in serious need of a paint job. Below each window the colour of the exterior had been washed grey by rain mixed with dirt dripping over the sills. There were many rooms above the butcher shop, and any one of them could house Han Hong.

When he looked down again, the old woman was no longer standing beside him. The sea of people made it impossible for him to pick her out in the crowd.

He took the stairs in twos. The first landing opened onto

a long, narrow corridor lined with numbered wooden doors. He tried the handle on the first and found it locked. Same with the second and the third. The final door, at the end of the corridor, pushed open at his touch. He entered, noting first the Persian rug on the floor, and then the unmistakable scent of early decomposition. Finally he noticed the pair of legs extending out from behind an armchair in the corner.

Damian took a breath and fought the urge to vomit. He hadn't known what he was going to find when he came here, but he certainly hadn't expected it to be a dead person.

JUSTIN WAS pulled up in a traffic jam when he saw her. Too late he realised she had also seen him. He had no opportunity to hide. And worse, she was heading this way. Justin honked his horn, urging the cars in front of him to move, but he knew it was useless. The traffic had crawled to a halt ten minutes ago and since then he had moved forward only about a centimetre. The flashing red of an ambulance up ahead told him that there had been an accident and it could be a while. Somebody was probably hurt. Injury? Death? He didn't much care. He cared only about returning home before Veronica did and forgetting all about this terrible mess. The stash of porn films burning a hole in his glove box right now made him feel sick. So did the knowledge of what he'd done to the girl in that room.

Destroyed her.

Or, by sharing the truth, had he in fact turned away from the sure-fire path to hell he'd been on for so long? He expected he'd never know. But one thing he'd decided upon – he was quitting.

A sharp rap on the passenger-side window told him she'd arrived. Justin forced his lips into a smile and flipped the switch to bring down the window.

Joy Lin grinned toothily in at him. 'How are you doing, Mr Holmes?'

'I'm fine thank you, Joy Lin,' he said. 'I can't say the same for the traffic.' He hoped the casual frustration in his voice would encourage the girl to show good sense and leave. Instead, Joy Lin opened the door and climbed into the passenger seat.

'I don't mind keeping you company,' she said, batting her eyelids in the way he'd begun to notice teenage girls did without thinking. Even his own daughter was guilty. Flirts, all of them. 'I'm on my way to see my grandmother but she'll still be at the market. I've got nothing else to do.' Joy Lin hauled her schoolbag in after her and rested it on a knee.

'Well, that's a kind offer, Joy Lin, but I'm rehearsing a presentation I'm giving at work tomorrow. I really could use the time to practise.'

'You can practise on me,' she said, her voice light and sweet. 'I'm on the debating team at school. I might even have a suggestion.'

Justin looked at her. Was this girl for real? What did she think she was doing, climbing into a strange man's car? Asking for trouble, that's what. He admired the creamy flesh of her thigh. She wore knee-high socks instead of stockings – purposefully erotic, surely. He wouldn't allow Isobel to dress like that. She wore ribbed stockings and lace-up shoes. And her winter skirt fell below her knee.

'You know, Joy Lin,' he said slowly, 'it's probably not a good idea to spend too much time in men's cars. You don't know me very well.'

If Joy Lin sensed the warning he was trying to give, she didn't show it. 'You're Isobel's dad. That's all I need to know, right?'

'If Isobel saw you here now, she'd probably think it was a bit weird.'

'Isobel said I left my earrings in your car. Did you find them?'

He saw her hand on the glove compartment and he reached out to slap it away. But she was too quick in her movement and he was too slow in his. She'd opened the hatch before he could stop her and a DVD case fell forward. The DVD cover was particularly graphic and the next moments passed in slow motion. Joy Lin stared, transfixed, at the image, her mouth frozen open in shock.

She did not move her eyes as Justin took the case from her and gently closed the lid on the compartment.

'I think it's time you went to find your grandmother,' he said softly and the girl nodded.

'Say anything about this to Isobel and I'll have to come and see you.' Justin heard the threat in his whisper cut through the air like a blade.

'I didn't see anything, Mr Holmes,' Joy Lin said slowly. 'I didn't even see you.'

And she was spilling out of his car and picking herself up and trudging into the evening light without looking back. Justin watched her for a while, turning back to the road ahead of him only when she had disappeared around the arc of the overpass.

The traffic had begun to edge forwards and he pressed his foot against the accelerator and moved on.

SOPHIE MANAGED to bluff her way through the first period, armed with a grammar game that took the best part of an hour. As she sieved her way out through the morning tea throng she fell in beside Janie, a young teacher from the Shire with a thinly disguised contempt for foreign students.

'I've got her,' Janie said, her narrow face aglow.

'Who?' Sophie asked.

'Come here.' Janie grabbed Sophie's hand and dragged her into an empty classroom. Sophie glanced through the windows at the rapidly emptying corridor. The last thing she needed right now was to spend her break listening to Janie's mindless prattle. She couldn't wing another class with games and free talk.

'You won't believe this,' Janie said. Sophie detected a conspiratorial tone in her voice. 'I'm filling in for Tim, who's on holidays somewhere hot.' Janie paced the room as she spoke, as though she were thinking out loud or testing a theory with Sophie as her audience.

'On the roll is a girl called Mei Li. I know her because I taught her last term.'

Sophie tuned in. She guessed she knew what Janie was going to say.

'But this is where it gets interesting,' said Janie, raising a bony finger in the air. 'The girl who shows up each day isn't Mei Li.' She stared at Sophie, her eyes shining bright, hands clasped together, an expression of sheer pleasure illuminating her thin face.

'You just said Mei Li was in your class,' Sophie said.

'That's the thing,' said Janie, grasping Sophie's hands with her own. 'She *says* she's Mei Li, but it's not her! It's a different girl.'

'What did you do?'

Janie smiled widely, unable to contain her self-satisfaction. 'I marked her name on the roll and continued on as usual.'

'Yeah?'

'Yes! It's exactly what Pete was talking about. You know, with that poor Wendy girl ...' Janie trailed off, lost in a thought. But in the next moment she snapped back, eyes again gleaming. 'I can't believe it, Sophie. I've caught my own fraudster. I can't wait to spring her.'

Sophie knew she should stall for time. She needed to talk to this girl, and she needed to see if she could establish some connection between the missing Mei Li and the others: Su Yuan, Wendy, Han Hong.

'Are you going to tell Pete?'

'Of course!' said Janie. 'But I'm going to wait until lunch. Make sure I have enough time to sit in on any interview with the student. I wouldn't want to miss out on that.'

Sophie smiled. 'Good on you, Janie. You're a right detective, aren't you?'

'Maybe I'm in the wrong industry,' Janie said with a smile as she followed Sophie out to the corridor. 'Keep it to yourself, hey?'

Sophie nodded. 'Cross my heart.'

Sophie followed Janie into the staffroom but turned sharply

to her left after passing through the door. The sounds of mid-morning chatter faded behind her as she stalked down the hallway towards the row of grey filing cabinets lining the back wall. The cabinets stored copies of student files. Sophie knew Janie took elementary English and it didn't take her long to find Janie's elementary class folder and Mei Li's file within it.

Sophie glanced at the form listing Mei Li's personal information. She was eighteen and Chinese. She planned to study at language school for one year. After that it was her intention to study at an Australian university. She wanted to study business. She flipped through the file to take a look at Mei Li's test results. She was only one term in, but her first test results showed her to be a student with potential. She hadn't aced it, but she'd done well enough in her reading, listening and writing sections. Her oral section, the only subjectively assessed part of the test, had let her down. *Speak up!* Janie had scrawled across the examination page. *Don't be shy. Enunciate!* Mei Li had probably needed to use her dictionary to decipher that last word, Sophie thought, annoyed on Mei Li's behalf. Janie was always complaining that she couldn't understand 'them' properly. It was as though she expected her students to adopt a broad Australian accent when they stood up to speak.

Sophie flipped to the plastic pocket containing Mei Li's introductory essay, the piece that had determined her class placement. The topic again was 'My Hometown'; Mei Li had titled her piece 'Kunming'.

Noodles like my hometown.

Su Yuan had also come from Kunming. She'd written about her hometown in her entrance paper and Sophie had looked at it only last week. Two missing girls from the same town. This had to be the connection she was looking for. There was one way to confirm it.

女孩

TAE HUN sat slumped at the back of the classroom hoping his teacher wouldn't call on him today. His left cheek still throbbed despite days of painkillers and a bottle of soju last night. Actually, he thought, shifting in his seat, maybe the soju was the reason his head throbbed. He would lay off the booze and get to bed early tonight.

His phone rang.

The other students groaned, several twisting in their seats to shoot accusing glares his way. Tae Hun scowled back at them as he fumbled with the zipper on the pocket of his army pants. His teacher, a weedy, balding guy named Jake, stared at Tae Hun, crossed his arms and tapped a foot impatiently against the floor. Tae Hun's fingers grasped the thick wedge of the handset and he tapped madly at its keypad, hoping to turn the damn thing off. He succeeded, and the synthetic pop cut out as suddenly as it had begun. The room was silent but for the sound of Jake's sneakered foot beating against the floor.

'Are we done?' Jake peered over the top of conservative spectacles that were at odds with his T-shirt and jeans. This school was much less classy than United. The teachers here were less organised. Half of them were washed-up surfers making a little money to fund their next surfing binge. Tae Hun thought Jake was a strange-looking surfer – he had neither the build nor the bleached blond curls of the surfers he saw down at Bronte where he sometimes hung out. 'Surfers come in all shapes and sizes,' Jake had said when Tae Hun questioned him on this. 'Don't judge a book by its cover.' And Tae Hun hadn't quite understood what that meant.

Tae Hun placed the silenced phone on his desk but Jake wasn't yet done with him. 'See that sign?' Jake pointed to a grubby piece of laminated paper tacked to the wall. *Turn phone's off*, it said, and Tae Hun couldn't help wondering why the administrators at an English school couldn't ask someone to help them with their punctuation.

Jake was waiting for Tae Hun to speak, his arms still crossed and his eyebrows raised expectantly.

'Sorry,' he mumbled and Jake's face softened.

'I'm not asking you to apologise, mate, just turn it off in future, okay?'

Tae Hun nodded, feeling foolish.

'Go take the call if you need to,' Jake continued. 'It's not like you're doing much here except distracting everyone with that banged-up face of yours.'

He was joking, or trying to make a joke, but Tae Hun felt the throbbing in his head intensify with rage. He pulled himself out of his seat and strode through the desks to the door. What did teacher Jake know about anything? What did he know about what went on out in the streets and backyards of the real world? They were so fucking self-righteous, these language teachers, particularly here in Australia. It was as though they thought their students were stupid or juvenile or both. It was as though they mistook language difficulty for intellectual incapacity. They'd use patronisingly slow speech patterns and speak loudly, almost to the point of shouting, as though addressing a room of stupid deaf people. The stupid ones were these teachers, Tae Hun thought. Here in their homeland, teaching their native language – anyone could do that. These teachers seemed to think they were doing something special.

Tae Hun looked down at his phone. The screen flashed green to signal the missed call. He checked the name of the caller and, with a sinking heart, saw the call had come from Sophie. And then the phone began to ring again. As Tae Hun watched Sophie's name flash on the screen he contemplated switching the phone off. But the memory of how Sophie had tenderly cared for him, bathing and disinfecting his cuts and giving him a place to stay, was still fresh. There was no point blaming her for what had happened out at the house.

'It's not one o'clock yet, I know that,' Sophie's voice at the end of the phone sounded desperate. 'I really need to talk to you.'

'Now?' Tae Hun knew he'd already said and done too much. If he'd only kept his mouth shut, none of this would have happened and he would be living his regular life, worrying about the rent and school fees and work and learning English. He wouldn't be worrying about the possibility that some crazy S&M club owner would hunt him down and kill him.

'I need to know where Han Hong came from,' Sophie said.

Tae Hun leaned against the wall. That was easy enough. He could give her that.

'China,' he said, shrugging his shoulders instinctively. He would have thought that was obvious, but perhaps Asians all looked the same to the Aussies. A lot of Aussies looked the same to him.

'Where in China, do you know?'

Tae Hun thought. He did know, they had talked about their hometowns one day early in the term. He couldn't remember the name of Han Hong's town, but she had said something about the name of her province that had struck him as beautiful. He tried to remember the English.

'South of the Clouds,' he said finally.

'Pardon?'

'She lives South of the Clouds. It's the name of her province, not her town. In English.'

鬼

AFTER SOPHIE disconnected the call she closed her eyes and leaned against the filing cabinet. South of the Clouds was the English translation for Yunnan province in China's south-west. And the capital of Yunnan was Kunming.

A commotion in the hallway stole Sophie's attention and she glanced up to see Janie hauling a female student down the corridor. Sophie slipped the class file back into its drawer and hurried to catch up.

'Janie, a moment please.'

Janie stopped and threw an exasperated hand in the air. 'I know I was going to wait,' she said. 'But then I thought she might do a runner. I figured this was my only proper chance to catch her.'

The girl squirming under Janie's fierce grip was a frail-looking thing with greasy hair and pimples on her chin. A long fringe fell down over her eyes but Sophie could see the curl of her lip as it formed a snarl.

'Can I speak to Mei Li in private, Janie?' Sophie asked.

Janie shot her an incredulous look. 'Did you not listen to me before, Sophie? This *isn't* Mei Li. That's the whole point.'

'Sure, Janie, but can I have a word with her before you speak to Pete?'

'Why?' Janie's eyes narrowed. 'You're not trying to steal my thunder, are you?' She stepped closer and lowered her voice. 'I worked this out and I want Pete to know that.'

Sophie did her best to sound sympathetic. 'I know, Janie, and you did a great job.'

'You can speak to her after we've talked to Pete,' Janie said.

On hearing his name, Pete poked his head out of his office.

'What's all this then?' he asked, his eyes darting from Janie to Sophie.

'Pete,' said Janie, stepping forward.

In a flash, the girl had twisted and slipped past Janie and back out into the corridor. As she did, Sophie stuck out a hand and grabbed the girl's fleeing elbow. The girl snapped her head back, agitated.

'Let go,' she snarled.

'What's going on?' Pete shot a glare Sophie's way.

'I've got her, Pete, no worries,' said Sophie.

Janie pulled Pete into his office. Sophie ducked her head and whispered into the student's ear, 'I need to find Mei Li. Tell me where she is.'

But the girl just stared back, confused. 'I am Mei Li,' she said, the words stumbling out of her mouth in a whimper.

Sophie shook the girl's arm. 'No, you're not. You know that and I know that. I need to find the real Mei Li, where is she?'

The girl searched Sophie's face, bewildered. Sophie noticed her pupils were the size of pins.

'Let me see your arm,' she said, but before she could reach for the sleeve to push it up, the girl opened her mouth and drenched the carpet in vomit.

'That's just great.' Pete leaned on the open door to his office, rubbed a hand through his hair. 'Get her to the bathroom, Sophie.'

'I'll take her,' Janie lurched forward but Pete held up a hand.

'No, let Sophie do it,' he said. 'Thanks for alerting me to your concerns, Janie. I'll check the paperwork while you get someone to clean this up.'

Janie scowled, shot Sophie a glare. Sophie positioned her body close to the student's and started to half walk, half drag the girl down the corridor to the bathroom. Six blue-doored cubicles stood opposite a narrow wall-length sink. Grey signs against the grey walls reminded students not to stand on the toilet seats. Automatic deodorisers pumped sweet, artificial smells into the air throughout the day but the tangy scent of urine remained an ever-present bottom note. Two young girls at the end of the communal sink giggled at their foamy-mouthed reflections in the mirror. *Why anyone would brush their teeth in this space is beyond me*, Sophie thought, as she helped the student to the basin.

The girl leaned against the mirror and fumbled with the tap. As the water gushed out, she studied it for several seconds before uncurling a clenched palm and cupping the running water in her hand. Sophie grabbed a roll of toilet paper and unravelled several sheets.

'Here, let me help you,' she said, as the girl gulped down fist after fist of water. The girl gripped the edges of the basin and slowly lifted her head. She allowed Sophie to wipe her face and the front of her shirt, but she kept her eyes down, refusing to meet Sophie's.

The skin on the girl's forehead and chin was blistered with sores. Sophie brushed them gently with the paper and they wept. Beads of perspiration bubbled around her hairline and on her upper lip, and her skin, sallow and yellow, smelled faintly of cleaning chemicals.

'What have they given you?' Sophie said so quietly it was almost a whisper.

The girl didn't respond. The two girls brushing their teeth had started shooting nervous glances their way.

'Can you tell me about Mei Li?'

A small moan slipped out of the student's mouth. Was that the sound of defiance or defeat? Sophie decided to prod some more.

'I'm really worried about Mei Li. Please tell me what you know about her.'

'I am Mei Li.' The girl's voice, little more than a childish whine, rang loud and craggy in the confines of the bathroom. 'I am Mei Li.' She bucked her head as she heaved out the words, grasping the rim of the sink with two palms and rocking her body in a slow rhythmic dance. Sophie glanced at the girls with the toothpaste. They shoved their belongings away, their cheeks glowing an embarrassed red. They shot shy smiles and lowered their heads as they pushed past and out the door.

'I am Mei Li,' the girl moaned again and it seemed to Sophie as though she were writhing with the pain of this lie. Her instinct was to take the girl into her arms but she feared frightening her further. Instead she reached out a tentative arm and placed a hand on the girl's back, spreading her fingers like wings, pleading for calm through her touch.

'Stop,' she whispered. 'Please stop this.'

It had an effect. The girl leaned back into Sophie's touch and as she did Sophie brought her body behind the girl's and slipped her arms down and under her armpits, pulling her back, carrying her weight, cradling her in an awkward embrace. 'It's all right,' she said. 'It's all right.'

'I am Mei Li,' the girl whispered, exhausted.

Sophie lowered the girl gently to the floor and she crumpled there, folded into the space between Sophie's thighs. 'It's okay. You are Mei Li,' said Sophie, glancing at the bathroom door. 'Stay there a moment.'

Sophie pulled herself up and pushed open a cubicle door. She grasped the sanitary towel disposal unit and lifted it out, surprised at its weight. With some force, she wedged it under the handle of the bathroom door, jamming it closed. They needed privacy now.

When she again sat close to the girl and placed an arm on her shoulder, there came a low guttural murmur.

'It's my job to say that.'

Bingo.

Sophie took a bony hand in her own. 'Who tells you to say that?'

'Every morning and every night they make me say it,' the girl mumbled, her nose running with snot.

'Who tells you?'

'My boss men.'

'You're working for someone?'

The girl nodded her head.

'They pay you?'

'At first they paid me. Then they give me drug. At first I say, no, I don't want to take it. I don't do this kind of thing. But they give to me anyway. Now I need it. I take payment in drugs.'

Sophie suppressed her rising indignation. 'Who are these men?'

The girl wiped her nose with her hand. 'My boss. They are my boss.'

'They drug you?'

'Yes. At first I don't want. But now I need. I come here only to study English. I thought the opportunity was a good one. To make money for my family. But these people are not good people. They ruin my life.'

'Did you tell the police?'

The girl recoiled in fright and anger. 'No. You don't tell police. I don't tell you to tell police. The police get involved, my family is hurt.'

'Your family here?'

'In China. My family.'

Sophie feigned retreat. 'Okay,' she said. 'But these men are doing the wrong thing by you. And by your family too. They threaten you.'

The girl shook her head. 'It's not so bad for me. Only this game.'

'Do they hurt you?'

'No, no. Only the drug and the game. Other girls, they do worse. They strip, they do S&M, they make videos ...'

'Videos?'

The girl nodded. 'For sale in Chinatown. I've seen the shop. Upstairs there are rooms with beds. Downstairs there are yellow movies. They wanted me to work there but I said no.'

'What is your real name?'

The girl looked up, a crooked smile on her lips. 'I have no name. No passport. I belong to them. I am only Mei Li.'

'But where is the real Mei Li?'

'She's working. Maybe at the video shop. I don't know. She's making money, right now. The drugs come later. Please, let me go. If I make mistake and the school catch me, then my boss will hurt my family.'

'We need to stop them.'

'I must protect my family. I nearly paid back my debt. Then I can go home. Dizzy said so.'

'Dizzy?'

'My English teacher. In Kunming. He helped me here.'

Dizzy. She fished her wallet out of the back pocket of her jeans and started flipping through the cards. Among the copier and restaurant cards she found her business card stash. She flicked through it.

Sophie settled on something green – the card belonging to Michael Disney.

MICHAEL DISNEY passed through immigration without a problem and now he was seated on the plane. A new life in South America beckoned. Now it was his turn to disappear.

He'd known it was over as soon as he discovered Zhou dead. He'd left the room as he found it and closed the door behind the butcher's body. It wouldn't be long before rotting flesh was discovered. Not even a ground-floor butcher shop could disguise the smell of a decomposing human body.

Where had it all gone wrong? It had been a smooth operation, illegal yes, but smooth. He'd operated for years but cracks had appeared in recent months and in the time since his substitute jumped from the window of the English school, things had fallen apart.

He'd leave the mess behind. The tracks would lead back to the language schools and the bent administrators there. None of them knew the real game they'd signed up to. Wouldn't Pete get a shock when he discovered just how far from decency he'd fallen?

The English teacher. What did she have to do with all this and why hadn't Zhou taken care of her, like he'd asked?

More to the point, who had taken care of Zhou?

SOPHIE MET Tae Hun at a sushi shop on Castlereagh Street. He sat at a kerbside table smoking a cigarette.

'I don't have a long time,' Tae Hun said, as Sophie sat down. 'And after this I don't want to talk to you again.'

'Tell me about the image, Tae Hun. You told me you took that photo.'

'I needed your help,' he said, not looking at her.

'If you want to help Han Hong you need to tell me the whole truth now.'

'Will you inform the police?'

Not a chance in hell. 'You know I won't,' she said. 'Tell me what you know about Han Hong.'

'I helped get her the job,' he said softly.

Sophie resisted the urge to interrupt. She sat back in her chair and forced her hands under her thighs.

'There's, how can you say it, a lot of opportunity here for foreign students,' Tae Hun said. 'For girls especially. I know people, groups of people, they run clubs like the one in Ashfield, they run strip clubs, dance venues, pornography shops, brothels.' He paused to take another drag on his cigarette. 'The girls, they go into the business of their own choice.' He looked up and met Sophie's eyes for the first time.

'And where do you come in?'

'You know the welcome parties?'

Sophie nodded. She knew them well. Every pub or bar at the Haymarket end of George Street seemed to run weekly welcome nights for the foreign student crowd. The nights were famous for their discounted drinks on presentation of an international student card, and Sophie had, on more than one occasion, helped stumbling teenagers with bellies full of cider back to their city share apartments after a night of good times and very little food.

'The parties are loaded with people like me,' he said. 'We tell the boss's girls about the opportunities available. We buy them drinks and show them a good time. We tell them how beautiful they are and how much money they can make, how easy it is, how safe they will be, how we will protect their visa.'

'Who's "we"?'

Tae Hun shrugged. 'I don't even know the names of all the people I work for. I get a message from Cho, the guy you met the other night. He tells me who to target, gives me a name and a picture.'

'Is the boss a man named Michael Disney?'

'I told you, I don't know. I got into it because of Wendy.'

Everything is connected.

Sophie sat back in her chair. She studied the boy sitting opposite her. Wendy's death and Han Hong's disappearance were connected and Tae Hun was the common denominator between them.

'Don't look at me like that,' Tae Hun said, his voice low. 'I don't know anything more about Wendy, or why she killed herself.'

'Did you know she was pretending to be someone else?'

'I know she was working for the same people as me, the same people as Han Hong. Substitution is a part of the game.'

'Was Wendy involved in sex work?'

'Probably. All the girls were. Sometimes they went to the clubs to work as dancers, sometimes they sat in on other student's classes for a term. They were paid in cash and drugs. Eventually, just drugs.'

'So did you know the real Wendy Chan?'

Tae Hun shook his head. 'I knew Wendy and I knew Han Hong. When Han Hong stopped showing up at the clubs, at first I thought nothing about it. But then I missed her. I realised I liked her, I wanted to see her again.'

'So what did you do?'

'I went to see Cho. He sells DVDs and sex toys in Chinatown.'

'And what happened when you went there?'

'He was busy with a customer, so I started flipping through the latest DVDs, the ones our girls make.'

'And you found a movie with Han Hong in it?'

He nodded. 'I took it without him knowing.'

'What makes you think she didn't make that movie of her own accord, and get paid for it, like all the others? What makes you think there's a problem?'

'Because the film isn't like the others – it isn't sexy. It's scary. And on the screen she looks afraid. I think someone's taken her and is making her work against her will.'

'Did you ask Cho about it?'

'You saw what they did to me for taking you to the club,' he said. 'You don't question the people I work for. I didn't want to get involved.'

So you involved me instead.

'And besides,' he said. 'If the film was in his shop, don't you think he might know something about what's happened to her?'

'You mean he's behind it?'

Tae Hun fidgeted with his cigarette packet, trying to find the right words. 'I think someone in the organisation is cheating the boss.'

Sophie worked hard at trying to decipher the boy's meaning. 'Let me get this straight,' she said. 'The business you're involved in is illegal, but everyone's there of their own accord.'

'Yes.'

'But you think one of the operators of the business has gone rogue?'

'I don't understand that word.'

'You think someone is operating behind the boss's back, holding women without their consent and making films of them.'

'I think so.'

'And they're getting away with it because of the whole substitution set-up and the fact that the girls consented in the first place.'

'That's right. The other students don't give a fuck, they just assume the girls are off working.'

Sophie considered this. 'But the boss must know his workers are going missing?'

Tae Hun looked at her. 'What's he going to do? Phone the police?'

Sophie's phone rang. She slipped it out of her jeans and scanned the caller ID. Damian. She guessed he was calling to tell her the butcher stocked more than just meat.

女孩

'I HOPE you have a decent alibi,' Damian said when she met him at a coffee shop overlooking Railway Square.

'Beg yours?'

Damian pulled out a wooden chair, indicating that Sophie should sit. 'For me, not the cops. I checked out your butcher shop.'

'And you found some kind of dodgy sex shop as well?'

Damian studied her. 'No,' he said, with a slow shake of the head. 'Missed that one. But I did find your Zhou character.'

'And?'

'Couldn't get much out of him. It's kind of hard to make someone talk when they're dead.'

Sophie stared at him. 'What the fuck?'

'I don't know who did it or why.'

'Are the police onto it?'

Damian shook his head. 'I left him there and I closed the door. I went out, took a walk, tried to figure out what was going on. I went back later. The body was gone.'

'Someone moved it.'

'No shit.' He stared at her. 'That's not to say the police won't get onto it.'

'Yeah, right.'

Damian's gaze penetrated her. 'It looks like it was a woman who did him in – there was an earring lodged in Zhou's throat, a cheap red plastic thing, shaped like a rose.'

Sophie's heart skipped. 'Must've been a woman then,' she said.

'He was a big guy. My theory immediately is that there were two people.'

'Have you told anyone about my story?'

'Nobody knows about your involvement yet.' His eyes searched Sophie's face. 'There's no reason they should, is there?'

She eyeballed him, said nothing.

'Another thing,' said Damian. 'When I asked about Zhou at

the butcher shop, the man behind the counter said he might be working at a restaurant. A place called Firewater.'

'The Sichuan place?'

Damian shrugged. 'Never been there. But the guy said it was spicy.'

Firewater. The night out with Wendy. The restaurant next door to Brad's.

Our storage room shares a door with the Sichuan place and so they think we should let them use it.

Images of her recent encounters with Brad flashed through Sophie's mind. The meeting with Jin Tao at Brad's restaurant: exactly how much of their conversation had he overheard? Brad appearing out of the blue on her doorstep, rushing off before she could invite him in. The animosity between him and Jin Tao…

'My friend works at the restaurant next door to Firewater,' Sophie said.

Damian smiled. 'You mean Brad?'

Sophie stared at him, surprised. 'You know him?'

Damian looked down at his hands. 'You could say that,' he said, and Sophie's heart lurched to her throat.

'He was hanging around my house when I came home to find a noose on my bed,' she said, her voice weak.

'A noose sounds pretty intense.'

'Someone left it there to scare me.'

Damian frowned. 'You mean when you came back from the mountains?'

Sophie nodded.

Damian rocked back in his seat. 'And you think Brad might have something to do with this?'

Wouldn't be the first time I've been betrayed by someone close. Nausea gurgled in Sophie's stomach. 'He never visits.'

Damian smiled. 'You've got it wrong.'

'What?'

'He was in your street because of me. We'd just had lunch together and I decided to stop by your house and talk to you some more. Brad decided to push on because he had a shift to work.'

'You ate lunch together?'

Damian nodded. 'We've been seeing each other.'

Sophie worked hard to stop her jaw from hanging wide.

'It's actually why I stopped you in the street on the day Wendy died,' Damian continued. 'I'd seen your photo at Brad's house and I knew you worked at that school.' He paused. 'I also know about your past.'

'My past?'

'Your father. The private investigation business. What happened.'

Arsehole.

'When I saw you there taking notes, I thought maybe you were back in the game.'

Sophie eyeballed him. 'Why didn't you come clean?'

'Career habit.'

'You're sly as they come and Brad can have you.'

'Trust me, he has.'

Sophie held up a hand. 'Way too much information.'

They laughed. The tension lifted.

'So Zhou's dead and it looks like a woman killed him,' Sophie said. 'It sounds like someone decided to fight back, so whoever is behind all this is likely to have their defences up by now. You've already been nosing around the butcher shop, so why don't you take the restaurant? Go out there and see what you can find. I'll get Jin Tao to help me hunt down the porn shop.'

'So there is some investigator left in you after all,' said Damian, his eyes sparkling.

鬼

'I LIKE your roses,' Joy Lin said when she looked up from her assignment.

Sophie looked at the bunch of roses in the glass jar on her desk. They'd seen better days and the edges of the petals had taken on a brown hue. 'I should hang them upside down to dry,' she said. 'You ever tried that?'

Joy Lin shook her head, thoughtful. 'I think I flunked the exam,' she said. 'I practised so hard but during the test I couldn't concentrate, couldn't find the words.'

'You probably did better than you think.'

'I probably did worse.'

'How about the lucky charms?'

'What?'

'The earrings.'

Joy Lin's face fell. 'I'm really sorry, Soph,' she said. 'I lost them. I hope they weren't expensive.'

'No,' said Sophie. She pushed her hair back, exposing her ear.

'You don't even have your ears pierced,' said Joy Lin, breaking into a relieved smile.

'So you don't need to stress,' said Sophie. 'I'm sure they'll turn up.'

'I don't want to find them.' Her lip quivered.

'Why not?'

'Because last time I looked for them, I saw something I can't unsee.'

女孩

THE HOUSE at number 60 looked like it belonged in a home decorating magazine. Beyond a low hedge and carefully manicured garden sat a two-storey house, all red brickwork, latticed windows and slanted gables. It appeared to be a warm home – *not unlike the one I grew up in* – but Sophie knew appearances could be deceiving.

Joy Lin had told Sophie everything: losing the earrings en route to the audition; the gear in Mr Holmes's car.

The connection had clicked for Sophie: hardcore porn, red rosebuds, a dank room in Chinatown. Justin Holmes had to know something.

Sophie left Joy Lin in the passenger seat. 'Don't tell him I'm here,' the girl had pleaded, and Sophie had done her best to reassure her that everything would be all right. But as she walked up the pebbled path to the front door, her cheeks carried the burn of her lie.

A woman answered on Sophie's first knock. Perfectly straightened hair, warm smile, lipstick on a front tooth.

'I'm here to see Justin Holmes,' said Sophie.

A puzzled expression crossed the woman's face. 'Are you selling something?'

'I just need to talk to him. It's quite urgent.'

The woman took this in. 'Who shall I tell him is here?'

'He doesn't know me,' Sophie said. 'I'm here about one of my students, a girl named Joy Lin.'

'Joy Lin Tan?' A new voice. A man appeared in the doorway. 'That's her.'

'She's my daughter's best friend,' the woman said.

'What's this about?' The man, Justin, placed his hand

protectively on the woman's shoulder and Sophie's glance fell to the wedding ring bound to his finger.

'I wondered if we could have a word in private?'

'Private?' The woman's voice had the shrill ring of concern to it now.

Justin gave her shoulder a squeeze. 'I think I know why she's here,' he said to his wife in a low voice. 'Just give us a moment, I'll tell you later.'

The woman glanced from Justin to Sophie, unease in her eyes. Then, with a modest bow of the head, she slipped from under her husband's hand and moved back into the house. He watched her pad back down the hallway. When she disappeared into a room, he turned to Sophie.

'Who are you and what do you want?'

'I'm a friend of Joy Lin Tan's. She sent me to collect a pair of earrings she says she left in your car.'

'Earrings?'

'Yes.'

Sophie thought she saw the muscles in Justin's face relax. 'Oh, those.' He paused. 'I seem to have misplaced them,' he said quietly. 'But tell Joy Lin I'll send them to school with Isobel as soon as they turn up.' His eyes pierced hers. 'Was there something else?'

Hell, yes.

'A man was murdered in Chinatown and they found a red rose earring in his mouth,' she said, watching Justin's face pale. 'Joy Lin told me she found porn in your car, and because I happen to know the dead guy was involved in that business, I thought you might know something about who killed him.'

Justin looked Sophie up and down. 'You make a habit of turning up on people's doorsteps talking ludicrous shit like this?' he asked with a sneer.

'You're saying you have no idea what I'm talking about?'

'No idea at all.'

'So if I take Joy Lin to the nearest police station and we tell them what she found in your car and we mention she's missing a pair of red rose earrings, you don't think they'll be interested?'

'There must be thousands of cheap fucking earrings in Sydney.'

'The ones I gave Joy Lin had the Chinese characters for David inked on the back,' she said. 'It will only take one phone call to discover if the one found with the dead body is mine.'

Justin paled. 'Are you after money?'

'Did you kill that man?'

'I did not.'

'How did the earring end up in his mouth?'

'I don't know.'

'Some women are missing and I'm trying to find out what happened to them. I don't know how much involvement you've had with any of this, but I need to know where you got those DVDs. I need to know the location of that shop.'

Justin stared at her. 'And if I tell you, will you leave me alone?'

'I won't go to the police, if that's what you're asking,' she said. 'And I won't mention the characters on the earring.'

He seemed to consider this. Then, head bowed and hands in his pockets, he said, 'There's a butcher shop in Chinatown. The DVD store is in the back room. You enter via an alley that runs along the back. They sell standard stuff there. But they sell a bunch of under-the-counter stuff too. The guy you want to speak to has a lot of rings in his face.'

Rings in his face. Tae Hun in a headlock. The backyard bouncer. Cho.

'Right,' said Sophie.

'You breathe my name in connection with this to anyone and I will deny everything,' said Justin. 'And then I will come after you with everything I've got.'

Whatever, man. You've got nothing but guilt.

'Sure,' Sophie said and she turned to head back to the car.

鬼

'SO YOU and Damian decided to go it alone?' Jin Tao was at his workbench, massaging salt and Sichuan pepper into the pimply white skin of a chicken. He grimaced as he worked, although Sophie suspected the pained facial expression came as much from their discussion as the task at hand. 'A man's dead, Soph. This needs to be handled formally.'

Sophie glanced around the kitchen. They were alone aside from Stu, who sat on a stool in the corner chopping garlic. 'The police won't give a shit about a few missing foreign students,' she said, matter-of-fact. 'I'm willing to bet on that.'

Jin Tao grunted, unimpressed. He trussed the bird and placed it gently next to another in a giant bamboo steamer near the stove. When he turned to face her, Sophie noticed the red stain of an irritated blush creeping into his face.

'I'm surprised you didn't lose your job for letting that girl go.'

'Maybe Pete was happy about it. You said there had to be someone on the inside, right? And besides, she was sick on the carpet outside his office – I think that put him off.'

'Yeah, well, I wish it had done the same for you.'

'I can't let this go, Jin Tao.'

He turned to her, his eyes studying her face. Even in the harsh fluorescent light of the kitchen he was beautiful. When he spoke his voice was quiet. 'Go to the police.'

'I went to the police.' She could hear her tone, defiant.

Jin Tao had picked up his steamer and was walking with it to the burners at the end of the kitchen. 'Then find another cop who'll listen,' he said over his shoulder as he secured the steamer into position over a blackened wok bubbling with water.

'The girl asked me not to talk to the police. She's scared for her family.'

'Her family?'

'In China. They told her they'd harm her family if she went to the police or if she tried to escape. She owes them a debt. She says that they'll let her go when she's paid it off.'

Jin Tao removed the towel from his shoulder and wiped his hands with great care. 'You know that's unlikely, don't you?'

Sophie nodded. 'That's the thing about imaginary debts, you never can pay them off.'

A cry from the other end of the kitchen – 'Fuck!' Stuart gripped his left forefinger in a clenched fist.

Jin Tao spoke first. 'You right, mate?'

Stu nodded his head as he examined his finger. 'Thought I sliced the top off it,' he said. 'But it's just a cut.'

'The idea is to slice the cloves, not your fingers,' said Jin Tao. 'Your apprentice could teach you that.'

'Yeah, yeah,' mumbled Stu as he headed for the first-aid cabinet.

Jin Tao exhaled a noisy breath and raised his hands in the air in defeat. When he turned back to Sophie, his expression had settled into one of resignation. 'What do you want from me, Soph?'

'I want you to come with me to the butcher shop in Chinatown. It's a front for an illegal porn shop.'

'It is not a front – I buy meat from there, thank you very much.'

'Okay, well, the illegal business is using the butcher as a cover. Whatever, I just want you to come check it out.'

Jin Tao sighed. 'What are we looking for exactly?'

'We're looking for some missing women.'

IN THE kitchen, Justin drank from a tall glass of water. The liquid eased the dryness in his throat but did nothing to quell the rage boiling deep inside him. Who else had Joy Lin blabbed to?

He'd managed to subdue the curious questions from his wife with a story about an argument between Joy Lin and their daughter. He'd thought it had been resolved, he said, but clearly Joy Lin had told her English tutor about it. His wife had immediately wanted to talk to Isobel about the incident but Justin had placed a hand on her arm. 'I promised Isobel I wouldn't say anything,' he'd said, imploring her with his eyes. 'Don't turn me into the daddy who can't keep secrets.'

Now, as he looked out the window to where his wife tended her gardenias, Justin ran over the conversation with the English tutor in his mind.

Clearly he'd made a mistake up there in the room with that girl. He shouldn't have told her the truth. Things had gone very wrong and now he could be implicated in a murder.

He scanned his memory for evidence that could link him to the crime. There were the earrings, marked, according to the English tutor, and the DVDs he'd purchased, but he'd always paid cash and had burned the last of them the evening before. He thought about the phone calls he'd made to the mobile phone number – those could catch him out if the police ever found a reason to check his records. Justin thought hard about any other possible traces he might have left. He brought the glass of water down hard against the benchtop, cracking it. Fucking idiot. The real problem, Justin considered, as his rage gave way to fear and dread, was that he had given them his address. It could be on their database. The police only had to access it and they would be knocking on his door in no time.

Justin pummelled the benchtop with his knuckles. He had to get back to the shop and speak to the guy at the counter. He'd use the threat of what he knew if he needed to. He had to make sure they erased all trace of him from the system.

JIN TAO had insisted they drive into the city. As she watched the rain beat patterns onto the glass of the window, Sophie was thankful she'd agreed. Outside, Oxford Street was a smear of neon and black. In the dark, the saturated asphalt glistened like oil and bounced light from the brightly lit shopfronts and their fluorescent signs.

'Would have been a terrible ride,' she started, and threw a smile Jin Tao's way.

He wasn't buying. He'd hardly spoken in the hour since he'd arrived home from the restaurant and announced he would accompany her. Now he simply gripped the wheel tighter and clenched his jaw in a sullen scowl. Rain peppered the windscreen, turning it opaque.

'Aren't you going to use your wipers?'

Jin Tao switched on the wipers and they swished once across the glass to reveal the sodden night. 'You going to tell me how to drive, too?'

Sophie folded back into her seat, studied the tension in Jin Tao's jaw and neck. 'I didn't mean to coerce you into this.'

Jin Tao raised an eyebrow but said nothing. Sophie tried again, threading lightness into her voice.

'I mean, you can just drop me off. I'll be okay on my own.'

Jin Tao drummed his fingers on the steering wheel. 'I thought you, of all people, would understand.'

'Understand what?'

Jin Tao slowed the car as they cruised past Spice I Am on Wentworth Avenue. He caught Sophie's eye as he looked past her to check out the queue of hungry punters on the footpath. 'Pissing down and they still come.'

'Understand what?'

Jin Tao sighed and spoke through gritted teeth. 'That if you neglect to look after people, you live with the consequences.'

She was silent as her mind groped wildly to find the meaning in Jin Tao's words. And then the confusion gave way to rage.

'You don't need to look after me.'

'I do.'

And then they were pulling over and Jin Tao had placed a hand on the back of her neck. She jerked away and knocked her forehead against the window.

'Careful.' Jin Tao's voice was soft.

'Fuck off.'

'I'm quite serious, Sophie,' he said. 'What you're doing here, I think it's less to do with those girls and everything to do with what happened.'

Sophie didn't bother to reply. If she'd brought an umbrella, she'd get out and walk; as it was, she was tempted to make a break for it anyway. The car suddenly felt too hot. The carpet's damp scent flooded her nostrils and she thought that just maybe she would be sick.

'It's not going to bring him back, you know.' Jin Tao had withdrawn his attempt to comfort her and again his voice sounded pragmatic and cold.

Sophie pulled the muscles in her face taut. 'Really, I have no idea what you're on about.'

'Come on.'

'No, really. You're not making any sense.'

'It's no coincidence these girls come from China.'

'You're right about that, officer.'

'I mean it's no coincidence that you're attracted to their plight because of China. Fuck, Sophie, you're half Chinese.'

'That's got jack-all to do with it,' she said. 'You can't just pull out the race card when it's convenient.'

'You're right,' Jin Tao said. 'This isn't about race. It's about David.'

And he'd done it. He'd done what she'd begged him not ever to do. He'd brought her back there, raised the memory, dragged it to the forefront of her consciousness. The memory swamped her senses like a rotting carcass breaking the surface of a murky pond.

女孩

AFTER THE park, after the search and the police and the press conference and the photographs and the media frenzy that surrounded David's disappearance, it had been just the two of them. Sophie and Li Hua.

For days and weeks they had stood together, side by side, riding the media storm caused by the fact a foreigner had been in charge of the Chinese boy when he disappeared, using it to their advantage in their search for Li Hua's son.

But each lead had proved futile and each new piece of information had contributed more to the confusion than to a solution. The police quickly lost interest and the story soon lost its currency. Thousands of Chinese children go missing every year. David was simply another. And like the others, he was never found.

'I don't blame you,' Li Hua said one day, her eyes glistening with fresh tears. It was the first time she'd said it.

Sophie felt the air scream out of her lungs, leaving her empty, deflated, at risk of collapse. 'You should,' she said, her voice a shadow of its usual self.

'And what good would it do?' Li Hua asked. 'I'd only lose my son and my soulmate at the same time.'

Soulmate.

'Am I that?' Sophie asked.

Li Hua nodded.

'I should have watched him more carefully,' Sophie said. 'It's my fault.'

'You are right and you are wrong,' Li Hua said, eyeing her. 'Yes, you should have watched him more carefully. But it is not your fault there is evil in the world. You were not to know someone evil was lurking so close.'

'What would you do to him?' Sophie asked. 'If you found the person who took David?'

Li Hua contemplated the question for a long time. Then she took Sophie's hand and placed it against her heart. 'I'd take a cleaver and drive it through his spine,' she said, and Sophie felt the pulse of Li Hua's blood beneath her breast. 'I wouldn't hesitate. Not for a second.'

鬼

'C'MON, SOPHIE, I'm sorry. I didn't mean to upset you.'

Jin Tao's voice stabbed at her like a knife. She lifted a hand to her cheek and brushed the skin to find it wet. He'd made her cry and that made her mad. 'Let's go,' she said to the window as she pulled down the seatbelt and buckled herself in.

'Does this mean you're talking to me again?'

'I didn't share my past with you for you to use it against me.' Her voice contained the right amount of ice.

'Sure.' Jin Tao stepped on the accelerator. 'Sorry.' They drove the rest of the way in silence.

Liverpool Street smelled of wine and garlic. Plates of olives and chorizo smothered sheltered sidewalk tables where sangria-flushed patrons ate and smoked. Sophie sloshed past them along the puddled footpath and out from under the shelter into the open night. The rain fell hard on her head and neck.

'Stick closer to me,' panted Jin Tao as he again shoved the handle of the umbrella close to her face. 'You're soaked.'

Sophie stuck her hands deeper into her pockets and increased her speed. 'It's only water.'

The lane ran parallel to the street that housed the butcher shop. As they entered it, Jin Tao shoved the umbrella into the crook of Sophie's arm. 'Take this,' he said.

'But we're here.'

Jin Tao's voice was firm. 'And since we're here together, you'll not mind if I go in first.'

She started to protest but Jin Tao interrupted. 'It's as simple as this,' he said. 'If there is something suss going on here, then the last thing you want is for the wrong person to see you poking around.'

Sophie leaned into the wall. He was right.

'Let me go, ask some questions, check it out,' Jin Tao said. 'I'll report everything back to you and we can decide what to do from there.' His eyes searched hers for some acknowledgement. 'Sound like a plan?'

She shooed him with a flick of her wrist. 'Go on then.'

As soon as Jin Tao disappeared around the corner, Sophie turned a sharp left into the lane. She knew Jin Tao would ask for Han Hong by name, and she loved him for it, but she didn't think it would get him far. She'd give him five minutes then she'd follow him in.

There was the clatter of metal against asphalt. Sophie jumped, her body tensing. She listened to the whir of something metallic – a hub cap maybe – spin a lazy circle against concrete, its vibrations bouncing. Somebody else was in the laneway, she was sure of it. Sophie twisted to face the entrance to the alley. A familiar, fearful gurgle tickled her stomach as she strained to silence her breathing, ears attuned to the other sounds – the rhythmic patter of rain a backdrop to the more brutal rush of gutter water, the low flat drum of an air-conditioning system, the splat of footsteps moving through puddles, the click and roll of an umbrella letting down, a low-pitched curse as ...

'Fuck!' He was upon her and she whacked him with all her strength. The stick of her umbrella connected with bone and the man lurched backwards, his own umbrella clattering against the wall as his hands swooped to his head for protection.

'What the fuck!' He crouched low in the gutter like an ambushed soldier, one open palm stretched out in surrender, the other massaging the side of his head. 'You can have my wallet, man. You can have it,' he yelped, his last words catching in his throat. 'Just don't hurt me. Don't hurt me, please.'

Sophie crouched low to the ground. The man glanced up and Sophie reeled back.

'You.'

It was Justin Holmes. He groaned.

'What are you doing here?'

'I could ask the same question of you,' he said.

'You had something to do with the murder. The earring. It really did belong to Joy Lin.'

'I thought you knew that,' he said. 'You told me it was initialled with some bloody Chinese name.'

'It's called a bluff,' Sophie said. *Seamus's favourite PI trick.* 'There must be thousands of cheap fucking earrings in Sydney. I just wanted to make you sweat.'

Justin groaned again and rubbed the side of his head. 'Did you have to hit me with that thing?' he said, nodding to the umbrella.

'Tell me what's going on.' Sophie pointed the tip of the umbrella at him. 'Why are you here and what do you know about the operations of this place? A whole bunch of girls are missing, kidnapped, sold into the sex industry, used as slaves and prostitutes. Someone killed Zhou. Don't tell me it was you.'

The man laughed. 'What are you? A cop?'

'No, but there's one just inside the store.'

'He won't find anything. They've gone.'

'Who's gone? Where?'

Justin shrugged his shoulders. 'The whole shop's shut up, moved out, as if it never existed.'

They were too late. Sophie felt tension drop into her stomach like a lead ball. 'So you came here because I told you about the murder?'

Justin nodded. 'I freaked out. When I met the girl in that room I had the earrings in my pocket. I was going to get her to wear them but we never got to that. They must've fallen out. I didn't kill anyone. I can't be implicated. I came down to make sure they took my name and address off the records. If my wife finds out about any of this, I'm screwed.'

'Where did you lose the earrings?'

'An upstairs room. They had a girl there. I gave her some information.'

'What information?'

'It's none of your business. I did the right thing but the information I gave her made her very upset.'

'Was this room above the butcher shop?'

'No idea,' he said, backing away. 'But it was up some stairs. Look, I'd appreciate it if you forgot you ever saw me here. I can pay you, give you whatever you want. I didn't do anything to any girl and I have never cheated on my wife.'

Sophie lowered the umbrella. Justin scrambled to his feet, turned on his heel and broke into a run. Sophie watched him reach the corner, take a sharp left and disappear. She was alone again – now with not even the rain for company. She tilted her head to the snatch of sky striking black between the outlined edges of the buildings. It hung dark and starless and Sophie knew it would not be long until it started to pour again.

And then she saw her.

Sophie's gaze fixed on a crooked fire-escape serrating its way up the brickwork to the sky. At the lower landing, light burned a triangle into a first-floor window, escaping from curtains that did not quite meet. And framed in the triangle, squashed up against the glass like a tanked puffer fish, was Su Yuan.

女孩

THEY SAT at a corner table in the food court near the Happy Chef. The place bustled with night diners sucking on noodles and watching the overhead TVs. They were safe enough here, Sophie reasoned, at least until the crowds thinned out. Jin Tao had positioned himself several tables away at Sophie's request, when she realised his presence made Su Yuan nervous. They needed to get some answers fast and for that Sophie guessed she'd need to speak with Su Yuan alone.

Su Yuan twisted a paper napkin between her fingers. She'd taken two tentative sips of her wonton soup when it first arrived, but it now sat untouched, an oily slick glistening on the surface.

'What's going on?' Sophie tried again, hoping the girl would talk now that Jin Tao had excused himself. 'I need to know why another student took your place at the school, where you went and why you decided to come back. I need to know what's happening.'

Su Yuan bit into her knuckles with enough force to draw blood.

Sophie leaned forward and took Su Yuan's free hand in her own. 'I thought maybe they'd killed you.'

A slight smile appeared on Su Yuan's lips. She picked up the soup spoon she'd laid carefully at the edge of her bowl and used it to scoop up broth. She sipped a tiny amount, as though eager only to moisten her lips. Then she began to speak.

'My sister disappeared from my hometown last year,' she said.

'Kunming?' asked Sophie, jumping in before she could stop herself.

'A town near Kunming. Actually, disappeared is the wrong word. She left my hometown last year. She won a scholarship to study English in Australia. It was called Golden Opportunities Scholarships. They advertised on the noticeboards around my hometown. The scholarships were open to girls under twenty-four only.'

'Was that fairly unusual?'

Su Yuan shook her head. 'Not really. With the one-child policy, there are many more boys than girls in China. So it can be harder for girls to compete. There are many opportunities like this for girls. To give them a chance.'

'But your parents had two children.'

Su Yuan nodded. 'My parents are farmers. There are exceptions for farmers if the first child is a girl. A chance for them to have a boy.'

'And so your sister applied for one of these scholarships?'

'She went for an interview. They filmed her. She told me it felt like an audition. But then, maybe only two weeks later, she got a message that said she'd won a scholarship. We were so happy for her. I'd started training in the police academy. It's not much of a job but it's more interesting than farming or factory work. But my sister, she had a chance at a proper education – it was a dream come true.'

'Who gave her this message?'

'The man who ran the business, an Australian.'

'Do you know his name?'

'Yes,' said Su Yuan. 'It's Michael Disney.'

Sophie tried to quell the anger rising within her. 'So what happened next?'

'My sister went to Australia. Mr Disney organised all the passports and the visa. My parents were so excited for her.' Su Yuan paused, twisting the napkin. 'At first my sister called home maybe one time a week. My mother would go down to the corner store and wait by the public telephone every Sunday afternoon. Sometimes she would wait there for three hours. My sister always called.'

'And then that stopped?'

'One day my mother came home very late in the night. She had waited for my sister's call all afternoon and most of the evening. But it never came. The next week was the same. We never heard from her again.'

'But you must have had contact details for her?'

'I'd been emailing her but I didn't have a street address and my parents never thought to ask. This was such an unusual thing for them. My parents have only left the province once, on a pilgrimage to Beijing. They've never been overseas, they can barely read or write. They trusted my sister knew what she was doing.'

'Did you report that she'd stopped making contact?'

'I knew there was more to the story. My sister had emailed me and indicated she was thinking about doing something to do with sex work. She didn't go into a lot of detail but I was shocked. I encouraged her not to do it. I told her it would devastate our parents if they found out.' Her voice caught in her throat. 'She said they wouldn't find out unless I told them. So even though I'd been training with the police, I decided to keep her secret. How fucked up is that?'

'It's called loyalty,' Sophie said.

'So after she stopped calling I left the police academy and I visited Michael Disney's language school. I wanted to speak to him to find out what he knew or if he had a contact address for her.'

'And did you find him?'

Su Yuan shook her head, a gleam in her eye. 'No, but I met his wife.'

Sophie's heart sank as she contemplated the idea of a woman being in on the disappearance of these girls.

'Australian?'

'Chinese. She told me everything about Disney's operation. She hated him. She married him because he promised to take her away from China, to Australia.'

Sophie nodded. 'My father took my mum away to Australia, too.'

'Only I'm sure he loved her.'

Sophie nodded. 'I think so,' she said. 'He promised to protect her.'

Su Yuan smiled. 'Disney didn't keep his promise to his wife,' she said. 'He kept her in her mother's home and visited every so often for sex.'

'But he told her about his business?'

'His wife made it her business to find out. She told me that the scholarship program is all a scam and that the girls are basically auditioned for the sex market. The girls don't know anything until they get here and are introduced to a party lifestyle with lots of opportunities for making money.'

'As prostitutes?'

'Prostitutes, strippers, waitresses, stars of skin flicks.'

Sophie sat back. 'That's quite a business,' she said. 'Although he'd have to be pretty sure the girls would be up for it.'

'He targeted poor girls through his scholarship program and I guess enough of them were interested in the work on offer to make it worthwhile. He had connections with most of the language schools, paid off the administrators in charge of timetables to make sure their visas stayed intact.'

'Do you think the administrators knew what the girls were up to?'

Su Yuan wrinkled her nose. 'I think they just took care of the schedules.'

Sophie thought hard. 'But it doesn't make sense that the girls disappear,' she said. 'I mean, why bother bringing them all the way out here just to have them go missing?'

'According to the wife, until recently nobody did go missing. Disney had everything under control, the girls were introduced gradually to the lifestyle, not forced into it. The hard part for the girls was getting out once drugs and debt were involved. But she said things had changed and that Disney himself was stressed and anxious and not sure what was going on. It all sounded very bad to me. I decided I had to use the scholarship program to come out here and find my sister.'

'Why didn't you go to the police?'

Su Yuan snorted with disgust. 'For what? What were they going to do? What proof did I have? And if they did believe me and word got out that the police were onto the operation, what would happen to my sister? Would they kill her? Of course. And I would never see her again.'

'You took an incredible risk coming here.'

Su Yuan nodded. 'Maybe stupid. But I can defend myself,' she said. 'I've been trained and I know how to fight. I know the element of surprise is what counts. I decided I just had to wait for an opportunity.'

'And if it hadn't come?'

Su Yuan shrugged. 'I couldn't do nothing. My mother is in so much pain.'

'So what happened?'

'The opportunity came. I treated it as an undercover operation and started working the same job that my sister had. I sold my body, not for money, but for my sister. I had to find her.'

Sophie tried to stop the shock from appearing on her face.

'And I asked every client I met about my sister. Most men wouldn't listen, wouldn't look at the photograph. But one man did.'

'And he gave you some information about her?'

Su Yuan nodded. 'He said she was dead. He said she'd died on film. That he'd seen her.'

A wave of nausea shuddered through Sophie's stomach. Bile threatened to spill its way up her throat and into her mouth.

'A snuff film?'

Su Yuan nodded, her eyes wide. 'I believed him. I was too late for her. I cried and cried. He untied me and left and

I decided to kill the next one of them that came into my room.'

'The next client?'

'The next boss.'

She said it with no emotion, as though she were talking about finishing a school assignment or sitting a test. Su Yuan had admitted to murdering someone and now she had gone back to eating her soup. Sophie leaned back in her chair. Fucking full-on. Could she do it? Kill a man if she had to?

'You killed him? Just like that?'

Su Yuan continued spooning broth into her mouth. 'I had to avenge my sister,' she said between slurps. 'It wasn't easy, but he didn't see it coming. I kicked him where it hurts and then I took his head in my hands and I snapped it.'

'I've met Zhou, he's strong,' Sophie said.

Su Yuan shrugged. 'Not strong enough,' she said. 'I left the red rose in his mouth for my sister. She was beautiful and he took her – I wanted to leave a mark on him.'

Sophie sat, speechless.

'You're so brave, Su Yuan,' she said finally.

Su Yuan stared deep into Sophie's eyes. 'If it were your family, you'd do it too,' she said.

You're wrong. My mother disappeared. I didn't look hard enough. I ran away.

'Besides,' Su Yuan said, 'I knew I had an alibi.'

Sophie's heart skipped a beat. 'An alibi?'

Su Yuan nodded, a smile curling at the edge of her mouth. 'I cheated them at their own game. They sent a substitute into the class, to replace me. The school's records, they're official documents, right?'

'Yes, but ...'

'So it is officially recorded that I was there, in class, at the time Zhou was killed. If someone checked my name off, it means I was there, right? I have an alibi.'

The brave woman sitting opposite her had risked everything for her sister. She'd done her research, checked the details, used her knowledge of the system to protect herself. And Sophie, with her ham-fisted detective work and the questions she'd raised, had ruined her alibi.

She took a deep breath. 'Su Yuan, we have a problem.'

'What?'

'Your alibi might not be so watertight.'

鬼

AT JIN Tao's suggestion, they travelled to Blue Lotus. There was no way Su Yuan could show her face anywhere she was known now. The gang would be looking for her.

'Why were you still hanging around the building?' Sophie asked. 'What if one of them had found you?'

'I've already lost everything,' Su Yuan said. 'I went back to hunt down the others.'

The kitchen was empty save for Stuart. He sat on a benchtop in his casual gear, a not very dashing ensemble of tracksuit pants and polar fleece. He rolled a cigarette between two fingers.

'Don't you usually do that outside?' asked Jin Tao, the disapproval clear in his voice.

'Too fucking cold, mate,' said Stuart with a grin. 'You'd kill me if you knew I smoked one in your room when I picked up that shiraz.' He jumped off the bench and stuck the cigarette in his mouth. 'Better change the location of your spare key, mate.'

Sophie suppressed an urge to whack the rollie out from between Stuart's lips as he passed. She was annoyed to find him still here – the fewer people to see Su Yuan, the better – but Stuart clearly didn't pick up on her vibes.

'Who's the pretty one?' he asked, indicating Su Yuan.

'A friend,' said Sophie, issuing her warmest smile. 'Service good tonight?'

'Always,' he said, his eyes still fixed on Su Yuan's face. 'You're gorgeous,' he said, his voice catching, as she passed. A blush crept across the girl's cheek and she looked at the floor. Stuart winked at Sophie. 'Feel free to bring your friends around whenever you want.'

'Right.'

A pause and then Stuart said, 'Well – I'm off. Ooo-roo, chefo.' The kitchen door banged behind him as he stomped out into the night.

'Sorry,' said Jin Tao to Su Yuan. 'He's not shy, our Stuart.'

Su Yuan's hair fell away from her face as she shook her head. 'It doesn't matter,' she said. 'It's nice to hear a friendly voice after all this time.'

'Did they talk to you?' Sophie ventured. 'The people you worked for?'

'Not much,' said Su Yuan. 'But I didn't care. I talked to the customers.'

'Which is how you found out about your sister,' said Jin Tao.

Su Yuan nodded. 'The customer, I could tell as soon as he walked into the room that he wasn't an evil man. He was shy, he was nervous, he didn't know what to do. I manipulated him. I talked about his family and my family. I told him he was handsome, that men like him were usually fat and ugly and old. I stroked his ego instead of his dick and he started to like me.' She paused. 'I think that's why he told me the truth.'

Jin Tao exhaled a long breath. 'Who'd believe arseholes like that would have a conscience?'

Su Yuan started to say something and then stopped, as though turning the thought over in her mind. 'Even depraved people sometimes have a conscience,' she said. Then, with a shrug: 'And if he hadn't helped me, perhaps I would have broken his neck instead.' She said it simply as though stating the obvious. Su Yuan had made a plan and she'd carried it out. She hadn't found her sister, but she had killed one of the men who'd taken her.

Jin Tao slid open the door to the storeroom. 'It's not very grand, but you'll be safe here,' he said over his shoulder as he knelt down and began heaving away a six-deep pile of rice sacks. The sacks scratched against the floor as he shifted them slightly to the right to reveal a trapdoor to the cellar.

'Jin Tao …' said Sophie, her voice laced with alarm. She watched as Jin Tao pulled open the door to reveal a set of stairs descending to a dark space below. She hadn't known this room had a door to a cellar. What did he keep down there? What did he use it for? Why did he think that Su Yuan would be able to bear another stint in an enclosed room?

'Just a sec,' said Jin Tao as he descended the stairs. 'I'll head down and take a look.'

Sophie's heart began to race. This felt all wrong.

Su Yuan tugged at Sophie's arm, her face betraying unease. 'You're not putting me down there,' she said, her voice a firm whisper.

'It's all right,' said Sophie, doing her best to sound reassuring even though tiny alarm bells had begun jangling in her head. Why had Jin Tao suggested taking Su Yuan to the restaurant instead of their home? She hadn't questioned him at the time. Now it seemed ridiculous. And he'd also seemed annoyed to find Stuart still hanging around. Sophie had assumed it was because he didn't want Stuart to see Su Yuan, but was there another reason? Why hadn't Jin Tao ever shown her the cellar? Why was the trapdoor covered with sacks of rice? Why did he think Su Yuan would agree to hiding down there and how long did he plan to keep her?

Sophie felt her breath quicken and the storeroom suddenly felt hot and airless. She pressed at the latch on the door to open it and let in some air.

It didn't open.

Sophie tried it again. Harder this time. The door didn't give. Sophie spun around. Su Yuan's eyes bulged. Behind her, Jin Tao emerged from the cellar, a frown on his face. Su Yuan spun around, hands up, ready to fight.

'No good,' Jin Tao said, as though offering a defence. 'The last place you'd want to stay after the ordeal you've been through.'

Su Yuan lowered her hands. Her whole body shook with released tension.

Jin Tao stopped. 'What?' he asked, concern in his voice. 'You guys look like you've seen ghosts.'

'Jin Tao, why can't we open the door?' The question sounded accusatory and he threw her a querying look. He leaned past her and unsnibbed a small bar on the latch.

'Locked yourself in,' he said as the storeroom was flooded with light. 'I'm sorry,' he said, turning to Su Yuan. 'I thought it would be safer for you here than at our place. Our house shares walls with some very nosy neighbours. And they're thin, the walls. We reckon the neighbours listen in on us.'

Sophie stared at Jin Tao, his words crashing into her heart. 'The walls are listening.'

Jin Tao shrugged. 'It feels a bit like that sometimes.'

'Wendy used that expression.'

'Huh?'

'Lenny told me Wendy asked him how to describe the walls

listening. And that night of the Sichuan dinner, you told me she said it then too.'

'She was drunk.'

Sophie's mind tumbled over itself. What if Wendy had known the girls were kept behind the restaurant's walls, or in a cellar in a storeroom like this very one here? Kept at the Sichuan restaurant, and she had been trying to give them a message? It made sense. There were dozens of restaurants in Chinatown but Wendy had taken them to only one.

'Take Su Yuan to our place,' she said to Jin Tao. 'I think I know where the girls are being kept.' And before Jin Tao could ask any more questions, she was out in the kitchen and then making for the swing door at a run.

女孩

HE WAS waiting for her when the cab pulled up in Sussex Street and Sophie spilled out into the rain.

'You're a bit late for dinner but I can see what's left in the fridge.' Brad gave an easy smile and offered her the shelter of his umbrella as he pulled a set of keys from his pocket. 'You want to tell me what's so urgent?' he asked, as he turned the key in the lock of the iron grille.

'You said your restaurant shares a storeroom with the Sichuan place, right?'

'It does,' he said as they clambered up the stairs. 'You want to raid their stock or what? I get caught thieving dried chillis from the neighbours and I lose my permanent residency permit, I'm telling you that now.'

Sophie took the stairs two at a time. 'It's a long story and I might be wrong but I think your neighbours are dealing in something slightly spicier than chillis.'

'What could be spicier than chillies?'

'Sex.'

Brad stopped on the stairs, one hand on the banister, the other sliding through his thick, sea-salted hair. 'You mean the neighbours are running some kind of brothel?'

Sophie paused at the top of the stairs and looked down at him. And then it came out in a rush. 'There's a syndicate kidnapping foreign women, using them as sex slaves, abusing them, raping them, filming them, killing them.' The words caught in her throat. 'The girls are being kept in Chinatown somewhere. I think your neighbours might be involved.'

'And you want to check out their storeroom?'

Sophie nodded. 'Maybe there's a cellar or something in there. Can you help?'

Brad glanced over his shoulder at the stairs leading back down to the street below. 'Does anyone know you're here?'

Sophie waved the query away.

'You didn't think to call Damian?'

'It's just a hunch.'

Brad pushed past her on his way to the kitchen. 'This is heavy shit, Sophie,' he said. 'If you're wrong then I'm screwed for helping you to break in.'

'Damian'll forgive you.'

'Yeah, when I'm sitting in an immigration detention cell waiting to be deported.'

Sophie followed Brad through the darkened kitchen to a side door leading to the storeroom. Beside neatly stacked shelves he searched through keys for the one that would unlock the door. 'It's here somewhere,' he murmured. 'I wish you'd told someone else about this.'

'It'll be okay,' she said, trying to hide her impatience. 'If we find something, we'll call Damian or the police immediately.'

Brad turned the key in the door and it opened on creaking hinges, revealing a similarly sized space on the other side. The stench of dried shrimp and mushrooms hit Sophie with the ferocity of a punch. The smell of onions was subtler, but still present. The musty pungency made her want to hurl. She stepped sideways into the room, squeezing past the overloaded shelves on either side of the door. 'Someone needs to give this place a once-over,' she said.

But Brad didn't answer.

'Brad?'

He'd been just behind her, but when Sophie looked back into the cavern of the Uyghur restaurant's storeroom, she saw Brad flat on the floor, blood seeping from a wound to his head.

Beside him stood a man in tracksuit pants and a polar fleece.

'G'day, Sophie,' he said in his familiar drawl. 'Guess who followed you here?'

Sophie stared at Stuart, so shocked she couldn't move. She opened her mouth but no sound came out. How could she have failed to notice Stuart? And how could she not have heard Brad fall?

'Ether,' said Stuart. He nudged Brad's shoulder with his boot. 'Followed up by a swift blow to the head.' Stuart revealed the stone pestle he held in his hand. He wagged a finger at Sophie, a smile on his lips. 'You shouldn't have dragged your friend into this, Sophie,' he said. 'I reckon I can safely say your mate is well and truly out for the count.' As if to prove it, Stuart gave Brad a rough kick in the side. Brad didn't utter a sound.

The sighting of Zhou in the Cross near Blue Lotus, the disturbances to her room. It had been Stuart all along. He'd been to their place. He'd seen where the spare key was kept, he knew Jin Tao's schedule, all he had to do was get a sense of Sophie's. And anyone with a computer and an internet connection could find out information about her involvement in David's disappearance. If Stuart had wanted to haunt her or stalk her, he hadn't had to look very far for a way to do it.

Stuart raised his hands defensively. 'Hey, I just shoot the footage.'

'Of the girls you helped kidnap.'

Stuart smiled. 'I'll give you that one.' He shook his head, his free hand on his hip. 'You're persistent, Sophie, do people tell you that?'

'What do you mean?'

'I mean you just keep going,' he said, inching forwards. 'We've been watching you. We've been threatening you. Your mate Jin Tao told me more about you than he should've and he gave me the goods to freak you out. We've done our best to intimidate you, we've tried to confuse you, but you just don't bloody well give up.'

'Who's "we", Stuart?' She would try to buy some time. There was another door behind her that she guessed led into the Sichuan restaurant. If she could open it from the inside, put some space between her and Stuart, she would have a chance.

'I reckon you could probably tell me that, princess,' Stuart said, as Sophie edged her way back. 'You've got it sorted out. You know about Michael Disney, who's done a runner; then there's Zhou, the butcher your little friend killed; our front of house guy, Cho, who's split to who knows where; and there's me, the guy with the camera.'

'So you made sex films with the girls Disney and Zhou had targeted and then Cho got the footage out to interested buyers.'

Stuart nodded. 'Yeah, except Disney didn't know about the kidnapping and the snuff films. He'd never've bought into that.

The rest of us knew there was more money to be made in the hardcore stuff. You'd be surprised how many people have an appetite for horror.'

'So you undercut him?'

'We kidnapped a few of Disney's working ladies and stored them away for our film productions, yes.'

'Using the existing operation as a cover.'

'That poor bastard just couldn't figure out why his workers kept disappearing.'

Sophie took this in. So Stuart and his colleagues had been operating of their own accord and taking things further than Disney had ever envisaged.

'Was Pete involved?'

'Who's Pete?'

She'd try a different tack, follow Su Yuan's lead, appeal to his conscience. Even depraved people have a conscience, Su Yuan had said. 'You're not the psychopathic type.'

'It's purely business as far as I'm concerned,' said Stuart with a shrug. 'When I got into it with Disney, the girls weren't dying. We just made a few sexy videos, operated some nasty nightclubs. But then this one girl got real feisty and threatened to spill the beans. Zhou had no choice but to knock her off, and because Disney didn't ask any questions the whole thing kind of snowballed.'

'And you thought it would be a good idea to start filming some of these women in the last moments of their lives.'

Stuart shrugged. 'Where there's a market...' He trailed off. But then, pulling himself together, he said, 'Beats the wages your mate pays.'

'You're disgusting.' She guessed she'd almost backed her way to the door. There was another question she wanted answered. 'What about the girl who acted as a substitute for

Wendy Chan? She must have known something about what you were doing. Is that why she killed herself?'

'She had a friendly relationship with Zhou.'

'Friendly?'

'They were fucking. He bought her shoes and clothes and shit. My guess is he told her something he shouldn't have. Pillow talk.'

'And she jumped because she couldn't handle it?'

'Guess she had a conscience,' he said. 'Pity, because her topping herself started this whole thing off with you.'

Sophie found the handle of the door behind her and turned it. It jammed. Damn. She'd have to scare him. Make him think she wasn't alone. 'You're finished now.' She was surprised at the strength in her voice. 'I've already called the police.'

Stuart laughed and took another step. 'You fucking hate the police. And anyway, I know you didn't.'

Sophie stared him down. 'You sound confident.'

'Because I followed you here. I heard your Uyghur mate stressing that you hadn't told anyone.'

'Su Yuan saw you in the kitchen. She knows who you are and what you've done.'

Stuart continued his approach. 'Bullshit, sweetheart, she didn't have a clue. And as long as you're not around to tell, then there's nothing to tie me to any of this.' He finished his statement with a sudden lunge and before Sophie could dodge his attack, he was at her throat, his thick fingers wrapped tightly around her neck. She flailed her arms wildly, her fingers searching for a weapon to use against him.

'You don't know how long I've waited to feel your flesh between my fingers,' he hissed into her ear. 'Listen carefully, Soph, and I'll tell you what's going to happen.'

Sophie forced her body to go limp, to relax and roll with the punches the way she'd trained herself to do as a child when getting dumped by the waves in the surf. She concentrated on bringing air into her lungs.

'In a minute, I'm going to knock you out,' said Stuart. 'And when you come to, you'll be in the cellar. See, there's this nice little cubbyhole beneath this room. It used to be used for food storage until the rats got in. Now it's used for storage of a different kind. We'll have our own little party in front of the video camera. And I'll get to see what it's like to go all the way with the boss's female friend.'

A surge of panic gave Sophie renewed strength and she bucked her knees, trying to find some leverage. What had Su Yuan done? Gone for the balls. If she could aim a kick at his crotch she might have a chance. But the more she bucked, the harder Stuart's fingers pressed into the skin of her throat until she felt her windpipe might actually snap. A wave of disappointment flowed through her, along with the realisation that it might all end here. Death, in a back room in Chinatown. Fuck that. She forced her eyes open and saw Stuart leering into her face.

'What next?' The question came out as a wheeze. The pressure at her throat was so great she couldn't swallow. But she needed to keep him talking. The longer he talked the more time she had to figure out a solution.

Stuart loosened his grip. 'When I'm done, I'll fillet you and you'll feel every slice of the knife.' He released his grip and Sophie crumpled in a heap to the floor. 'It's going to be a sensation,' he said, driving a boot into her chin and sending her reeling against the wall. 'I'm going to make you into a star.'

He strode to the other end of the room and Sophie clutched at her jaw with her hands. The blow had been intended to knock her out and pain drove through her skull like she'd been branded. Through blurred vision, she saw Stuart bend over a rucksack in the corner. She placed a hand on the wall behind her and attempted to get up, but the pain in her jaw was spreading and her head was beginning to spin. It was no good. She looked around desperately, searching for anything at floor level that could help fight off another attack.

And then she found her weapon.

An open basket of dried chillies poked out from beneath the bottom shelf, the skins dark and crinkled and spilling over from the basket onto the floor. It wasn't much but it was better than nothing. She had to take a gamble. She drove her hand into the basket and pulled out a handful, sweeping her arm back to her side just as Stuart approached. She saw he carried a metal cleaver in his hand, a pair of plastic cuffs in his mouth. If he cuffed her, it was over – that much she knew for sure.

'Come here, sweetheart,' he said as he bent towards her, his breath adding a further sour note to the storeroom's stench.

It took every ounce of remaining strength for Sophie to shove the handful of chillis hard into Stuart's face. She took him by surprise and he dropped the cleaver with a clatter. She mashed the seed pods hard against his eyes and clawed at his skin, gouging it with her nails.

'Bitch!' he roared in pain and shock. He brought his hands to his eyes, leaving the cleaver exposed on the floor.

She hesitated only a moment once the cleaver was in her hands. Li Hua's words rang in her memory: *I'd take a cleaver and drive it through his spine. I wouldn't hesitate. Not for a second.*

Sophie raised the cleaver with two hands and brought it down hard against Stuart's right shoulder. She felt first fabric and then skin give way beneath the blade and then metal meet with bone.

Stuart opened and closed his mouth twice with no sound. Then he released a moan. He twisted his head to look at the object that had hit him, and when he saw the cleaver lodged firmly in his flesh, his face drained of blood and he passed out.

'Bastard!' Sophie leaned back against the wall. Relief pulsed through every vein in her body.

And then noise in the kitchen. Footsteps on the stairs. *More of them. Fuck.*

Sophie placed a hand on the handle of the cleaver. If she had to pull it from Stuart's broken flesh to use as a weapon, she would.

But the people who came running through the door were not here to capture her. Sophie saw Jin Tao's face.

'Soph!' He rushed straight to her. Behind him, Damian bent to examine Brad.

Su Yuan stood in the doorway, straight as a guard.

'I thought we might be too late,' said Jin Tao, his arms around her shoulders, folding her into his chest. Sophie sank into him. He smelled like sweat and spice. 'I thought we might be too late,' he repeated, his breath heaving, pulling her closer, running his lips against her hair.

Su Yuan moved past them. She checked Stuart. 'He's dead.'

Sophie forced herself to focus, to drive away the emotion that threatened to engulf her. 'Are you okay, Su Yuan?'

The girl took Sophie's hand in hers, held it tight. 'You did it,' she said. 'You killed a man that hurt my sister. It means you are a kind of sister to me now. We are connected.'

Sophie blinked away hot tears. She brought Su Yuan's hand to her mouth, kissed it. The girl smiled and turned away.

Sophie leaned into Jin Tao. 'How did you know I'd come here, and about Stuart?'

Jin Tao pointed to Brad, sitting up with Damian's help. 'Thank the tea guy. He sent Damian a text.'

Brad smiled weakly and gave Sophie a wave. Damian held a bag of frozen dumplings against his head and the image, coupled with Brad's goofy smile, dried Sophie's tears and forced a laugh. 'You were passed out!' she said.

'I faked it,' Brad said with a wink. 'I had to try to save you, didn't I? I meant it when I told you I owed you my life.'

DOWN IN the cellar, Han Hong sensed something was happening.

She'd been alone for too long down here. She was freezing and starving and she had hardly the strength to strain her ears for unusual sounds. But she'd heard them.

She knew she'd heard the dull warble of distant conversation, the high pitch of a woman's voice, followed by a moan and a thud.

Han Hong guessed a new girl had found the strength to fight and received her punishment as a result. And if they were bringing in another girl, it meant her time had come. This was her time to disappear.

Han Hong shifted. She'd lost weight and her bones ached from her long confinement on the floor. Her skin itched and she suspected there'd be a weeping rash on the underside of her legs if she ever saw them in the light again.

If she ever saw the light.

Han Hong realised the terror of her situation had long passed. *With time, comes acceptance*, she thought. Even in the most horrific of circumstances. She no longer had the strength to fight so she would die at the hands of these people. She had long stopped hoping that she would be set free. These people had a purpose. They made films and they were always looking for their next star. She guessed what it meant now. They would come and they would take her and she would simply cease to exist.

She would never see the mountains from her mother's balcony window again.

The door opened and Han Hong readied herself for the masked man to make his entrance.

But the sound that came to her ears caused her heart to pound.

'Hello?' said a woman's voice. 'Is anybody there?'

Acknowledgements

IT TAKES a team to produce a book and I'm so deeply thankful to all the talented and supportive people on mine.

My sincere gratitude to everybody at Echo Publishing, particularly Angela Meyer for believing in this story and for her insightful structural suggestions; Kylie Mason, for her astute and sensitive editing, Sandy Cull for her visually striking and tonally perfect cover design and Shaun Jury for making all the letters look just right.

Thank you to my agent, Sheila Drummond, for taking on *Ghost Girls* and representing me. Big love to writer Angela Savage: without her encouragement and advice this book may still be a large, untidy file on my hard drive.

I had a supportive and perceptive team of early readers: Claire Berry, Carolyn Collins, Marcia Gardner, Lucy McCarthy, Di McElroy, Karen Reid, Charmaine Smith and Genevieve Wallace – thank you. Thanks to Mum and Marg for early writing time. Appreciation also to Elizabeth Schiavello Photography and Kelly Merritt for photos and friendship.

I am so thankful to have grown up in a family where the joys of reading, writing and creativity were valued and nurtured. I read books in trees and saw the 'spookies' and talked to an imaginary friend named Nat. Thanks Mum, Dad and John for encouraging and supporting my wild imagination.

To He Wen Bin (Winnie), my dearest friend, thank you for your love, stories, feedback, translation skills and eye for detail. Despite the distance, we are connected.

To Eugene, your endless support, patience and love beats through me every day. Thank you for your unceasing optimism and your own beautifully creative energy – it inspires me.

To Florence and Rocco, I love you.